ABOUT THE AUTHOR

GB Williams specialises in complex, fast-paced crime novels. Born and bred in Kent, GB moved to South Wales as a supposedly first step on a year around the world. Then she met a guy. Kept the guy, kissed the travel goodbye.

Since then, she's worked, married, had two great kids – the usual. Now working as a freelance editor and writer, she lives with her family and the world's most demanding cat. And she hates every photo ever taken of her. Find out more at www.gailbwilliams.co.uk.

Published in Great Britain in 2022
By Diamond Crime

ISBN 978-1-915649-25-6

Book design: jacksonbone.co.uk
Cover photo: Arno Senoner/Unsplash

Printed and bound by
Ashford Colour Press Ltd,
Gosport, Hants PO13 0FW

Diamond Crime is an imprint of Diamond Books Ltd.

For Bobby and Queen

PLAY THE GAME

GB Williams

GB WILLIAMS

CHAPTER ONE

"I need a library."

What Elaine actually needed was a bibliothèque. It was one of the few French words that had stuck in her mind, mostly because it had sounded a lot more fun than any discotheque could.

Unfortunately, her French was extremely limited. She could ask "où est la bibliothèque?", and she did, several times. The problem was, she didn't understand a word of the answers and relied on hand signals instead. This would be so much easier if she could just Google it, but she had to avoid being traced, which meant having to do things the non-electronic way. The battery wasn't even in her phone right now, just in case.

Which all added to why it took an hour to get to the library that was, had she known the route, only about ten minutes from where she'd been when she'd first thought about finding one.

The worst thing was that hour had given her far too much time to think. Thinking about her situation didn't improve it. Exactly one week ago she had discovered that her husband, Jason, had lied to her for the entire twenty-five years that they had known one another. She'd long ago come to terms with the fact that the man she'd married for security was, in fact, a manipulative, controlling, abuser, but she hadn't realised how consummate a liar he was. It took his death for her to find out what he did for a living. He was a spy. It wasn't as glamourous as it sounded.

In keeping with her appalling luck, it turned out that he might even be a double agent. Jason was supposed to have had evidence that a lot of people wanted, people from all sides. The problem was, all those people now thought Elaine had that evidence. She didn't. She didn't even know what the evidence was.

The mistake they had made was trying to use one of her foster-children against her. Lazlo Zakis. He'd come to her as a scared little boy, ten years old and totally out of his depth. She'd taken him in and loved him, tried to help him in every way she could. He hadn't been terribly receptive, but she hadn't expected him to be the kind to stab her in back either. Which is what had happened. She didn't have the evidence, but she had found what she supposed to be the key to finding it.

So, when Lazlo indicated he was in trouble, she'd been ready to do whatever it took to free him. And that included leaving her home and all the security she thought she had, travelling to Paris, figuring out that Lazlo was a turncoat, faking the evidence to have something to pass over, and then having to fight for her life not to be captured by the people Lazlo was clearly working for.

And somehow the most terrifying thing about all that, was that her get away was achieved about seventy minutes ago.

Still, she was at the library now, things to do.

She stepped inside.

The next question was where to start. A librarian took pity on her looking lost and since the hipster young man spoke flawless English, she explained what she was doing, asked him the question and thus got the answer much faster than expected.

Elaine blinked at him. "Switzerland?" How on earth did Switzerland get abbreviated to CH? She could probably find out, but it was one of those interesting but not important questions. She'd expected to find the answer by trawling through books. This was much easier. She had got lucky – again. Just as Ladderman had accused her. Ladderman, the British secret agent who had been on her tail since she left home. She'd lost him for now, which avoided him trying to send her home, as that was the last place she wanted to go. But he had turned up to help in that final confrontation, and she kind of missed him already, although she wasn't sure she could trust even him. Too much of her life was built on lies, and what else could a spy do but lie to her more? She pushed thoughts of him aside and looked at the librarian again.

"Any idea how I can find out what a bank code is within an IBAN code?"

"Do you have a code?"

"That part is C-O-U-T."

Again, he didn't need to check. "Probably Coutts Bank."

Of course! If she'd had her brain switched on, she probably could have figured that one out for herself. Though in her defence, until about an hour ago, she was pretty much fully occupied with trying to stay alive. Something to think about later. Right now, she needed to focus.

"I think," the librarian said, "it's either based in Geneva or just has a well-known branch there. Do you want me to double check?"

Given how much sense the answer made when added to everything else she knew, that felt unnecessary. She thanked the man in English, then German, then remembered where she was and reached French as she left the library. At least she knew where she was going now.

Geneva, Switzerland.

* * *

Special Agent Madison Turner put the phone down. Her contact in Paris had reported and it didn't feel good.

Elaine Blake, the woman she called Mom despite the foster relationship and only a ten-year age difference, had survived an encounter in Paris with people Madison wouldn't want to face if she could avoid it.

Hearing how Elaine had used a pencil to incapacitate one potential captor, and then used the depth of a holdall on her back to make the grip so awkward for a second man, that she had been able to near bite through the skin between his thumb and forefinger, impressed Madison beyond belief. Elaine had even paid a group of local teenagers to run interference for her. Elaine had escaped capture. She'd also lost Madison's contact and Cormac 'Mac' Letterman, the MI6 man following Elaine.

Elaine and Jason Blake had fostered Madison after her own parents were murdered. She was one of twenty-one children they had fostered over the years. Madison had been in protective custody, Jason Blake being one of the men assigned to protect her. Jason had taken her home. Despite Madison's initial resentment and grief, Elaine had always been there for her, seeing her through some of the darkest hours of her life. A wonderful, warm woman, Elaine had welcomed Madison into her home and her heart. Elaine making herself at home in Madison's heart was something the younger woman hadn't expected. She wondered again if Elaine knew that every child she had fostered had a link to espionage.

A text message appeared on her phone, pulling her from her memories. The boss wanted to see her.

Only not her immediate boss, but Regional Director Alan Bromstad. He had taken a personal interest in this case that officially they, the CIA, had no interest.

In his office, Bromstad waved her into the seat before his desk. She sat before that poker face, hoping her worries didn't show.

"So, where is she heading?" he asked.

"I'm not sure. From the report, it's clear that she now knows that Lazlo Zakis is working for those he claimed were his captors. So, being a logical woman, Elaine will consider the original mission to save Lazlo as complete. There's nothing to save him from." Madison sighed. "There's no obvious driver at this point to suggest where she might go."

"What about a less obvious driver?" Bromstad asked.

Madison took a slow, steady breath in as she considered that. "Well, given how long Mom's been kept down, she probably needs to kick out and take some time. And she has the money to do it now."

"Yes," Bromstad agreed. "Have you found out why she was given that money?"

Madison nodded her head. "As far as I can make out, MI6 believed she was working with Jason. When she asked for the money, they wanted to know what she would do. They thought they'd follow the money and find Jason, or they would follow Elaine and she would lead them to the evidence."

"Will she?"

Here, Madison was on difficult ground. "I'm not sure. You see, she told me she hadn't found the evidence, which was technically the truth, but not the whole truth. The report says that Elaine handed over a falsified cypher and a key. Which suggests that what she meant was that she hadn't found evidence but had found clues to it."

"Why would she lie to you?"

"She didn't lie. She was frugal with the truth. To protect me." Of that, Madison had no doubt. "She doesn't know who I work for. She probably thought that the less I knew, the safer I'd be."

"Which doesn't help us. If she's given the opposition the cypher and key."

"She gave a falsified cypher and a different key. At least that's what she told Letterman. What he told us."

"You trust that she told the whole truth there?"

Madison nodded. "She isn't much of a liar. She's never needed to be. If she lied to me, it was through omission, not outright. Yes, I think she told him the truth."

"And you trust this MI6 agent to pass that truth on?"

"Not entirely." Madison had met Letterman twice, on matters of business. It wasn't so much that she didn't trust him. He seemed a nice enough type. It was more that she didn't have a good reason to trust him.

"You're the analyst, Agent Turner. What do you think is going to happen next?"

"I think Mom found something in the house she hasn't shared with me. It's probably not the evidence, but it could be clues to finding the evidence. Mom's not stupid. If she faked stuff to hand over, it's possible that she's deciphered what she found. She may well be on the way to wherever that leads."

"We have no idea where that might be."

"No, sir," Madison admitted. "We do, however, know that Agent Letterman is still on her tail."

"So are our opponents," Bromstad added the less hopeful truth.

Worst of all, they weren't even sure exactly who their opponents were. Criminals from the Eastern Bloc with deep pockets, was as close as they could tell.

"There is one possibility," Madison said. "I found out that Lazlo had booked two airline tickets. One departed yesterday from Paris to Frankfurt, the one booked for today is to Geneva. It's possible that she'll go to Geneva in case that's where Lazlo has gone."

"You think she'd follow him even if he's turned against her?"

"It's possible. His defection wouldn't stop her loving him. And she'd want to know what was really going on. Yeah, I think there's a good chance she'll try to follow him."

Bromstad considered her again. "Why have you never told her that you work for the CIA?"

Madison shrugged. "I told her I was a data analyst. I just didn't tell her who for. Somehow it felt..." She couldn't really explain it. She shrugged. "I know we're not the secret service, but it felt like I should keep it secret. Mostly because what Mom knows of the CIA, she's got from books and TV, and she's never been that impressed with Jack Ryan." She shrugged again. "She'd worry if she knew the truth."

His eyebrow twitched. "So, you were just protecting her?"

She nodded.

"You protect each other by omitting to tell the truth?"

"Well, I admit it's not a great standpoint, but I guess we both work on the idea of what you don't know can't hurt you."

A softness entered Bromstad's eyes. It didn't stay long. "What do you plan to do?"

Test time again. "I'm going to keep watching, see if anything turns up. And I'm going to hope she calls me so I can find out where she is. I need her to call."

"I think it's her who needs you," Bromstad said. "Would you follow her out there?"

Madison frowned slightly at the idea. She'd never been a field agent, though she found the idea appealing. "I don't consider that necessary at this point.

"Why not?"

"I have changed my perspective. Elaine already has a highly trained MI6 agent after her and she's running rings around him. Even our man said she gave him the slip easier than he liked. I don't think she needs me out there. I think she needs me in here, analysing, researching, finding the data she needs. Doing what I'm good at."

* * *

A twenty-seven-year career in MI6 had left Cormac Letterman unprepared for this last week and Elaine Blake. He stalked through central Paris to retrieve his bag from the Gare Saint-Lazare, as he wondered what his next step should be.

Exactly one week ago, he had received what seemed like a simple order: go to Cardiff and search the Blake house. The only oddity in that was that the house was owned by Jason Blake, another MI6 agent. Ten days ago, Jason Blake, colleague not friend, had gone missing and was now dead. At least he was officially dead. Reality remained unclear.

Elaine hadn't even known until last Friday that Jason worked for MI6 when he and Steve Southgate, another agent, had disappeared from Prague. The problem was that Jason had evidence of treachery across the borders of Europe and Russia. In response MI6 had sent Mac to find that evidence.

Instead, he'd found that Elaine Blake was not the bland little mouse they had all believed. She was a talented artist, a loving foster mother, fiercely protective of her children, and a damn sight better in a fight than he would ever have predicted.

Automatically, his tongue touched the rough line of his lip where her punch had split it. Nothing in her background checks had indicated a history of her being violent any more than it had shown a history of violence against her. Knowing now that she had been a beaten wife made him wonder what else Elaine Blake was hiding. What he really hadn't expected was to like her. He hadn't liked a woman in that way in a very long time. If ever.

It was galling to admit that Elaine was also a very smart cookie. She'd found something he'd missed. From what she'd said, it was a cypher that decoded to Watch Tower. From what he surmised, the cypher said more than that. And there was a key, a physical key. He didn't know what it meant. As far as he could tell, neither did Elaine.

Now hefting his bag from the locker to his shoulder, he reviewed the last seven days, in particular, the last 36 hours, and realised that everything Elaine had done made perfect sense when considered in the light of her being a mother acting to protect her son.

While hearing a man on the concourse bid farewell to his companion, the one illogical thing Elaine had done, popped into Mac's mind. She had spent time in Charles de Gaulle Airport waiting on a Frankfurt flight. Or more accurately, watching the line of people checking into the Frankfurt flight.

"Who was she looking for?" Mac asked himself. "Who was supposed to be on that flight?"

CHAPTER TWO

Elaine bought a business pro ticket for the train from Paris to Geneva. She decided it was worth the money for the legroom alone. The decent drink on arrival didn't hurt either, for all it wasn't exactly free.

She stowed her holdall and kept hold of her handbag, dumping it in the neighbouring seat as she luxuriated back into the comfortable padding of what might actually be a leather seat, and which offered plenty of room to move in.

Once the train was underway, the sense of relief washed through her. As lovely as Paris had been, she was glad to get away from it. She'd escaped Ladderman and foreign thugs. She wished she could think of him as something other than Ladderman, only she hadn't asked his name, and it was unlikely he would have given it. It was so weird. A week ago, she hadn't even known him. Now he often appeared in her thoughts. When he had come to her home to look through her loft for the evidence they were after, he'd been carrying a ladder. Hence her calling him Ladderman. She only wanted to call him that more because he'd reacted oddly the first time she'd said it to his face.

She'd never forget that look, or his face. It was one she needed to be vigilant for in case he found her again. Finally, she had the sense to look around the carriage: plenty of business types and high ends. No Ladderman. Hers weren't the only jeans in the place, but she'd lay money on them being the only ones costing under a tenner. Come to that, they were also probably the only ones under a hundred pounds and not from a named designer.

Today was Friday. It was only on the previous Saturday that she'd changed the lagging of the hot water tank, and found the cypher hidden along with a key. The key now lay safely zipped into a pocket of her outsized handbag; she had written the cypher in her notebook, which was also in the handbag. She'd solved the cypher on the Sunday. That her husband had picked the name of their friend and his lover, Keira, to be the key to that cypher had stung. The sting had disappeared quickly. How much hurt could a man she didn't really care about do her? She was emotionally stronger than that. At least she was now.

She'd gained enough strength to talk openly to Madison. They'd always been close, but now they were closer. She itched to call Madison again now, although they had agreed it wasn't safe, and she shouldn't be dragging another civilian into this game of spies. Of course, her mind flitted through all the other children she'd fostered over the years, all twenty-one of them, she could list them without pause, but that was its own special form of torture. She had no idea what was going to happen in the coming days, but everything was changing, she was changing. What if she never got to see any of them again?

The urge to call Madison grew stronger, but Elaine resisted. Madison was helping her. Lazlo had betrayed her. The one thing she really regretted was that she hadn't tried harder to stay in touch with some of the others. Especially Utku. She missed him. She'd accidentally insulted him, and he'd stormed out of the house, hadn't spoken to her since.

She should have tried harder to reach out to him. Another lost opportunity.

Pushing back the past, she focused on the here and now. The cypher still nagged her. None of it made sense yet. She wondered if Ladderman was getting on any better. There again, she had told him she had decoded it to 'Watch Tower'. It wasn't a lie, but the full cypher read 'Water Tower Godiva North Gate Spell', so he was missing pieces of the puzzle.

The IBAN number she had found hidden in a picture. There might be other copies of it, but she wasn't worried about them, mostly because she (a) didn't know they actually existed, (b) couldn't control them if they did, and (c) it was so hard to spot there was a good chance it wouldn't be found. Not to mention point (d) she was already on her way to Geneva to find out about it, and if it was a wild goose chase, she had half a million from MI6 to spend chasing that goose.

Of course, there was the other reason she was going to Geneva. Lazlo Zakis. He was her son. Okay, her foster son. And he had betrayed her. That didn't stop her loving him, like she loved all her foster children, but it did temper what she would do for him. Madison had told her he had made bookings in his name to Frankfurt and Geneva. She'd watched the check-in of the Frankfurt flight. He hadn't got on it. That she had seen him since, argued against his going there.

That made her consider what she was doing.

If the IBAN was Coutts in Switzerland, there was likely to be a reasonable to considerable amount of money involved. From what little she knew of Coutts, it wasn't your everyday kind of bank. No scraping-by current accounts there. She couldn't go to a swanky bank dressed in any of the outfits she had with her. She just didn't look the part, and she was going to need to. For a start, she had to prove she was Jason's wife.

That was fairly easy. When she'd picked up her passport, she also picked up their marriage and birth certificates. She even had Jason's death certificate, taken in case Madison refused to believe her. In other words, she carried everything any bank would need to give her access to a dead husband's bank account. Unless Jason opened the account in a name other than his own. She assumed Jason Blake was his real name, but that seemed increasingly questionable. Or her paranoia had kicked in again.

Hang on in there, you can do this.

If the bank agreed she was Jason's widow, the only other obstacle she could think of was wills and probate. Even that wasn't an issue. One thing she had done on Tuesday was go to the solicitor, where she'd had Jason's will read. Thankfully, they'd arranged their wills some time ago, so that whoever survived the other, got everything. Because she'd done that before heading to London, without returning home, she had a copy of his will with her too.

Arrival time for Geneva was after six that afternoon. The bank would be shut. The shops would be shut, or possibly not, she didn't know. She'd have to find a hotel and do some serious shopping in the morning. Today being Friday, meant she wouldn't get to the bank until Monday.

A weekend in Geneva. She smiled. *Yeah, I can do that.*

Shouldn't.

No, she really shouldn't. This wasn't a holiday.

Since she had a table seat, she replaced the battery in her phone and put it on the table. Her pen went down beside it, and she looked through her notebook. An extra small Moleskin notebook in turquoise, a present a few years ago, she forgot who from. It didn't really matter. It was a part of a past that was growing ever more distant, like a nightmare she had finally woken from. Unlike a nightmare, however, she remembered it all too clearly. She opened the book, the second page.

The cypher. Another page, and another. The bloody code key. She turned another page to the answers she knew off by heart. Watch Tower. Godiva. North Gate Spell. *What the hell does it mean?*

Her trip had started because Lazlo called her. He had claimed, and she had believed, that he was under duress, but was he? Not from what she had seen at lunchtime.

Then there was the claim that Jason was alive. She picked at that scab and found it didn't hurt at all. It was odd that the man she'd been married to, and controlled by for twenty-five years, would no longer be there. Odd and liberating. Jason's death left her sorry for that in much the same way that she had been sorry to hear about David Bowie's death, a distant sorrow and no real impact on her day-to-day life. But right in her heart of hearts, she really didn't believe Jason was dead. She might have his death certificate, but certification wasn't necessarily a fact. It would hardly be the first lie she had swallowed.

Besides, Jason's continued life was irrelevant.

The problem was that some very bad, and as yet unidentified, bad guys wanted evidence that they believed she had. She didn't know what the evidence was, or what should happen to it. All she knew was that it proved treachery. Nothing she had yet seen indicated who the traitor was or what they had betrayed. Only when she knew that could she decide what she would do.

Which meant that she had to get to the evidence first. But how? She looked up and noticed the discrete little sign in the corner of the window. Free Wi-Fi. Had to be worth a try.

She picked up her phone and checked the cypher.

Watch tower. Godiva. North Gate Spell.

* * *

The Starbucks outside the Gare Saint-Lazare provided Mac with a comfortable place to use the shop's Wi-Fi to do some virtual snooping. Eventually, he accessed the flight passenger manifest, and he didn't recognise one name. Then he found the booking registration. The name leapt out.

Lazlo Zakis.

Elaine had gone to the airport in search of the foster son she believed was in trouble. Now that made sense.

What made little sense, was how she'd known about the booking. One thing Elaine wasn't, was a hacker.

Mac looked out over the street outside, sipped the now lukewarm coffee, and considered.

All the children that Jason and Elaine Blake had fostered had come to them via the agency – MI6, not adoption. They had been the children of agents or persons of interest. Did Elaine know that? The brief said not; what he had learnt of the Blakes' marriage said not. Unfortunately, reports of Elaine and reality were proving wildly contradictory. The reason it mattered was that the first child the Blakes had taken in was now Special Agent Madison Turner of the CIA, based in their London Office. And Elaine had dropped in to see her on the way from Cardiff to Paris.

A glance at the screen in front of him showed that the Frankfurt flight booking had been made on Wednesday evening. That was after Elaine had left the UK. That meant either she had found out on her own, which seemed unlikely given everything else that she had done after arriving in Paris, or someone else had found out and told her. Madison was the most likely person to do that. The temptation to phone London and ask her was great. It was also impossible. Not because they worked in different agencies and different countries, but because he was supposed to be on radio silence. His orders were to find the evidence on his own, no backup, avoid all contact, and don't come back until the job's done. Such fun.

If Madison had made the discovery, she had to have contacted Elaine to pass it on. How? Phone was the obvious answer.

He took his phone from his pocket and dialled the number he had for Elaine. It registered as 'phone not in use'. Had she dropped the number for a new one? Not have roaming on her plan? No – he'd read the file, the detailed background checks. She had roaming on her phone plan. Though given that she hadn't left the UK in over twenty-five years, not even for a honeymoon, it seemed unlikely that that resulted from anything other than it being included in the package she was on. Maybe she'd simply turned her phone off. There was no way for him to tell.

He gained access to her email account simply enough. There were lots of emails. Mostly spam. All of it unread for the last three days. Nothing from Madison, nothing that looked encrypted, and nothing with awkward phrasing to suggest a coded message. He checked the Spam, Junk and Trash folders, just in case.

No phone, no email. Not that he could trace, anyway.

Just to be on the safe side, he checked if her phone contract was still active.

It was.

Then he checked for activity in her bank account.

Nothing.

Mind, given that she'd taken ten thousand in cash and a banker's draft for £450k, it was hardly likely she'd be running short of funds in three days.

Sitting back, he had to admit to a grudging admiration for Elaine Blake. She was a total amateur, and yet she was running rings around him. Then there was just how lucky she got for no obvious reason. She didn't have to charm barmen to tell her about their customers. She was just her; honest, natural, genuine. The word mumsy sounded too twee, but she kind of was. It was obvious when she talked about her family that she cared. Deeply. That would give people a reason to confide. He wished he'd met her in better circumstances. Though, in all fairness, he had. Part of checking up on her a few years ago. He'd written her off as a mousy suburban housewife and paid little heed.

He shook that point from his head and went back to the computer. Elaine was looking out for her son, Lazlo. Though she now knew he wasn't as loyal to her or the UK as she had originally believed. Fifteen more minutes and he found another point of interest. Also on Wednesday, another booking made in the name of Lazlo Zakis for a flight to Geneva.

He closed the laptop.

That was as good a choice as any other he had.

CHAPTER THREE

An hour on Google did little to enlighten Elaine. The answers made no more sense than the cypher.

Though getting nowhere with her quest, she remembered how much money she currently had access to. She might as well use it while she could. She had a plan and a smile on her face by the time she put the phone away.

That smile broadened as she stood outside The Grand Hotel Kempinski and looked up at the impressive frontage.

Wow!

Wow!

Just wow!

Maybe not.

Oh, go in. What kind of rainy day am I saving the money for? Memories are more important than cash and let's face it, it's beyond time to make some good memories. Even eye-wateringly expensive ones.

Despite wearing jeans and being a touch grungy, Elaine held her chin high and walked confidently. She quickly amended her gait as her weight seemed too heavy on the bridge from the pavement over what appeared to be an open-air dining area below. A blue-uniformed young man looked her up and down. She clearly fell short of the expected dress code, but he offered a smile and opened the door for her.

She moved forward and stepped into the most opulent foyer she had ever been in. Highly polished beige marble flooring stretched before her. She was glad she wore trainers – she feared she might go skating otherwise. The lighting was subdued, but sufficient. The occasional furniture, muted and relaxed, looked comfortable. A grand piano shone to one side. Even the check-in desk had been designed for elegance as well as function. The back-lit privacy shield glowed golden.

Black-shirted receptionists stood behind the desk, one looking down her nose at Elaine. "Are you lost?"

If that look was intended to cow Elaine, it had the opposite effect. The worm had turned. She wouldn't allow anyone to treat her that way again. She was as good as anyone. *I'm better than Ladderman, better than his decisions for me.*

"No." Elaine didn't like the young woman's attitude. "But if you'd like to lose your job, keep up that attitude and I'll be having words with your boss."

She saw the girl's eyes narrow and her lips purse.

"Perhaps I can help?" The slightly older man moved from the other side of the desk, and the first receptionist offered a saccharine smile and moved away.

Elaine's own narrowed glare relaxed as it moved away from the girl and to the young man now in front of her. "I'd like a room overlooking the lake for three nights."

"Let me check our availability."

As she appreciated the fluency of his English, Elaine prepared to be told the hotel was fully booked. If so, this boy would need to give the girl lessons on how to brush off unwanted guests with style.

"Ah, yes." He looked up at her. "We have a Deluxe Junior Suite with lake view available for three nights." Then he named a price that surprised Elaine. She believed the Savoy in London charged more than that per night for a standard room. She might not travel, but she had always enjoyed getting on the internet to dream.

"That's great, thank you." She smiled as she placed her prepaid card on the counter: somehow getting out wads of cash here seemed rather crass.

The receptionist, whose badge named him Kurt Weiner, smiled as he took the card and processed the check-in. As they completed the paperwork, Elaine put her holdall on the floor, resting it against the desk. The way her back ached from carrying it, she resolved to get herself a decent backpack tomorrow.

"If there's anything we can do to help, just call on us. The concierge is here twenty-four hours a day and if you need anything more, the Lady in Red will be happy to help."

Elaine frowned. "Lady in Red?"

Kurt pointed discretely across the way. Elaine did indeed see a lady in red; she was currently talking to another lady, that one in a hijab and a trouser suit from Donna Karan.

"The Lady in Red is our guest ambassador. It's her job to develop a personal relationship with our guests to best anticipate their needs."

Personal anticipation of guest needs, huh? A warm idea of luxury seeped through Elaine. Indulgence, but why not? "So, if I need to go on a proper spending spree and have a pamper session, she's the lady to help me arrange that?"

Kurt smiled. "She certainly is." He picked his hand up, his crooked finger the classic gesture of calling someone forward. "And I'm sure our spa would be more than happy to help you relax during your stay." A uniformed porter arrived. Kurt passed over her room key and spoke in French to the man, before turning back with a smile. "Enjoy your stay, Mrs Hyde."

She smiled, accepted back her payment card, and followed the porter to a generously proportioned lift. On the third floor, he led her to the right and at the third door, used the key to open it, allowing Elaine to enter first.

She thanked him and took three steps before she stopped and gaped at what lay before her.

This sitting room area alone was bigger than her lounge in Cardiff. Double sliding doors led into the bedroom area, but what stood before her caught her attention. Floor to ceiling windows offered the most incredible view of the Jet D'Eau. The astounding pressure defied gravity. The jet shot up at least a hundred feet into the air, to send the water high before curving back to the lake in a graceful arc of white and rainbow mist before the clearest indigo sky. It seemed October, and Autumn, had decided to be clean and crisp. Grey and damp had been left behind in Blighty and Paris.

"I like Geneva," she breathed.

"Glad to hear it, Madame."

She jumped at the sound of the young man's voice and turned to face the porter, who had taken her pack into the bedroom for her. He faced her with a smile.

"Is there anything I can get for you, madame?"

"Actually, yes. A little information, if you wouldn't mind. The boutique in the lobby. What time does it stay open to?"

"Seven, but I'm sure they'll stay open longer for the right customer."

That idea just made her smile wider. "I'm sure they would." But she wasn't sure she was that kind of customer.

"One other thing, I've not been to Switzerland before. What's the etiquette on tipping?"

The boy smiled. "If you think you've had excellent service, feel free to tip, but we're all paid a living wage here, so it's not compulsory, and we include service charges in restaurant prices."

"That's good to know." She smiled. "I've never been good at figuring out what percentages were." Which was a complete lie because she'd always been very good at maths. "So, I hope this isn't an insult." She had reached into her pocket and pulled out a twenty euro note.

He stepped closer and took the note. "Thank you, madame. Shall I let the boutique know you will be down?"

Now this was service she'd like to get used to. "Yes, please. Thank you."

Left alone again, she took off her shoes and socks to enjoy the sensation of the deep pile carpet. Ever nervous, more so now, she checked the suite door had locked before entering the bedroom. She'd never seen a double bed so wide—three pillows wide! Luxury indeed, but to be savoured later. For now, she had other things to do. With the hotel looking over the lake, no one could look in, so she didn't worry about the wide-open curtains as she stripped to her underwear.

From her bag, she pulled a simple black jumper dress. Opaque black tights, and low-heeled shoes with matched shoulder bag. A quick brush neatened her hair; she added mascara and lip liner, ready for what lay ahead. She checked she had the room key, then headed out. The boutique was still open. She browsed to find that not only did they carry some classic pieces she liked, but they also actually had her size. They even had the trousers pinned for hemming to the exact length, promising that they would be ready by ten the next morning for her. She took her other items and headed out.

A glance around showed the Lady in Red was free. On approaching, she felt rather odd, awkward, but the lady welcomed her and put her at ease.

An hour later, Elaine was sitting at the bar on the second floor. Her purchases safe in her room, she sipped perfectly chilled white wine, feeling at peace in a way she hadn't in years, possibly ever. The terrace doors stood opened, but it was too cold to sit outside, so instead she swirled her drink and looked into the darkness, the bright spots of light across the way unfocused.

What am I doing?

The excitement of the train journey, her arrival in Geneva, the hotel, the shopping, her arrangements for tomorrow – had all been fun distractions, but there was no getting away from what was going on. Whatever might be going on – that was the big problem. She really didn't know.

Evidence of treachery, but what evidence? If she decoded the results of the cypher, would she understand? What about Lazlo? And-

A tanned male forearm appeared in the left of her vision. It seemed golden against the shining pristine white of the bar, a left arm. Which meant that its owner was standing facing her. And closer than was strictly necessary, given that she was the only one sitting at the bar. Others luxuriated in the seductive lighting and soft comfort of the leather couches. Some brave souls had even gathered on the terrace, but as far as she knew, until now, the bar had been solely her territory.

He said something, but she didn't recognise the language, didn't understand.

She turned her head to look at him. Nice looking, if you liked chisel-jawed handsome. The almost complete lack of lines suggested Botox or a facelift, teeth so white and perfect they couldn't be natural. He wore tailored black trousers, a white silk shirt, and the untied bow tie was straight out of the last Harlequin romance she'd read. She bit her lip not to laugh in the man's face.

"Hello." She'd tried for neutral, but the urge to laugh had put such a wide smile on her face she didn't think she'd hit it.

"Ahh, English?"

His accent sounded generic European, like received pronunciation that didn't originate anywhere, but wandered all over the place.

"May I buy you a drink?"

She glanced meaningfully at the large glass in front of her. "Seems this one hasn't evaporated yet." When she looked back at him, his features were fixed in that same smile, but his eyes screamed confusion. "It's okay, people say I don't have a sense of humour. It's not true. I do. But it's kind of weird and most don't get it. Never mind. Thank you, but no, I have a drink."

Back on ground he understood, he gave her come-to-bed eyes. "Perhaps the next one?"

Elaine was still trying not to laugh. "Perhaps." Turning to the bar, she looked away to sip the wine. She could have fun with this, but she really didn't want to. The idea of what she needed to do weighed too heavily.

"What brings you to Geneva, lovely lady?"

This time her stomach turned over. She swallowed, placed the glass carefully back on the bar before she presented a serious face the man. "My late husband."

The million-candle smile dimmed somewhat, but he recovered. "Will you scatter his ashes on the lake?"

I'd rather dance on his grave. That thought surprised her, she hadn't realised her emotions ran so venomous. "No. Just sorting out his last affairs." Unfortunately, that word brought up pictures of Keira, and the memory of betrayal. Being able to look back now without the pain, she realised just how much she had learnt from Jason. Like not to let anyone walk over her again.

"It is a recent loss then, non?"

She looked down at her wedding ring. "Very."

"I am sorry."

The arm on the bar moved a fraction of an inch further away. He was looking for an exit strategy about now.

"I'm not." When she looked into his brown eyes again, she saw surprise. "But let's be honest here." She kept her voice friendly and light and leaned in speaking for his ears only. "You don't fool me. Your hands clearly state that you've never done a day's work in your life. Your looks are too clean cut to be entirely natural. Your accent is wandering all around central Europe. I'd suggest sticking with the Italianate, you do that best. And while a dalliance with you might be fun, you wouldn't get the purse from it that you're looking for. If you strike out elsewhere, and I'm still around later, I'll be happy to share a drink with you, but right now, all I want is to be alone."

He offered her a smile, a small salute, and then sauntered away. She watched him go. *Nice butt. Shame really.*

* * *

Mac looked at the phone like it might turn into a cobra. This might well be the stupidest idea he'd come up with yet. Problem was, it was pretty much the only idea he had come up with.

Radio silence was all very well, but that didn't mean he was without contacts. They heard things, told him things. That was how the game worked.

Jason was double crossing his wife, not just bedding Keira and beating Elaine, but, if the rumours were true, by squirrelling away that extra in a secret Swiss bank account. And where did he get that money? A favour for a favour was the grease in their gears, but if these stories could be borne out, there was more to Jason's little extra. A bribe here, a back hander there, withholding and fencing recovered goods, failure to surrender seized funds.

If people knew about those activities, and the agency didn't, what more didn't they know?

This had started with Jason supposedly having acquired evidence of a traitor in their midst. He hadn't entrusted that evidence to anyone, hadn't passed it on to his superiors. Why not? Was he so arrogant to think that he could bring the traitor in alone?

Mac thought for two seconds. Yes, Jason was that arrogant.

Was Jason stupid enough to try blackmailing a traitor? Quite possibly, that went hand in hand with arrogance.

The next question, where was the bank account? How much did it contain? Did anyone else have access to it?

Jason, obviously.

But what about Elaine?

She might not be named on the account, but his second search of the Cardiff house showed that she'd taken her passport, her and Jason's marriage and birth certificates, and Jason's death certificate. A little snooping uncovered the fact that she'd procured a copy of Jason's will too. That was the kind of official documentation that would get even a Swiss bank manager to pass things to a wife.

So that meant it was possible that two people could get into that bank account, and Mac wanted to get his hands on either of them. Preferably Elaine. A live Jason would lie, and dead men told no tales.

More importantly, it was clear Mac wasn't the only one now looking for Elaine Blake. Jason hadn't had the evidence with him in Prague. The agency didn't have it and it seemed the people it implicated didn't have it either, or they wouldn't have tried calling Elaine for it. If all sides thought Elaine had it, everyone would be chasing her.

He had to get to Elaine first. Good as she had already proven herself to be, he had to get her out of this game. She didn't belong and she could get herself killed.

That shouldn't matter to him, but it wasn't his job to look the other way when random British Citizens got themselves murdered. Elaine Blake definitely fit the description of random, so he had to do something.

He made the call.

CHAPTER FOUR

Heart pounding like she'd run across Europe, Elaine sat up in the bed and cursed the repeating bad dreams. Her head spun in turmoil from nightmares dreamt and real. Restful sleep was impossible.

Go home, you're useless.

The words echoed in Elaine's ears as she sat in her suite and looked out over the growing dawn. Jason's voice in her head usually spurred her to defiance. In these early hours, with her confidence at its lowest, she wondered if he was right.

No, she couldn't afford to think that way.

It was Monday morning. *The* morning.

After a weekend of some extreme pampering and increasingly cold sightseeing, shopping and spending more freely than she had ever allowed herself to do before, Elaine now had to face reality again. She looked in the mirror, pleased by what she saw. She looked better than she had in years. Actually, after shaping wraps, a facial, a proper dye job and haircut in long layers to bring out her curls, with light makeup, and the subdued trouser suit, she didn't just look better than she had in years; she looked better than she ever had. The fact that the pounds were dropping off because she hadn't eaten a full meal in days wasn't hurting, either. Dieting didn't come into it. She'd been skipping meals because she wasn't getting hungry. She had gone to dinner each night, ordered but picked rather than eaten. There was a nagging suspicion that she should apologise to the chef. The food was fabulous, each new dish tasted delightful, she simply couldn't eat. A few mouthfuls, and she was done.

Not like me at all. But then, neither is that reflection.

Packing was quick. She hadn't actually brought as much as she might have – mostly thermal underwear and thick socks, which she now wore, and thankfully, a lovely new lady-back rucksack. Unlike standard rucksacks designed for men, the lady-back metal supports were shorter, so it didn't dig into her glutes as she walked. Her black boots looked good enough, but she'd need extra padding to walk in them all day. As she reached for her pack, she looked around the suite, enjoyed the view one last time. The bed was so wide she'd actually slept in it sideways on Saturday just because she could. A bed, and a night, made in heaven. Shame then that the nightmares had been so hellish. She gave a sad smile as she picked up the rucksack. It would have been nice to have shared the weekend with someone, but...

But it did no good to dwell on such things. As she stepped into the elevator, she grinned with surprise to see the man from the bar on Friday night. He looked tired for nine-thirty in the morning.

"Hello," she said as she stepped in. The doors closed. "Good weekend?"

"Si, signora, molto buono. E tu?"

She nodded and smiled. "Not bad, not bad at all."

He laughed. "You English. Always the understatement."

He allowed her to leave the lift first as she headed to check out and he simply left the hotel. For a moment, she waited for a receptionist to be free, only to be surprised again by the cordial greeting.

"How can I help this morning, madame?"

Elaine wondered if the congeniality was because the girl didn't recognise her or because she got a ticking off on Friday. Not that it mattered. She slipped her key onto the counter.

"I'm checking out but would like to leave my baggage here for the day. Can you manage that, or do I need to see the concierge?"

"I can arrange that for you, Mrs Hyde."

The voice came from the man who appeared at her side. She turned to the porter from Friday night. "Thank you." He took up her rucksack and headed for the concierge's area. Elaine turned back to the female receptionist again. She smiled, agreed her stay was wonderful and thanked the girl for helping her as she took the receipt, since she didn't want to give an email address. As she turned away, the porter returned, giving her a ticket to collect her bag later.

"Can I call you a taxi?"

She shook her head. "No, thank you."

"It's very cold."

She looked out of the glass front of the building. "It's a beautiful day. Besides, I enjoy walking."

Elaine thanked the man again, then stepped out into the day.

Bracing!

Ice blades sharpened in her lungs as she breathed deep. November had arrived with a bite and the frigid air stung with every lungful. Still, not far to go. About five hundred metres, in fact. With the lake on her left, she walked calmly down the pavement, even if her heart beat a tattoo and her throat dried at the prospect of the approaching meeting. The sightseeing over the weekend had more than tourist value, she'd figured out a thing or two walking around.

As she reached the crossroads where she could go to the Pont du Mont-Blanc, she looked up at the building. Overly square and a little out of place on the corner against the more traditional architecture, the seven-storey building which housed Coutts & Co SA bore a massive sign near its roof that said 'Rolex.'

"The Watch Tower," Elaine said as she stopped for a moment and looked up at the sign. "Sometimes, Jason, you are far too literal."

She didn't have an appointment, which might have been a criminal offence given the way the receptionist reacted.

"Don't have a relation working in the Kempinski, by any chance, do you?"

That didn't impress the woman either. After half an hour of waiting, she showed Elaine inside to what seemed less a bank and more a paperless office. Another hour passed and finally Elaine sighed and sat back. This really was going exactly as expected. Badly.

"So let me get this straight," she said, shifting to sit up again. "You believe I am Jason's wife. You believe he is dead. And you believe I am his sole beneficiary."

"Of course, Madame Blake. You have provided all the necessary documentation." Herr Schmidt waved his hand over said documentation. Thank God this man had accepted the copy of the will and not demanded the original. He had also said that as Monsieur Blake's widow, she had the right to the money.

"And you are happy to transfer his account balance into my account?" She had opened a new account here, and transferred in all the funds from London, knowing that this would be harder to trace than that was.

"Already done."

"Tell me again," *because I will never get over it*, "how much was that?"

"Four million, one hundred and three thousand and twenty-eight Euros, eighteen cents."

Over four million. *Four million!* She'd spent the last twenty years scraping to pay off the mortgage on a house worth a tenth of that. *Jason, you are a selfish bastard. Hopefully, were.*

"Okay, then what's the problem with the safe deposit box? I have the key." That lay on the table with the paperwork. "You admit that it's one of yours, the one for Jason's box, so why can't I have access to that?"

The man looked uncomfortable. "Monsieur Blake, he put the caveat of a password upon the box. I cannot give you access until you give me the password."

"But Jason never told me the password."

The man shrugged. "My hands are tied."

"I don't know the password."

He offered the ghost of a shrug. "But you knew your husband."

Don't bet on it.

"What would he use as a password?"

Good question. A memory surfaced. Now she shrugged. "The Big One?"

The banker's brows raised. "He'd use that?"

She nodded. He'd typed it so often, she had figured out his home computer password. She'd used it a few months ago when she'd needed administrator rights to do something while he was away. Why, oh why, had she ever given him such control? Still, those days were over now. "Whatever else you can say about Jason, he wasn't lacking in ego. But I take it from your reaction it's not the right password?"

Sadly, he shook his head. "Non. May I offer you a coffee while you think about it?"

She suspected she would need something stronger. "That would be most welcome."

Schmidt was gone long enough to grow the coffee himself, so she was a little surprised when he came in without any. "Forgive me, I was called in to consult with another of the partners," he said as he moved back behind his desk. "Have you thought what the password might be?"

She nodded, uncertain she'd picked the right one.

"Godiva."

He shook his head.

"Coventry?"

Another negative. She went through several variations. Nothing.

The stern-faced gatekeeper interrupted them with two coffees. Bone china cups, with elegant silver milk jug and sugar bowl. Once the woman left, Schmidt asked Elaine how she'd met Jason. Honesty was easy, she'd met Keira a couple of days before at the Uni orientation, they shared halls, and they had become friends. Accepting an invitation to a foreign film night struck Elaine as a good thing to do, even though she didn't like many foreign language films, unless in German, because she just didn't get the nuances of what was going on. But it had all been part of the plan. *Fit in, be normal. Never, ever even think about what you did.*

She hadn't revealed it then, she didn't tell Schmidt now. They chatted as they sipped the refreshingly strong coffee.

"So, what did he love most?" Schmidt asked at last.

Lying. But she couldn't say that. "Keira." The name slipped out as she remembered the only fully naked photos Ladderman had passed her were of Keira. Jason's Lady Godiva. *All makes sense when you think about it.*

Elaine watched Schmidt move to the tiniest smile.

"That's the password, isn't it? Keira?"

A head tip confirmed it. "You see, you do know your husband."

She considered him. "That's why my name being Elaine surprised you. You expected Mrs Blake to be Keira."

"My apologies. I hadn't meant to display the reaction."

She shrugged. "It's no problem, and you didn't exactly show it, no raised brow or dropped jaw. You held too still a heartbeat too long. I take it that I can have the box now?"

He nodded and stood. "This way, please."

Elaine followed Schmidt to a private room, through more security than she expected in a building that looked the way this one did. But there again, bank, safe deposit boxes, had to be secure. She mentally shrugged it off and tried to be normal – which remained foreign territory for her.

"If you would wait here, I'll retrieve your box."

It was a comfortable room with a table and executive chairs, good carpet, and stylish decoration. It felt more like a home than a bank. Two doors led off; the keypad operated one she had stepped through and another identical one on the opposite side. Schmidt carefully hid the number he entered into the door control. Even so, as it opened, she saw yet another door, thick vertical bars, and solid crossbars. Soon he came back bearing a long thin box which he placed on the table.

"When you are ready, knock on the door and Monsieur Fischer will open for you."

Monsieur Fischer was a big man Schmidt had introduced her to on the other side of the door. The second she'd seen him, the word 'bouncer' screamed in her head. She nodded and thanked Schmidt as he left.

Once alone, Elaine dragged in a deep breath and looked at the box. She didn't know what she expected, but this was about seven centimetres by twelve, and probably about fifty centimetres long. There was an obvious lid, but for a moment, Elaine wasn't sure that she wanted to open it.

Don't be stupid. You've come this far. You can't stop now.

She checked the door, not in the least surprised when it just looked blankly back at her. Her hand was as steady as a rock as she unlocked the box. The lid came up easily. She didn't know what she was expecting, but it hadn't been another security box. Reaching in, she realised it wasn't actually a box. It was a bag, and that was inside a wire mesh anti-theft bag. She shifted and twisted it, pulled it from the steel box and placed it on the table. Inside, she saw nothing else, when she tipped the box up, nothing moved. She put the box aside and looked at the parcel. And the wire securing it was itself secured by a tumbler combination lock.

She would open it, but not here.

It was definitely a book. A fairly large one, though soft-covered. She picked it up and put it into her shoulder bag. She'd always had a penchant for large shoulder bags, being a reader and often taking a book with her. The package fit easily and snugly into her bag.

I'm doing the right thing.

CHAPTER FIVE

Mac pushed his worries aside as he looked at the woman now with him. As always, his first thought on seeing Keira Southgate was that the woman needed a good meal. Now wrapped up in a thick wool coat, a big fake fur hat on her head, she looked like a walking coat rack, lost in the bulky items. He grew more concerned to see how sunken her eyes had become.

"Where is she?"

He resisted the temptation to say 'Geneva,' since he was picking Keira up from Geneva Airport.

"She's staying at the Grand Hotel Kempinski."

"Sounds nice." Keira's voice sounded odd, raw.

"It is."

"What's she doing?"

Mac didn't respond. His research suggested Elaine had taken a train from the Gare Saint-Lazare to Geneva. Only on Saturday, when he caught a glimpse of her on CCTV near the Geneva train station had he realised she remained in the city. It had taken all of Sunday to track her down. He still didn't understand why she was here, but he needed to get her to give him the cypher and key and go home. Only that would get her out of this dangerous game. It might not make her safe, but she would be off the front line, a damn sight safer than wandering aimlessly around Europe. Not that she was aimless, he just didn't know what her aim was. "Just get her to return home with you."

"Why?"

"You know better than to ask questions." And he knew better than to answer them. Especially when he couldn't.

They pulled up outside the Kempinski. Mac paid the fare and slipped from the car, turning to offer Kiera a hand out. A skeleton would be fleshier. The thought juddered through him. He dropped the touch.

He nodded his thanks to the doorman as they crossed the bridge and entered the reception area marked out in warm and inviting hues. He pointed Keira to an area of brown leather chairs. Without a word, she moved across and sat down. Several people waited at the reception, but he could get his information elsewhere. He spotted a lady in a red jacket, clearly a member of staff. He considered what the best approach would be. Roughly his age, she seemed professionally happy to see everyone. As she handed some paperwork to the couple she spoke with, Mac noticed she wore no wedding ring. Schmoozing, it was then.

But even as he approached the woman, he heard the voice behind him.

"Keira?"

A glance over his shoulder revealed Elaine. Whilst definitely Elaine, she looked like a new woman. A more attractive woman. The redder hair, cut to a more flattering style, suited her. She wore a trouser suit that showed her figure, hugged it, enhanced it. It made her generous curves obvious. She held herself with a confidence previously missing. She could purchase a new outfit, even a new hair-do, but self-esteem wasn't for sale. That she'd found somewhere else. Something had changed her. Keira stood and the two women embraced.

Good. This is good.

Elaine might do for a friend what she would not do for him. She might go home. Mac shifted even as he tried to blend into the background. Elaine sat beside Kiera, so staying behind Elaine, he moved closer, and sat in the cluster of chairs behind the pair.

"… more me again."

"If you haven't been you," Keira asked, "who have you been?"

"A very scared, trapped little mouse."

From the sound of it, Elaine didn't plan on going back to that. The idea filled Mac with unaccountable pride.

"So, what now?"

Even Mac heard the bitterness in Kiera's unhappy tone. Grief finally catching up with her? Or was it the loss of Steve's income she missed since finding out that she wouldn't be getting the generous pay out Elaine had? Not that Keira hadn't grasped at every opportunity for a free ride up to – and including – now.

"Are you going to roar all over Europe?"

The rustle of fabric told Mac that Elaine shrugged.

"Maybe. Might even go further than that. Roar across the globe."

Mac spotted movement and looked to his right; the polished finish to the wall acted as a distorting mirror, but it showed him that Elaine reached out to touch Keira's arm.

"Look, Keira, I think it's way past time we were truly honest with each other. I love you like a sister. I love you more than my sister."

"You have a sister?" Keira sounded surprised.

Her surprise surprised Mac. The background check had revealed more than just a sister.

"Yeah, and a brother. But we don't talk any more than my parents and I do."

"I didn't think you had family." Keira sounded genuinely shocked. "None came to your wedding."

"They were invited but declined, well, they didn't even bother responding. Which was, frankly, something of a relief, and I've not reached out to them since. Nor do I want to. They have made it perfectly clear that they want nothing to do with me, and I couldn't be happier about that. But we're getting off topic here. I grew up a very different person to the one I am now. Something happened, and I decided I had to change. So, when I went to uni, I took that chance. I completely reinvented myself. New wardrobe; cut my hair to get rid of the dye; stopped with the makeup; threw out... I threw out what I could."

Mac had seen what she hadn't thrown out, her art. The thing that displayed the very heart of her.

"When I met you, I basically tried to mimic you, be you. It never worked, of course. It's not natural. I wanted to study art, but needed to support myself quickly, so I studied maths."

"You got better grades than I did."

Resentment hollowed that statement. Mac found himself learning as much about Keira as Elaine. Vindication of his never having liked Mrs Southgate.

"Yeah, well, I'm an excellent student, but I never loved the field. When you started seeing Steve, and Jason and I tagged along, it was just proximity. I remember thinking at one point, quite early on, that I wished you'd break up with Steve so I could dump Jason, but you never did. Slowly, I

started caring about Jason. He was nice to me. He seemed...
normal, kind, safe. I figured he wouldn't be like—"

Mac wondered what she hid by cutting herself off.

"He wouldn't be like the guys I had known before. I
thought he'd be good to me, good for me. And he was. For
a time. When Jason proposed, I said yes out of obligation. I
was thinking it was the normal thing to do. Not love, not
romance novel love, but it was safe, and I needed safe. I
figured it was good enough, that I'd cope with it for a lifetime.
If my family taught me anything, it was that relationships take
effort, you have to work at them to make them work, and I
was convinced Jason and I could manage that. I realised how
wrong I was before our first anniversary, but I stayed to try to
make it work. Turned out the only way to do that was fake
it, fake everything, constantly. It was exhausting. The only
good thing about my life was all the kids we took in."

Keira made a noise.

"What's that for?"

The sneer sounded before Keira spoke. "You have no
idea."

"What?" Elaine asked. Her voice by contrast was totally
relaxed. "That at least two of them might be Jason's?"

That floored Mac. Definitely not something the agency or
he were aware of.

"Oh, don't look at me like that," Elaine told Keira. "Just
because I don't say, doesn't mean I don't see."

"But it meant living with definitive proof of being
betrayed."

Elaine shrugged again. "No man can betray what isn't
there. Besides, I don't *know* they were his. Timings suggested
it. There again, Jason being blond with no outstandingly
notable features made seeing his image in the faces of kids

fairly easy, even when they definitely weren't his. Add to that the fact that I can't have kids, taking in other peoples was my only chance at motherhood, I found it all rather easy. Whoever their parents were, it's not the kids' fault, can't blame them. Things didn't always work out so well, but not because I didn't try. Things might have worked out better for you had you'd tried harder to accept LaTrice."

Keira gasped. "How did you know?"

"Jess and LaTrice have the same profile. They have to be sisters."

"Half-sisters," Keira bit out the words.

"Keira, are you really alright?"

Mac heard genuine concern in Elaine's voice.

"Of course I'm not," Keira snapped. "I've lost my husband. One I loved."

"Really?" Laughter bubbled in the tone. "So how come you were fucking my husband?"

"Elaine!"

"Oh, don't, Keira. I've seen photos. I found them when looking at stuff after he'd gone missing."

Mac frowned. Why would she make it seem like she'd found them on her own? Why not blame him? She had no reason to care about driving a wedge between Keira and the organisation.

"I suspect those guys sent to search the house found them, too. Maybe even took copies. Probably put them up in the office loos to wank over."

Keira didn't respond to that, something to be grateful for. But Elaine was spot on. Jeff had taken copies and had pinned and used them as guessed.

"You know what?" Elaine sighed. "It's okay. I don't actually mind that we shared him. Not that it was just you and me. It has to be said, Jason was an incredible lover. It seems he had a lot of practice."

Silence fell heavily. Mac started re-evaluating some of his past interactions with Jason and Steve. The thing about their line of work was that you never really knew who you were working with. They all had to be consummate liars.

"I miss Steve."

"Oh honey, of course you do."

The distorted image on the wall showed Elaine pulling Keira into a big hug. They had been friends for a long time, and that didn't just go away. Elaine held Keira as she spoke softly, and Mac had to concentrate to listen.

"The difference is you actually loved Steve, and he loved you."

"I did love him."

Elaine sighed. "What about Jason? Did you care for him, too?"

Keira nodded. "It was different, but I loved being with him."

"You mean having sex with him? Well, you know what they say; Too much love will kill you." Elaine forced a laugh that she clearly didn't feel. "Keira, Steve loved you. He loved his country, too. LaTrice was an accident in the line of duty, one he couldn't completely walk away from which, by the way, is a good thing. Though I suspect there were professional repercussions for him too. For you, Jason was convenient and fun, a distraction. I get that, and I don't blame you. I guess the first time for you and him was some spat with Steve, an act of rebellion?"

Mac saw movement in the big fur hat Keira still wore as she leaned on Elaine's shoulder. "I was drunk and angry."

"And once he'd had you, Jason had all the leverage he needed to keep you coming back. And all the skill to make it feel good despite any guilt."

Low-level guilt, Mac assumed, and realised that Elaine was giving Keira an out, forgiving her trespasses. If the small sobs that escaped Keira were anything to go by, it was exactly what she needed – and a demonstration of Elaine's generosity. A few moments later, Keira sat up again. Mac saw her wiping her eyes.

"When are you coming home?"

Elaine sighed. "Not sure. It hasn't felt like a home for some time."

"But I miss you. It's like I've lost my best friend as well as my husband." Keira sniffed. "I'm not sure how to cope."

"You haven't lost me, sweetheart. I'm just somewhere else right now. We've been friends for twenty-five years, and that doesn't disappear overnight. Besides, you've got Jess, and if you opened your heart a little bit more, you'd have LaTrice too."

"But you have to come home."

Keira sounded like a whiny kid.

"Why?"

"Why not?"

She shrugged. "Things I need to sort out first."

"Like what?"

"My head." The laugh in Elaine's voice didn't detract from the obvious pain.

"What about your job?" Keira asked. "You need to get back to that."

"Well, no, that's not going to happen. I hereby give you a month's notice, which is covered by the remaining five days including today, of compassionate leave that I am entitled to, and the eleven days of annual leave I've accrued and not taken this year, which would leave four days unaccounted for and I am sure HR will tell payroll to deduct that from my final salary payment. I'll find a way to send an email to that effect sometime today, they'll need it in writing."

A pause hit him; Keira was probably gaping at Elaine.

"But… You can't… I mean…"

"Keira, I just did."

"But what are you going to live on?"

It looked like Elaine shrugged.

"Half a million won't last long if you keep staying in places like this."

"True, but why did I get it in the first place?"

Mac struggled with that one too, but his superiors had promised they had their reasons. He figured the reason was seeing what Elaine did with it, who she led them to.

"I'm kind of waiting for them to come grab it back, which is why I moved most of it to a personal off-shore bank account they can't touch."

"Is that why you're in Geneva? For banking?"

"Yes."

"I don't understand you."

"That's okay. Keira. Hate to say it, but you look exhausted. Guess it's all the travelling. It's lunchtime, and I for one am starving. There are some fantastic restaurants here. Shall we get some lunch and talk? I think we have a few things still to discuss."

Mac was in two minds whether to follow the women as they stood and headed for food. Another day he might give it a miss. Their chat was personal, it told him nothing useful, but the conversation might change at any moment. Besides, he was hungry too.

Five minutes later, Elaine and Keira were seated at a corner table where they read menus while Mac propped himself by the bar and ordered a pint of lemonade and a steak sandwich. The women made an odd-looking couple. Both head to toe in black, Elaine's red hair stood out vibrant and alive, while the blonde of Keira looked washed-out and tired. They were beyond earshot, and lip-reading was difficult over this distance.

An attractive woman sauntered into the bar, and Mac's concerns instantly redirected. The woman glanced at him, offered a barracuda smile, before she sat at the table right next to Elaine and Keira.

Shit.

Illyana Kuznetsov. Probably not her real name, but the only one he had for her. A mercenary. With the spread of Russian oligarchs and what they were prepared to pay to get their job done, she was rarely out of work, and her work was his business to stop. The fact that she was the one in Paris who had held Lazlo in check and tried to trap Elaine was just one more misdemeanour to hold against her. Would Elaine recognise her now she wasn't wearing the disguise she'd had on in the Trocadero? Regardless, with both Illyana and Keira knowing he was here, if either highlighted his presence in any way, Elaine would notice. He did not need that.

The waiter served Elaine and Keira, then moved on to take Illyana's order. His order arrived. He ate from habit rather than hunger. Always eat when you can, you never know when you won't be able to. Keira ate; Elaine encouraging her to do so. He saw Elaine moving things around her plate, but not actually eating. He'd known a girl who did that once. She'd been anorexic. He scrutinised Elaine's figure. She had visibly lost weight since he'd first seen her. Some of that was the clothes, some of it the posture. She didn't wear that dragged-down-by-life look any more. She sat straight rather than hunched. It wasn't just the subtle makeup enhancing her cheekbones; it was fewer pounds. Had she stopped eating? Combine that with greater activity, and anyone would lose weight. But she was still at a healthy level. There was nothing to worry about yet.

As he watched, Keira stood, Elaine pointed, and Mac realised Keira needed the ladies. He tensed to move, but Elaine moved first. She placed cash on the table and walked out. As tempting as it was to follow her, he glanced to Illyana, who hadn't moved. So, he couldn't. If Illyana was here for the same thing he was, keeping her away from Elaine was more important than following Elaine. So far, he'd always caught up with her, no reason to think he couldn't do it again.

Illyana's eyes switched from Elaine at the exit, to the door Keira had gone through. She wasn't certain which to follow. The waiter appeared, asking Illyana if the meal was acceptable, getting between Illyana and Elaine. For a moment, Mac had the upper hand. He saw what Illyana could not: Elaine didn't leave the hotel. At least, not through the front door. Suddenly, Illyana started complaining loudly in French. The waiter reared, somewhat taken aback, then she stormed out without paying.

"What happened?"

Mac turned to Keira, who had appeared at his shoulder. "Wait here."

He followed Illyana, as she all but ran up the stairs to ground level. He shifted position again and saw her move out into the street. She looked both ways, and spotted something, someone she followed.

What now?

Even as he wondered, he stepped aside for a porter in hotel livery. Mac was fairly sure Elaine remained in the hotel, which meant Illyana had taken off on a wild goose chase. What would Elaine do next? What had she told Keira? Moving back into the bar, Mac automatically nodded his thanks to the porter who stepped out of his way and moved to the corner table where Keira sat reading a note.

"What's that?"

She swallowed and looked up at him. She looked on the verge of being happy for the first time in a long time. "It's a note from Elaine." She handed it over.

Keira, love you dearly. Sorry I can't be around for you right now. I need to work out who I am. Tell the man who came for me in Paris that the Watch Tower is just down the road. It's Coutts Bank. Stay strong and I'll call when I can.

Your friend forever,

Elaine.

A note quickly scrawled on hotel stationery. Without a word to Keira, Mac turned, taking the note with him, and raced up the stairs to the lobby. The porter must have passed the note on, and Mac needed to speak to him. In the lobby he saw the man carrying a bag to a car for a stout older gentleman. After handing the bag over to a chauffeur and accepting a tip, the porter returned to the lobby. Mac intercepted him.

"Excuse me," he said, not giving the man chance to avoid him. "You gave this to my wife downstairs, what happened to the lady that gave it to you?"

The porter looked at the note and then up at Mac. "She left, sir."

"Did she say where she was going?"

"She said Rome might be nice this time of year."

CHAPTER SIX

The price of direct flights from Geneva to Frankfurt was prohibitive. So, Elaine took the advice of the travel agent and travelled by train which gave her the chance to log into their Wi-Fi and her email to send an official notice of resignation to work. She ignored the stack of unread emails in her inbox. The first leg of the journey from Geneva to Bahnhof Olten had been an easy two hours. At Olten she started shivering. Time spent with Keira had meant no time to change into warmer clothes. These trains might be better than the British ones, but changing in toilets was never fun. She'd probably end up putting her foot down the pan, or flushing while lacing her shoes, or knocking the tap and getting water all over herself. She'd rather freeze.

The second leg, to Frankfurt, was much worse. Not entirely the fault of the train company; they could have turned the heating up, but she soon had reason to be grateful they didn't. Passengers packed the train and a rather large man sat beside her. Gag-worthy body odour. Then at Freiburg, a family got on; two women with seven children between them. Seven children all of whom seemed to have a bell in every tooth, and not much in the way of good manners.

Sweaty man got off at Baden-Baden, but the family stayed. As did his stench, which appeared to have a life of its own. As the train pulled off again Elaine, unable to stomach anymore, went to find another seat. As she walked through the carriage, she caught sight of a mono-browed man in a thick black overcoat. His face didn't look like it understood the word smile and the way he scowled left her uncomfortable. Still, she couldn't read his thoughts and it wasn't her place to judge. She walked past and kept going to the next carriage, ignoring the idea that she'd seen him somewhere before under the assumption that he looked like pantomime villains everywhere.

She told herself not to be paranoid when she spotted him again half an hour later. He walked through the carriage, looking at people. Ice ran down her spine.

Probably nothing. She hunched into her seat. *He's not 'The Mono-brow Murderer', you've just got an overactive imagination. And paranoia.*

Paranoia doesn't mean they aren't out to get you.

STOP IT! He probably just needed to stretch his legs. He didn't look at me any longer than he looked at anyone else. He also didn't seem to move back down the carriage.

Paranoia crawled under her skin and wriggled like a thousand prickling bugs. Ladderman found her in Paris and he was with Keira in Geneva. Elaine didn't know how, but someone must be tracking her. Ladderman, yes. But was he the only one? Her not seeing Mono-brow before, didn't mean he hadn't been there before. She sat and worried about it all as they moved. Two minutes before they reached Mannheim Hauptbahnhof, Elaine headed for the toilet. She'd stowed her backpack in the luggage rack near that end of the carriage and when she came out of the toilet, other passengers had already stood, preparing to get off. She asked, in her best German, if the guy standing closest to her bag wouldn't mind passing it down to her. He did so with a smile and an expression that suggested surprise at the weight of the thing. Elaine thanked him and hoisted it onto one shoulder. Not having to go back into the carriage, reduced her chances of being spotted by Mono-brow. She left the train at the same time as the other passengers, using their mass to hide. This was one time she was happy to be below average height.

Stomach knotting as she disembarked early, she hoped that wasn't a fineable offence. She hoped for nonchalance as she scanned those around her and recognised no one. Once off the platform, she held back and allowed the crowd to pass. No sign of Mono-brow. Over-cautious had its dangers but beat the stupidity of under-cautious.

On stepping out of the station to the wide concourse in front, Elaine stood in awe of the station's impressive, classical, and well-maintained architecture as she slipped her arm through the second strap of the rucksack. Off to her left stood a tall grey building, but the red signage stated it to be the InterCityHotel. Part of her wanted to scream at the inappropriate use of Camel Case; the lack of spaces between capitalised words. Still, mostly she just wanted to get off the street and hide, the hotel looked as good an option as any.

The long-winded check-in stretched her nerves, thankfully, they didn't snap before she got the key. The bland beige and brown room on the fourth floor was more than adequate for her needs, yet Elaine found herself mourning the Kempinski. She didn't, however, mourn the room rate. While having money was great, with no idea of final destination, likely actions or activities, or even time frame, she had to control her spending. She dropped her bags on the floor, deadlocked the door, drew the curtains and undressed. The hot shower worked wonders to ease her tense muscles. Soft, fluffy towels even made her smile.

Dressed in joggers and a sweatshirt, she sat on the bed and pulled the bag from the safe deposit box onto her lap and grabbed her little notebook. Over the weekend she had started a journal, a timeline of all that happened. Somehow, writing it down made it less unreal. She added today's events. She needed a drink. Preferably a bottle, but human interaction struck her as too much trouble, and they didn't do room service here. Her stomach grumbled. She opened the minibar.

Peanuts and a tiny cola. *Oh joy.*

As she ate, she wondered what to do.

Keira wanted her to go home. That implied the organisation Jason and Ladderman worked for wanted her back in Wales too; Keira couldn't have found her on her own. Could she?

Elaine didn't think so, but a week ago she didn't think she'd be travelling across Europe with money from a secret bank account and a book of mysteries in her hand, so what did she know?

All irrelevant. She was pretty sure that Ladderman had been the bloke at the bar trying to blend into the scenery. The big question for her was, why would they want her to go home? They'd found nothing in the house. Did they think she had their evidence? In Paris, she'd told Ladderman about watch tower, and in Geneva she pointed him, well Keira, to the bank. The bank would have to stay within the bounds of confidentiality, but Ladderman might have the pull to overcome that. If it was still Ladderman doing the pulling. Mono-brow's interest was probably just a figment of her imagination. She remembered what else Ladderman said.

I want that evidence too. But I don't want either one of us to die for it.

A chill skated down her spine. She hadn't dwelt on that prospect until now. But if Ladderman followed her without her knowing it, who else might have? Lazlo had lied. His actions in Paris showed he was working for the people he had claimed held him captive. She remained unconvinced of Jason's demise, but she had his death certificate so unless he turned up, she would act the widow. And if he did turn up, there was a good chance at this point that she'd kill him. She'd want to. Hell, she already wanted to.

She shuddered as memories she'd been repressing for over twenty-five years resurfaced. That face. That bastard. The hand that reached for her even as—

No! She would not let her past control her any longer.

She had to deal with the here and now. Ladderman and Lazlo, and the different people they worked for, wanted the evidence Jason allegedly had. Evidence they clearly thought she now possessed. Well, Ladderman might not, he might believe she had nothing, which would explain why he wanted her to go home. Of course, if she did go home, everyone else would know where to find her, and everyone else might not be so ready to believe that she didn't have the evidence. She looked at the secured book on the bed.

She checked her notebook.

Watch Tower – the Coutts building in Geneva.

Godiva – a naked lady, Jason's mistress Kiera. And a password.

North Gate Spell – Even written out in front of her it made no sense.

What she'd discovered was that the North Gate Spell originated from a book by Steve Jackson, a role-playing book called *Sorcery!* The spell, as she'd copied from a fan page she'd found, read:

By Courga's grace and Fourga's pride
One lock made of golem's hide
Tumblers two sealed deep inside
I bid you portals open wide!

It didn't mean a bloody thing to her. She'd never played a choose your own adventure book.

With a huff of frustration, she read it again and again. Maybe the book itself would make it clear, only she didn't have a copy.

She took a breath and considered the cypher. Watch Tower held the safe deposit box. Godiva held the key to the password for that box. Logically then, the North Gate Spell would be how to get through this last layer of security, the combination to the external lock.

Of course, she could go buy a set of wire cutters, but that would look suspicious, and if she figured out the combination, she'd be able to open it before the shops opened tomorrow. She glared at the locking mechanism; she needed a combination of three numbers.

She reread the four lines of the spell.

Oh, you bloody idiot!

The numbers in those spell lines were now so obvious it was hard to credit that she'd not spotted them straight off.

She cursed herself, as she took up the security bag and turned the number disks to read 412.

It didn't open.

Balls!

What now? She couldn't think of anything else. Why would Jason have used the reference if it didn't mean anything? What if the fan site was wrong? Right numbers, wrong order? Well, it might make sense, wouldn't want to spoil the game, she supposed. If she remembered her maths correctly there were $3 \times 2 \times 1$ permutations of three numbers, so six possible combinations to try. It really would not take her that long to try the other five possibilities. She sighed and shifted the tumblers. Nothing. Next combination.

The lock snapped opened.

She wondered if this was how dogs who chased cars felt when catching one – she'd got what she wanted, but had no idea what to do with it. Fear washed through her. She wanted someone else to look first and then tell her everything would be okay. The memory of kissing Ladderman came unbidden to mind. Whatever else he might do, reassuring her seemed unlikely.

Carefully, she reached inside the bag and her fingers gripped... a book. The second of pause. What was she waiting for? The book to turn into a scorpion and sting her? She was holding a book in a bag. She pulled it free. Aware that other paperwork came with it.

Soft black textured leather covered the book, the page edges glittered old gold. She'd seen this kind of thing before; her grandfather had a Bible like this. She turned the book to view the spine. Indented lettering, Cyrillic. Uncertain what to do with it, she took its weight in both hands and allowed it to fall gently open in her hands. The paper was so thin she feared to touch it. Unable to read the script, she judged by appearance. This must be a Bible; no other book was set out like this. Since a couple of the pages had collapsed rather than opened, she carefully uncurled them to flat again. She saw no reason for the pages to open at this point, other than it was the middle of the book. She saw no signs of frequent reading, no bookmark, no marks on the paper.

Why would Jason consider a Russian Bible important enough to keep in a safe deposit box? She turned the bible over in her hands. Given the obvious age, it might have some intrinsic value, or Jason might be more sentimental than she gave him credit for. No, that didn't ring true. Jason had no family, and he was even less sentimental about that than she was about being estranged from hers. She looked at the other papers.

The photograph was obvious, even face down. A very worn, frequently looked-at photograph. Uncertain, almost afraid of what she would find, hoping it wasn't anything like Ladderman put on that damn memory stick, Elaine reached for the image. She chewed her bottom lip, turned the photograph over and saw a black-and-white photograph of a family. Mother, father, and two sons. She frowned at it. Not black and white, just very faded. A thin sliver of the edge retained stronger colour than the middle, suggesting it had once been framed and kept in sunlight. In the background she saw a lake or sea and part of a place sign. '"YANS'K"'. That told her nothing. She had no idea who these people were, but the man bore a strong resemblance to Jason. The clothes the couple wore suggested to her that the photo had been taken some time between the 1950s and 1970s. Possibly later if it was Eastern Bloc. Which would suggest that one boy could be Jason.

She looked more closely at the image. Was one Jason? The boys looked about four or five. She looked closer again. Not twins, but not many years between them, if even a full year. None of the family looked happy. The picture didn't match anything she knew or imagined of Jason's past. Though looking back, she had never really imagined much of Jason's childhood. When her parents had ignored their wedding invitation, Jason had told her he didn't have family. He always shut her down if she asked about his childhood. She put the picture on top of the Bible and turned to the other paperwork. The first thing she picked up was in Russian, a mystery she'd need help to translate. The second one looked official, possibly a birth certificate.

She placed each on the Bible. The last remaining letter lay crisp and white, trifolded into a standard DL envelope, addressed to Jason Blake. She opened it, shocked to see the logo of their local health authority, stunned when she read what the letter said.

The air ripped from her lungs – inhalation made impossible.

The letter confirmed a successful vasectomy, resulting in a zero sperm count and that unprotected sex would not result in pregnancy. She could only stare at the words as they swam before her.

Tears pushed forward. She forced them back to focus on the date of the letter. Two weeks before their wedding.

You bastard!

Pain exploded in and around her. Instinct told her to tear it up, but she couldn't. The letter crumpled in her hands as she crumpled forward, screaming out in agony, sobbing and shaking and unable to credit what he'd done. She'd told him well before the wedding that she wanted children, and he'd made sure she never had them before they even got married. God, all those years when she'd sobbed and apologised for being unable to provide an heir. All the times he'd thrown that inability at her!

Bastard!

The pain was so deep she found new furnaces of hate to incinerate them both.

Falling to her side on the bed, she was capable of nothing but crying. This betrayal beat all betrayals. This betrayal she would never forget, never forgive.

CHAPTER SEVEN

Rome might be nice this time of year.

Mac could virtually hear Elaine saying it. And she'd say it with that twinkle in her eye which guaranteed her not going to Rome.

Did that make her a bitch or a smarty-pants? Should he throttle or applaud her?

It made little difference when he hadn't been able to trace Elaine or Illyana after they left the Grand Hotel. He had seen Keira back to the airport and a return flight to England. Being rid of her and her maudlin brought relief. Her suggestion that she stay and keep him company hadn't appealed in the slightest.

He found a coffee shop and sat down with a latte to think.

Elaine had whatever money Jason had tucked away. That might be very little, or more probably, a whole lot. No way of knowing now the account was closed. So, the world was her oyster. Coutts kept safe deposit boxes at that Geneva address too, so it was possible, though Mac had no proof, that she'd taken something else from there as well. The evidence he wanted? If it existed. The safe deposit box, not the evidence. Though at this point he questioned the existence of the evidence too.

Stop overthinking.

Okay, in Elaine's place, what would he do now?

She might be rich. She might go anywhere she wanted to. But Lazlo would still shadow her. She clearly hadn't returned to the Jardin du Trocadero. Did she believe that Lazlo was trouble? Mac didn't have any evidence of that either. And there lay the real problem with this whole situation. No evidence. Not much in the way of certainty, and his job on the line if he didn't find some fast.

What did Elaine know?

1 – Jason was dead.

2 – Lazlo was lying.

3 – Mac wanted her to go home. So, she probably wouldn't.

Did she know Mac wasn't the only one after her? There was no way to tell, so he assumed not.

She must have suspected he'd get the message about Rome, or she wouldn't have left it. Which made Rome the one place she wouldn't go, just in case he did.

She knew Jason was dead.

But did she? Lazlo told her he and Jason were together. That put a huge question mark over Jason's death.

What would Mac do now if he wanted to know about Jason? He'd phone the boss, but Elaine didn't have the choice, and right now neither did he.

Start where the question arose. Where did Jason die? After this length of time, that scene would have been washed clean of any corroborating or disproving evidence. Would Elaine think that way though? Probably. She wasn't an idiot.

How much did Jason keep Elaine in the dark? Had she known Jason's itinerary? If so, she'd know about the conference in Frankfurt. In her position, he'd go there on the assumption that a live Jason would go there to make contact with his former life.

Mac drained the dregs of his coffee as he stood.

* * *

When Bromstad called the meeting, it wasn't in the office, something that surprised Madison, but she could hardly refuse it. They met on a bench facing the fountain of Bessborough Gardens, on the far side of the Thames from Vauxhall Cross.

"Alan," she greeted as she sat beside the waiting man. It felt odd to call him by his first name, but he had insisted in his note that she do so.

He didn't take his eyes off the fountain. "It's nice here, don't you think?"

It wasn't a test, just a question. She looked around. The octagonal fountain was nice, probably looked great in summer when it was on, but now it was just a fancy grey construction of concrete and metal. The lawn was green enough, the trees very well established, the planting providing good, if monochrome green colour. "It's nice enough," she admitted. "Nothing special."

The smile eased onto his face. "I think that's why I like it." He turned to her. "Did you manage to tie your mother down?"

That image amused Madison. "I managed to find out that she was, until this morning, in Geneva. I found a booking at the Kempinski Hotel in the name of an alias she had set up. I can't find any bookings for her away from Geneva, but that could be because she's not using her real name or the alias I know of, or it could be simply that she's travelling in a way that doesn't require names, like by train."

"Did you check car hire?" he asked.

She nodded. "I did, though in all honesty, I don't think Mom would drive. She's not that keen on driving in the UK, I doubt she'd enjoy being on the other side of the road."

"Never been to America then?"

"No. France is as far afield as I can find her travelling, day trips with the school and family when she was young, but back then, she was living in Kent, so Calais was closer than Oxford for her."

"If she was never a good traveller, she's taken to it well now."

Madison had to agree. "I'm not sure Mom was as bad a traveller as Jason made out. And I think she just needed a reason to travel and not to be with Jason."

This time Bromstad was frowning at her, and she wasn't entirely comfortable with the scrutiny. "Elaine is Mom, but Jason is Jason?"

Not something she wanted to discuss, and since there was no obvious question, she didn't respond.

"The rumours about his proclivities," Bromstad said quietly. "Did they extend to you?"

"I don't consider myself a victim, sir."

"I told you, Alan outside the office." It was a strangely avuncular tone, caring. "I'm glad you don't consider yourself a victim, Madison, but that doesn't make it right."

That she was the one who did everything she could to seduce Jason didn't absolve either of them of guilt, but she knew what had happened, as did Elaine. That they were both okay with that, relieved some of the guilt she felt for sleeping with her mother's husband. Emotionally, the fact that Elaine was her foster not birth mother didn't come into it. "No, Alan, it doesn't. But Mom and I are the ones that have to live with it. Jason can rot in hell for his actions."

There was a pause, Bromstad was clearly considering what he had to say before he said it. "Do you think he is dead?"

"According to all official sources, he's dead. However, Lazlo told Mom that he's not. Without a secondary reliable source, I'm not completely prepared to believe he's alive, but without seeing his body, I'm not completely prepared to believe he's dead, either."

Bromstad nodded, his thoughts engaged.

"Alan, I'm grateful that you're taking a personal interest in this case, but can you tell me why?"

Again, the pause for consideration. "When you brought the situation to my attention, every argument you presented backed up reasoning I've been presenting to my superiors. I don't have the personal connection you do, which is, in all honesty, the reason I didn't want you investigating the matter at the beginning. What little we do know about the evidence Jason Blake was reported to have, is that it relates mainly to the Eastern Bloc. Of most specific interest to the US of A, it relates to activities in Ukraine and Russia. The activities there, well, they should concern us all, but it's not my area. However, this case, this I can take an interest in. Sometimes I find I must focus on a small detail to see the larger picture."

Standing, he reminded her to keep him informed before he moved to step away. He stopped, turned back to her.

"You have to understand that this is a double-edged sword, Madison. Thus far I am impressed with your work, and indeed all that your mom is doing. But if I have to, I will use that sword against you."

CHAPTER EIGHT

Back in the comfort of jeans and multiple layers, including thermals, Elaine adjusted the pack on her shoulders. More research at the Mannheim Library had revealed that one of the conferences Jason had mentioned ran Thursday and Friday, so she booked herself a place under the name Heike Frisse – the German lady whose passport she had inadvertently picked up after a collision in Paris. She wondered a moment how that poor woman was managing without her passport.

The library also gave her the opportunity to message Madison. With the conference still two days away and figuring that being in any one place too long might be bad for her health, she'd moved on.

Paranoid, much?

Perhaps, but movement at least gave her the illusion of safety. It might be the reaction to having stayed too still for the last two decades, but now she wanted to move more. To travel. Hitch-hiking was probably not the wisest thing ever to do, but while no seasoned traveller, she was no wet-behind-the-ears teenager on a gap year either. She also lacked the qualities to make her much of a target—she was honest enough to admit not being sexy. Which might also explain why it took a while to get picked up. Finally, a middle-aged man in an expensive looking Audi pulled up beside her, electric window rolling down. The car was immaculate, leather upholstery and all the gadgets, not the type that usually stopped.

"Alles ok? Brauchen Sie Hilfe?"

Her time in Germany had improved her German somewhat, he asked if she was okay and needed help. She leaned down to speak with him.

"Ich bin Richtung Norden unterwegs. Ein bißchen ausruhen wäre schön. Können Sie mich ein Stückchen mitnehmen?" She hoped that made sense: she was heading north and could he help her out. He understood her imprecise pronunciation.

"Wohin genau?"

She blinked and searched her memory. Oh! He wanted to know where exactly she was going.

"Frankfurt. Aber ich muss nicht vor Donnerstag da sein." She hoped Donnerstag was Thursday; when learning she had forever been mixing Donnerstag and Dienstag, which should be Tuesday.

"Ich fahre nach Wiesbaden. Wäre das ok?"

Wiesbaden was, she thought, a short way west of Frankfurt. And she smiled. "Ja, das wäre wunderbar. Danke."

She opened the door, surprised by the sound of the boot popping open as the man himself stepped out of the car. He offered to put her rucksack in the boot, to give her more leg room. She smiled and handed him the baggage and they both got into the car.

As he drove, they talked. Elaine learned that Wilpert Ackermann was a pharmaceutical rep, which explained the boxes in the boot. After being in Stuttgart for a few days giving a training course to new staff, he was heading home. He couldn't wait to see his wife and children. It all sounded so nice, so normal. Elaine said she was travelling around Europe, largely aimlessly, taking time out from life, doing the gap year she missed as a teenager. She felt a total fraud. Not wanting to bring any trouble on this man's head she told him to call her Annie. Not exactly a lie, Annie being her middle name. Wilpert asked if she wanted to stay the night with him and his family. She demurred. He insisted. Besides, Frankfurt being all of three-quarters of an hour from Weisbaden, he would drop her off on the way to work on Thursday if she stayed the two nights.

"Let's wait until I've met your wife. She might not be so open to the idea."

Wilpert assured her that Ailse would be fine with it.

An hour later, Ailse was completely fine with the idea of her staying; in fact, she was surprisingly insistent. The boys, Stein and Dieter, turned out to be great kids. It helped that Elaine explained to Stein, working on his computing homework, what database normalisation actually meant and how to achieve it.

"Wow," the youngster said. "You made that seem so easy. Much better than my teacher."

Once she'd translated the fast spoken German, she automatically hugged the boy; that felt like the first praise she'd had in years.

As she sat in the spare room that night, she picked up Jason's Bible, fumbled it, shocked by what she saw. Knees shaking at the prospect of a new mystery, she sat on the edge of the bed, held the book properly and looked at it. Soft black leather and gold edged leaves. Then she twisted the edge, turning a straight edge into a wedge. Not only did it have a beautifully painted fore edge of a pastoral church scene, and more numbers, starting with 52, were written in black on the image.

"Jason, you really are a philistine."

She added the number to her notebook, then texted it to Madison. It was impossible to know what it was. Eighteen digits. That was four digits too many for account and sort code. At least it was in the UK, she had no idea what it would be in the other countries. Nothing else struck her as obvious.

A day spent in the company of a happy, functioning family was both boon and barb to Elaine. The Ackermanns were everything she had hoped she and Jason would be, with extra love thrown in. She was torn between wanting to stay forever and wanting to run away screaming. When Wilpert said he was ready to go into the city, she found herself reluctant to say goodbye.

The Ackermanns were the kind of people she could have made lifelong friends, in another time, another life. As things were, she'd never see them again, and that was surprisingly painful. For once she stepped out of being an uptight Englishwoman and actually hugged Wilpert. As she walked away Elaine realised that the last two nights had been the simple human contact she'd denied herself for years. *No, that Jason denied me for years.* Jason had never been keen on her so much as shaking anyone's hand. If she hugged a man, he accused her of infidelity. The recriminations had got so bad that she simply didn't touch anyone, ever. She hated that.

* * *

Madison heard the ping from her phone, but she was deep into an analysis at the time, her personal email could wait.

The tone of the reports suggested political gridlock ahead, but there were still things that could be done. She notified the relevant field office and closed the files.

It wouldn't take a moment to check her email, it might be from Elaine. She didn't however recognise MrsHeidiNgPC@gmail.com. Still, it only took seconds to set up a gmail account. She opened it. Got confused. Figured it out. Checked a few things.

"Well, damn Mom, go you."

Two minutes later she was sitting in front of Bromstad again.

"She's heading for Frankfurt."

Bromstad said nothing but indicated Madison should go on.

"She emailed me," Madison said, and passed her phone across.

"Mrs Heidi Ng P.C.?"

"Hiding in plain sight," Madison translated.

"Your mother has a twisted sense of humour. But wouldn't that be P.S.?"

"But P.S. has a standard meaning. Had she put P.S., I'd be looking in the postscript for a message. The C is there as a homophone, see as in sight."

"P.C. also has a standard meaning. Personal computer, perhaps she left something on her laptop?"

"Unlikely, given that a check in the house reported a broken laptop in the bin. Besides, as you pointed out, she does have a twisted sense of humour," Madison agreed. "And right now, it's serving her well."

"She clearly thinks highly of you." Bromstad read again. "'Hello my little superhero?'"

"I believe that is both a compliment and the key to the next line."

Bromstad read again. "'Bruce gave me a lovely big cushion.' You can decode that?"

Madison nodded. "When I was talking to Number Two —"

"You mean Agent Sarah Smith of MI6?"

"Apologies, sir. Yes, I do."

"Wonder why they call her that?"

Madison couldn't help smiling. "I could tell you, but then she'd kill me. The point is that Agent Letterman sent Agent Smith some photographs from my parents' home. Agent Smith shared some with me. Mom sent one of the same to me." Now Madison placed a printed copy of one on the desk in front of Bromstad. It was a photograph of Elaine and Jason's fifteenth wedding anniversary. Someone had taken it from an upstairs window. There were plenty of others in the picture, including she had realised when she'd really looked, Agent Cormac Letterman, and Agent Mustapha Tannek. "There are two superheroes named Bruce. Batman and the Incredible Hulk."

"She was talking about the Incredible Hulk," Bromstad deduced as he looked more closely at the picture. "Bruce Banner."

Madison offered another image, a close up of the banner, an extreme close up that just about revealed the twenty-two-character code.

Bromstad looked at it. "An IBAN number?"

Madison nodded. "Coutts Bank in Geneva. The account was in the name of Jason Blake. Apparently, his wife came with sufficient evidence of Mr Blake's death, including his last will and testament leaving all to Mrs Blake, and all monies have been transferred to her. The original account is now closed."

"Do you know how much?"

"Over four million Euro."

Bromstad reared. "How did he get that much?"

"Backhanders? Bribes? Pay offs?" Madison shrugged. "I don't know, but clearly, he is the traitor they were looking for. Or at least he was one of them."

"And apparently, his wife knew about it."

"No," Madison said. She took back her phone and used her fingerprint to re-open it so Bromstad could see the message again. "You see, she says, 'The scales are lifted from my eyes,' and later she uses the phrase 'ever more educational'. I believe she means that she worked this one out, that she didn't know beforehand, and that she believes there's more to learn. That's why she's still out there."

"It could just mean that she's finally seeing her husband for what he was. A using, manipulative liar."

"No," Madison said. "I'm sorry sir, but the conversation I had with her the night she was here, tells me she had already seen that and woken up to the reality of it. This is telling me she didn't know about the bank account."

"Perhaps so, but she's taking full advantage of it."

"After all he put her through, she deserves to."

"You mean the beatings?"

Madison nodded. "She said there were only two beatings, but I got the impression of more. There again, beating someone down isn't necessarily about fists. But I also mean the fact that Elaine Blake was born to be a mother, and he made sure she never was. That will have cut to the very heart of her. The absolute worst way he could ever have betrayed her."

Now Bromstad frowned at her. "Meaning?"

"The second part of that line. 'The scales are lifted from my eyes, the seeds were never there, always blanks.' Knowing that Jason enjoyed sex, knowing how active and with how many partners he was, I suddenly realised that it was odd that he never had any children."

"None that he's acknowledged fathering."

"The point is, I did a bit more digging in Jason's medical history. Not something I'd ever considered doing before. I discovered he had a vasectomy before he married Mom. Yet she believed she was the one with the problem. She couldn't have children because he wouldn't, and he forced that decision on her without consultation."

"So, he was adept at keeping secrets." Bromstad said. "That's a bonus in our line of work." He looked at the phone, scrolling up the screen to read the rest of the message. "You said Elaine is heading to Frankfurt then Berlin. How do you know that? This makes no sense. 'Still, I cannot read his good book. Need to see if IT is any good. Now all the shadows have gone, this should be ever more educational.'"

"I think what she's saying there is that when she emptied the bank account, she found out that he also had a safety deposit box. I think that he had a book inside that she can't read."

"The evidence everyone's looking for?"

"I can't be sure. You see the mention of a *good* book makes me think of a bible."

"Was Blake religious?"

"Not as far as I know, but I can't figure out any other reason to reference a good book."

"And you think she's gone to Frankfurt to get the book translated?"

"No sir," Madison said. "Sorry to keep contradicting you, but Elaine speaks German. She's not the most fluent, her pronunciation was always a little off to my ear, but if she had a book in German, she'd be able to read it. She must have something in another language. Besides, she also texted me a run of eighteen digits to see if they meant anything to me. It's taken me a while to figure it out, but I think it's coordinates for a place in Berlin, the first twelve digits anyway. The last six I'm not sure about, they could be a code for something, or a phone number. I replied to her message this morning."

"That would explain her going to Berlin, but why go to Frankfurt first?"

"You see that she's typed IT with capitals. She doesn't mean it, she means eye-tee. Jason's six weeks away started in Prague where he went missing but after that he was going to Germany for several IT conferences, the first of which is in Frankfurt, this Thursday and Friday."

"The line about the shadows?"

"Letterman was tailing her, she's lost him." Madison felt oddly proud of her for that. Even Bromstad looked impressed. "It also means she doesn't think anyone else is after her, which I think may be a problem, because from the chatter I've heard, there *are* people on her tail. And if one of them is Lazlo Zakis, then he knows her, not as well as I do, but well enough to spot her, possibly well enough to find her."

Bromstad's eyes rested on the screen as he re-read the message, considered Madison's interpretation. He passed her phone back. "Do we need to send someone after her?"

"Honestly sir, I'd rather not put that kind of target on her back. Besides, who could we send that she wouldn't give the slip the way she does Letterman?"

CHAPTER NINE

Elaine reached the conference centre and headed for the cloakroom, checking in her overcoat and rucksack. She brushed down the suit she had brought in Geneva and pulled her handbag over her shoulder. Time for coffee.

Her watch said ten to nine. The conference didn't open until ten, so a drink would fill some time. The smooth latte warmed her. Never having been to a conference before, excitement and fear warred inside her. She wasn't in any rush to finish her second latte even though the conference had opened. There was nothing she particularly wanted to see. Nerves had eroded her certainty that coming here could achieve anything. Paranoia argued this was a fool's errand. Did she expect Jason to be risen from the dead and manning a stand? The company she thought he worked for was a front for him, but it might still be real. Stomach clenching, she sat back and watched, waited.

Far too many people were far too eager to get in, crowding the entrance. Unable to stomach more coffee, Elaine visited the bathroom, then joined the queue to register. Her badge and lanyard, or Heike Frisse's, was requested and handed over. The badges each had a bar code and as she started to wander around the various booths and tables, Elaine wondered why the codes were being read. Of course, registration of who attended which stand. Security.

That wouldn't be a problem for her. As far as she knew Heike had nothing to hide.

Elaine wandered towards the corner of the room and found a quiet spot where she paused to peruse the event brochure.

She found Adept IT, the company Jason claimed to work for, easily enough – not surprising in an alphabetical listing. So, they weren't a total fabrication. The small Adept stand stood at the far corner of the hall. The conference was starting to fill up but there was still a lot of space and Elaine didn't want to approach Adept while the floor was too open. She decided to do what she normally did at a supermarket, she slowly wandered up and down the aisles until something caught her eye.

The something that caught her eye froze her blood and stopped her in her tracks. She turned her back, trembling, and stepped inside the nearest display booth. *Mono-brow man. Here? Why?*

"Guten morgan, Frau."

For a moment she blinked up at the woman.

"Wie kann ich helfen?"

She smiled and in perfect German said, "I'm sorry, but I just spotted an ex-colleague I would really rather not meet up with. Can you check if he's still there? Tall, solidly built. Short black hair, no parting of eyebrows."

"Ah." The younger woman shifted slightly to look down the aisle. "Ja, I see him. He is talking to a representative of Ohmnet." The woman, whose name badge said Delma, stood straight and looked down at Elaine. "Might I suggest you go down the other aisle?"

Until Delma pointed it out, Elaine hadn't noticed that the stand stood deeper than most, open to be entered from the aisle on either side. How easy to walk across the way and avoid Mono-brow, which, after thanking Delma, she did. But even as she walked in the opposite direction, the fear started building inside her. Her gut twisted and cramped; waves of nausea crashed through her. Someone coming here from the south might have been on the same train – but two days early? That seemed unlikely. She wished it to be a coincidence, but nothing about him suggested a job in IT. She had been working with IT and databases long enough to recognise 'the sort.' So, what was he?

Death on two legs.

Don't get paranoid!

Paranoia didn't mean no one was out to get her. She walked on, trying to stay inside the crowd, heading towards the back corner of the large conference hall. Towards the Adept IT stand. Well, she might as well have a quick look now she was here.

* * *

Mac did not enjoy conferences. Still, they made for a discrete rendezvous. Tannek looked no happier at Mac's presence than Mac was to be present. He guided Mac to the coffee station at the rear of the hall.

"Why are you here?" Mac asked as they waited for their order.

Only when they had their coffees did they move to a high table in the far corner of the shop.

"This is un-fucking-believable," Tannek said. "A message from Number Two, she sent me here. Orders are, find 'Mom' and bring her home, or rather find you and tell you to take her home. Preferably with the required goods. I'm not even sure what she's talking about, though I'm guessing this has something to do with Elaine Blake."

Did radio silence only work one way?

"How the hell does someone go off grid so completely in the middle of Germany?"

Mac had no idea. After Geneva, he had completely lost track of Elaine. Again. He'd managed to find the name and card she'd used in Switzerland, though the prepayment was almost all used, and the card hadn't been used since. Nor the name Elaine Blake, nor any of her cards. Coutts hadn't been much help. They admitted to having had a Mr Blake as a customer, that Mrs Blake had claimed her late husband's account and the contents of his deposit box, but that was all. They would not give details on active accounts. They would neither confirm nor deny if she had another account with them. Neither had Mac had any luck trying to get through their security walls to follow the money. That was tougher than the Pentagon. He knew how difficult it was to go off grid, so how was a rank amateur managing it?

"No idea," Mac grumbled. "But Elaine Blake is better at this than expected." He wondered if it related to her reading habits. When searching her belongings he had found boxes and boxes of books. He had opened every book and flicked through, just in case. She read masses of crime novels, spy thrillers, books that in no way related to the dull reality of Elaine Blake. In the end he'd become impressed with Elaine's packing skills: there were way too many boxes he just hadn't been able to get the same number of books back into.

"She's no one."

Mac looked across at his colleague's scorn. "She's the one that traced you. She found what I couldn't. Solved a cypher. Traced a bank account none of us knew about. And she's evaded us several times."

"And yet you remain sure she's a rank amateur?"

Mac shrugged. "Amateur, yes. Rank, no. There's no evidence of her being trained for any of this."

The silence stretched. No evidence didn't mean no training.

"Does she have the evidence?" Tannek asked.

Mac was starting to wonder if she was the evidence. Had Jason told her more than they realised? Was Elaine selling their secrets? Either she was amazingly good, a natural at espionage, or someone had trained her. Circuitous and contradictory thoughts ran around his head like a plague looking to infest. "She didn't have it in Paris, but I suspect she may have it now."

"Found in Switzerland?"

"Why else go there?"

"Jason's nest egg?" Tannek suggested.

Possible. Probable even. But not a full explanation. "Then why not go back to England and live off it?"

"Why not blow it on an amazing holiday, sounds like she's been denied one a long time."

"Maybe, but then why not use her real name and normal bank accounts to do it, it's a lot less hassle that way. Why go off grid at all if she'd not hiding somethi—?"

"What?" Tannek demanded.

Mac lowered his eyes and kept his coffee cup in front of his face as he turned from the man he had spotted. "Ulrich Demko is here."

Tannek shifted, putting his back to the direction Mac had been looking. As far as Mac knew, Tannek had never encountered the mono-browed Russian. He kicked himself for being surprised. Ulrich and Illyana in Paris, Illyana in Geneva, Ulrich here. A tag team made following someone so much easier than working alone, as Elaine's unknown location mocked Mac. Either that or he was getting too old for this game. 48 was only a few days away, and he'd been playing long enough to be utterly jaded. He looked the other way and couldn't believe what he saw.

"Crap."

"Mac?"

He turned back to Tannek. Behind him, Mac still saw Demko. Thankfully, the Russian was scanning the opposite end of the hall. "Elaine Blake is at the Adept stand."

Tannek's eyes widened. "If she's got the evidence, we can't risk Demko getting to her first."

"Agreed."

"I'll steer him away; you deal with her. Terminally, if necessary."

Mac didn't like that idea, and it wasn't Tannek's call to make, but now wasn't the time to argue. They moved off in opposite directions, Mac found himself caught in a crowd. Blocked. When he overcame the obstruction, he looked straight into Elaine's surprised eyes. He stepped forward, his foot kicked something, a glance down showed a cute robot rocking on its rollers. A man with a controller scowled at him.

"Entschuldigen sie." He stepped over the robot and hurried forward. Unsurprisingly, Elaine had disappeared, but he caught a glimpse of red hair rushing towards the front of the hall as she dodged into the next aisle. He rushed after her.

CHAPTER TEN

Elaine breathed heavily, clammy with sweat. What the hell was going on?

Mono-brow *and* Ladderman? Did they work together?

She'd done the only thing she could think of and dived into the nearest ladies, hoping they wouldn't follow her. Not much of a safety blanket, but all she had. Now she leaned on the sink shelf and tried to catch her breath, push the nausea down. The other women in the restroom looked at her like she was insane.

Accompanied by flushing, someone asked her if she was alright. She was far from alright, she felt cold and every muscle quaked. Terrified of every possibility, she struggled for what to do next, but shutting down wasn't an option. She turned to the voice.

The woman from the booth earlier. "Delma!"

"Lord! Did something happen? Did that man catch up with you?"

No, but what a fantastic explanation. She nodded. "I think he spotted me. He was certainly coming towards me, so I just ran."

Delma frowned. "Sorry, but this seems excessive for an ex-colleague."

"He's an ex-colleague because I had him fired after he assaulted me." The lie came out of nowhere, and she internally apologised to all the real victims out there, but it did the trick. Delma's expression told her she had an ally. A couple of additional gasping women helped.

"I will call security, have him thrown out."

Elaine shook her head, taking a last deep breath to steady herself. "No, that will just cause a fuss I don't need. Besides, I've actually seen what I came here for, all I need is get away. Is there a way out without going through the hall?"

Delma nodded.

"Shall we check that there's no man out there?" One of the gaspers asked.

"Bitte." Delma nodded, gave them a description. The woman went out, almost a minute passed before she came back in.

"There was a man waiting, but after a hard stare, he left."

Both Delma and Elaine thanked the woman, as they left the rest room and turned from the hall. At a rear security door, Delma used a pass card to swipe, and open the exit. One more door and they reached fresh air. Elaine thanked and hugged Delma, wishing her all the best before she hurried away. Right now, she just wanted to get away, she'd double back later for her bag. She moved from the conference centre as quickly as possible.

She found another coffee shop, this one with a payphone inside. Her hands shook as she dialled. Relief flooded through her when Madison answered. Keeping her voice low, Elaine gave Madison the Adept and Ohmnet company names and asked her to investigate. She had no idea what Madison should look for or what she might find, but it was all she had. Madison told her about the numbers, and reported that nothing new had come up on Lazlo. He seemed to have disappeared off the face of the earth, but she would keep searching.

"You realise there's no reason for you to continue looking for him? He's turned against you."

"I know," Elaine hated to admit it, but she had to. "But if I know where he is, maybe I can find out why. Maybe I can bring him back."

The silence from the line told her what Madison thought of that idea.

"I'll be okay, Madison."

"I hope so." Worry was clear in Madison's voice.

"You know Lazlo isn't the only one of my babies I worry about," Elaine said. "I hope you aren't taking any risks supporting me."

She found Madison's gentle laugh oddly reassuring. "Don't worry, Mom. I'm being careful. Besides, I'm safe at home, you're the one gallivanting around the world. You're the one taking all the risks. I'm not sure that careful is enough anymore. I don't want you in danger."

"I don't want me in any danger, either," Elaine assured her. "But I get the distinct impression things would be worse at home. I'd be a sitting duck."

"You know what, Mom? Hate to say it, but I think you're right. Don't worry about me, I know what I'm doing. Trust me."

"I do sweetheart, which is why I'm going to ask you to do something else. If things go pear-shaped, can you tell Utku I'm sorry and I love him?"

"Mom—"

"Please Madison, it's just a precaution. I fully intend things not to go that pear-shaped. But in case. Last I heard he was somewhere in Africa."

"Last I heard he was back in Turkey. I won't let things go so pear-shaped you can't be the one to tell him."

Hoping that last was even possible, Elaine signed off and moved away from the phone. She did trust Madison, but what kind of mother would she be if she didn't worry about putting her daughter at risk?

Elaine felt the pressure building on her – all the things she didn't know. She didn't know what Lazlo was up to or where; had no idea if Jason was alive or dead. She had been coming around to the idea of Ladderman as one of the good guys, but couldn't trust Mono-brow was. With both here, were they working together? On which side? She stood in the middle of a minefield with no idea which way to turn. Except towards Berlin. She had to go there now.

She also needed her bag. Which she couldn't get it all the time Ladderman was hanging around the exhibition centre.

Her order was called. She took it and sat down. Coffee sloshed into the saucer. Hands still shaking, she bought the hot cup up to blow across and cool. Fear and caffeine were not good for her. The absence of her coat wasn't helping either. She shivered. She looked over the rim of her cup at the haunted eyes of a girl begging on the cold street. Was she sleeping rough? Elaine's maternal instincts kicked in, she wanted to go to the girl and take her in, make her safe. Only that wouldn't make her safe, it would make her a target. She felt useless looking at the girl. A girl with red hair, wearing black.

Decoy.

* * *

Mac was stumped.

He had lost Elaine in the crowd. Now he had to hunt – be methodical. There was only one public entrance for the hall. He went straight to it and looked around. No Elaine. Maybe she remained inside. He moved away from the centre of the foyer and stood back, eyes on the exit. Several minutes later, he spotted Tannek.

A short whistle drew Tannek's attention, and the Arab joined him.

"What happened?"

"She saw me and ran," Mac said under his breath. "I don't think she left the hall, and this is the only way in or out."

"For the public," Tannek agreed.

"She's not likely to have a key card to get out the back entrance."

"No," Tannek agreed.

"Unless she bloody blagged someone to let her out. Urgh!" Could she have done that? Small innocent-looking Elaine Blake, dupe some poor sap into helping her? Probably. Only Keira said Elaine never asked for help, 'too independent by half' was her phrase. Elaine had certainly stood well enough alone since leaving the UK. Urgh. This woman tied him in knots.

"Do you want me to circle the building, check if she's out there?"

Mac sighed. "If she's left the building, she's gone. Long away. What happened with Demko?"

"He wandered past the Adept stand, then through the aisles, and made his way back to Ohmnet's stand. Illyana's there too, by the way, and I've met her, so I thought it best I keep away."

Mac nodded. A wise precaution.

"Now what?"

"Now we wait."

Whatever spy fiction might imply, spy fact was a heap more boring. Lots of standing around waiting, watching. Lots of going in circles trying to figure out how other people's minds worked. *Women!* No wonder Mac had sworn off them years ago. He'd realised young that he couldn't do the lying to a loved one thing after a terrible relationship with a woman in the organisation. It had been foolish to think they would work. They both understood the job. They shared one vision. They never fully trusted what the other said. The relationship had petered out. He hadn't bothered since.

Elaine was only a few years younger than him; what had age done for her? It certainly didn't seem to have dulled her wits any. He paced, needing to release some of the energy building up inside. Then he saw her. He looked twice, but there she was. The long overcoat she'd been wearing in Geneva, collar pulled up. Hat jammed on her head, but enough hair showing to reveal it as red and curly, and she was just now walking out of the building, walking fast, hands in pockets, and shoulders up, trying to be invisible and all the more visible for it. He slapped Tannek on the arm and ran after Elaine.

Outside on the street, he called her name, the sound almost lost under the rumble of a passing truck. Elaine moved faster; her hands came out of her pockets, and she ran. Mac pushed all his strength into powering his legs into long fast strides, as he raced after her. A couple of hundred metres down the road, he caught up, grabbed her arm, and swung her to face him. His jaw and his hand dropped.

Not Elaine. A young girl, filthy, not taking care of herself.

"She said to tell you, 'close but no cigar'."

* * *

Madison was surprised by the call to her team leader's office. Accepting the offer to sit, Madison noted it was smaller and neater than Bromstad's office, and the view over the alley at the back of the building was hardly attractive. She faced the woman opposite. Mrs Claudia Simpson had run to seed. Too much jowl, too many wrinkles. Too much padding for just middle-aged spread.

"You've been spending a great deal of time conversing with Director Bromstad."

It was a statement, and a truth. Madison didn't know what to say, so she said nothing. A move which did not improve Team Leader Simpson's mood.

"Why?"

Madison met her boss's eye directly. "I am not at liberty to say."

Hard eyes narrowed and thin lips clamped. "Have you forgotten that I am your superior officer?"

"Of course not, Agent Simpson." Though the fact that they were still both officially referred to as agent made it seem they were closer to equals.

"Then tell me what you've been working on, because you are not logging all hours on your assigned tasks."

"I'm sorry, ma'am, I can't do that." Bromstad had been very clear on the point.

They continued to stare at one another, an unbreakable impasse. "You're suspended from duty pending investigation, Agent Turner."

CHAPTER ELEVEN

Suspended on a Thursday, called back the following Wednesday, Madison sat and worried. She'd let Bromstad know she had been suspended pending investigation but would continue investigating for her mom. He hadn't been in touch. She didn't know what that meant but she was back, and Simpson wasn't.

"She got transferred to Washington," her colleague on the next desk told her.

Madison shrugged. "DC is nice."

"State," he corrected her. "Not sure she'll enjoy a city where it rains 163 days a year."

"Doesn't sound much different to here," Madison said without emotion as she turned back to her work. Average days of rain in London was around 156, and Simpson had bitched about every single one. Privately she thought, into every life a little rain must fall, but such pettiness wasn't where she wanted to put her energies.

Beneath the calm exterior, Madison worried. She hadn't heard from Elaine since Frankfurt. The research that she'd done on Adept and Ohmnet had taken her to unexpected, unpleasant places. Elaine was in greater danger than she realised, and the thought made Madison sick to her stomach. What if Elaine hadn't been in contact because she couldn't? What if something had happened?

She stood before the floor to ceiling windows, a glass of wine in one hand, and her arm around her waist as she looked over the River Thames.

Another set of arms wound around her waist, and she felt the warmth of the solid male pressed against her. Neil had proved to be her rock these last few weeks.

"Dinner's on. Nothing to do but let it simmer for twenty minutes," he said as he snuggled closer.

Though she didn't mind cooking, Neil really loved it. He'd never made a bad dinner. "Thanks."

"She'll be okay," he whispered in her ear.

A slight turn of her head allowed her a light kiss. "I hope so. But she's not been in touch for a week and I'm worried."

"Understandable." He kissed her neck again, trying to divert her. "All mothers worry when their fledglings fly the nest."

That made her laugh. "She's my mom."

"That only makes it harder. And though I've only met her once, in the lift, she seemed a lovely, sensible woman. And given what a lovely, sensible woman she raised you to be, I'm sure she'll be okay, and she'll be in touch just as soon as she can."

It couldn't be soon enough for Madison. Still, Neil was here, dinner smelled good. She twisted for another kiss.

The door buzzer sounded.

"It's probably a chancer," Neil said, joining their lips again.

The door buzzer reverberated with an annoyance no inanimate object had a right to. With a tut, Madison slipped out of her lover's embrace and went to the door cam. She had to blink and check.

"What's he doing here?" She released the front door.

"Who?" Neil asked.

She turned back to him. "My boss." Once Bromstad was inside, she looked between the two. "Mr Bromstad, this is Neil Dailey, my boyfriend. Neil, this is Alan Bromstad, my boss."

The men nodded in acknowledgement across the width of the apartment. Then Bromstad turned to Madison. "We need to talk in private."

"I'll pop out," Neil said.

"Sorry to drive you away," Bromstad said. "This is important."

Neil shrugged. "It happens." He moved over and kissed Madison's cheek. "Any more than twenty minutes and turn the dinner down, don't want it welding itself to the pan."

She nodded and thanked him, seeing him out. Once the door was closed, she turned back to Bromstad, inviting him to sit.

"This won't take twenty minutes," he said as they sat on the two facing sofas. "I just wanted to know if you've heard from your mom at all?"

"Not since last week when she was in Frankfurt," Madison admitted. "I'm quite worried."

Bromstad nodded. "Of course. What did you find after that call?"

"I looked into Adept and Ohmnet. As far as I can tell both are legitimate IT companies. The only thing I am sure of with Adept is that the British secret service uses them as a front when they need to get their own operatives into certain areas. Ohmnet might offer the same service to other powers, though if they do, I couldn't find any definitive proof of it. Ohmnet is privately owned, ownership recently changed hands. Haven't found who yet, Simpson pulled my access when she suspended me."

Bromstad nodded. It was standard procedure and clearly, he would not step outside standard operating procedure. It was unlikely he'd admit to having made this visit if asked. "Have you been able to get any details to Elaine?"

She shook her head. "It's quite difficult as I'm never sure where she'll be, what number she'll call from, or how long she'll have to talk. I'm thinking of another way to send information to her, but that will take time, which I'm not sure if I'll have, if you see what I mean."

"Honestly, no, I don't."

Madison tried again. "I have a brother, foster brother. I can send some things to him, more details than I could exchange in a phone or text conversation that may well be monitored, and then send Mom to him."

Bromstad nodded. "While you were out of the office, other data came in, and much of it is not good. Elaine was picked up on street CCTV in Berlin five days ago. Near the coordinates you gave her." He reached into his coat pocket and drew out a small slip of paper, passing it to her. "The details I can share are in there. Firstly, Mrs Blake may need to go to Prague. It may answer some of the questions she's likely to have. If she survives, then the other factor comes into play. I'll let you read and digest, then it's your call what you send to whom." He stood. "By the way," he said as they reached the door. "That dinner smells divine. I'll invite myself over properly some time."

"You'd be welcome, Alan. Just give me advance notice, because Neil's the cook not me."

He looked down at her, brows raised. "Then you're a very lucky woman."

* * *

Close but no cigar.

Though unsure he'd even received it, and even though it was now over a week later, Elaine felt rotten about sending that message to Ladderman. She felt worse about freezing feet and trying to sleep in what she assumed was a disused… In truth aside from disused, she had no idea what this structure was. Two meters square and brick with a rusted, holey corrugated iron roof, charring on the inner brick face suggested an attempt at a fire in the past. Tonight, it was the only shelter she'd been able to find, and literally anything was better than nothing at this point.

The rain turned to snow that blinded and the night here was so incredibly dark she'd been afraid to keep going. At least the snow wasn't settling, something to be grateful for. For safety's sake she'd decided to stay awake all night. Falling asleep risked never waking up, she might be found in months, frozen, but half eaten by wildlife. If found at all and not entirely eaten by wildlife.

Oh, cheery thought. Thanks brain.

She supposed she should be grateful that she no longer heard it whisper that she should slink home in that voice suspiciously like Jason's.

She looked around the small building. Not that she saw much, the cloud cover muted weak moonlight. In the UK, an estate agent would probably call it 'Bijou and ripe for development.' Though the place lacked the elegance of bijou. And the ripe came mostly from the smell. Which they might brand 'a distinct and interesting aroma.'

A laugh bubbled up to surprise her. She shouldn't be surprised any more, smiling and laughing was happening a lot more these days. She had tapped an unknown well of happiness within. Or possibly madness. *I'm going slightly mad*, Freddie Mercury sung in her head. And perhaps she was. In the nicest way possible.

If the two weeks since leaving home had taught her anything, it was that she could cope. She coped with more than she ever expected. She travelled well, found her way easily enough. Though admittedly today turned out a disaster. She had hitched a lift, unfortunately with two guys who thought her hitching meant they could hitch up her clothes and have fun against her will. Though not proud of what she'd done to get away, she wouldn't regret it, they left her no choice. She'd left one permanently blinded and the other probably needed a testicle retrieval operation, but it was their own fault for attacking her in the first place.

She got away, still in one piece, with all her gear, her health, her wealth, and just a modicum of pride. She'd have to make do without warmth for now, but she calculated she could manage that for one night. She'd layered as many clothes on as possible, and cwtched up in the driest corner.

Her biggest worry was the uncertainty of her location. Somewhere west of Nuremberg and heading for the Czech Republic. She hoped. The men had pulled off the autobahn on to unfamiliar and small roads, she'd instantly tried to get away, but child locks defeated her until the driver opened the door. They'd been all over her, pawing at her, laughing at her. When she'd got away, she'd just run and kept on running. She'd gone over fields and small tracks, by the time she'd calmed to a walk, she found no road nor another human being. She'd seen sheep, but only one or two. She wouldn't mind if this turned out to be an animal shelter, and at this point filling the space with sheep would add a woolly, if noisy and noisome, blanket.

Looking back, Frankfurt had been a surprise to her. Ladderman and Mono-brow proved shockingly simple to get away from.

The more she'd considered it, the less likely their working together seemed. Of course, certainty was impossible, but she remembered the way Ladderman warned her about the bad men in the Jardin du Trocadero. In that last conflict, she had spotted Ladderman. Knowing his face made that easy. But she'd got the impression he had seemed to be facing someone, but she didn't see who. If she had, would that someone have had a Mono-brow? Ice bloomed inside her.

She knew neither man was following her now, or at least she hadn't seen them, and she had been vigilant.

What would she do if they did catch up with her again? She supposed that would depend on what they tried.

What would they do?

She dreaded to think when it came to Mono-brow. It might be unfair to judge by appearance. Good could be ugly. Beauty could hide bad. But it was all she had to judge the man on, and now was not a time to be trusting strangers. As the day had reminded her.

If Ladderman ever spotted her again, she expected a confrontation. She'd almost welcome it. Her life had been more exciting since he stepped into it, and that started all the way back when he'd pressed her against a wall. If not busting for a pee, she would have jumped him then and there. Actually, it started before that, when he'd suggested frisking her and the image of his hands all over her leapt to mind. Her heart beat faster at the memory.

She laughed at herself.

A man like that would never be interested in a drudge like her.

Not a drudge now.

No, and never again.

She looked to her bag as she set it up to rest against, needing comfort no old stone wall could provide.

What she kept in there was precious, valuable, needed consideration. It made no sense, it was all beyond her, an amateur in this game of spies. She needed help with it. There had to be a way of contacting Madison, only that would mean flitting onto the grid, and she was afraid of putting Madison in danger if she did. There was another option, Ladderman.

She shook that pie in the sky from her head. If he found her, he'd just try to send her home, and she didn't want to go home. Not now. Maybe never. She needed another plan.

CHAPTER TWELVE

"Cigar?"

Mac looked at the man who made the offer. Petr Bartos revolted him, not for the fat, sweaty body, but the arrogance, self-indulgence, the abuse of the vulnerable. The man owned and frequented too many brothels, was known to indulge in practises illegal in just about every nation, and talk, cheap though it was, hinted with fearful breath, that he practised every way to kill there was.

Mac shook his head. "I don't believe we're allowed to in here," he said in flawless Czech.

That wouldn't stop Petr. All Mac needed was entry to the event and now he had it.

Close but no cigar.

That phrase haunted him – taunted him. In the nine days since Frankfurt, he had utterly failed to make inroads into his own mission. Twice he had traced Elaine by use of her prepaid card in the name of Mrs Hyde, but both times she had used it on leaving a hotel and he hadn't reached the place fast enough to find anything but her absence. The two points didn't even give him much of a trajectory. Elaine Blake was too slippery by half.

Oddly, tracing Lazlo proved to be easier than tracing Elaine. Lazlo had pissed off the wrong Frenchman, an attaché with the Latvian embassy. For reasons unexplained, the Frenchman investigated Lazlo, and found some connection to organised crime. Lazlo's behaviour had raised alarm bells with others, and he'd run for the Czech Republic.

Mac paused inside the great hall of the Rudolfinum Concert and Exhibition Hall, allowed himself to appreciate the sheer beauty of the place. The exquisite Neo-Renaissance building had a grand entrance, opening at the first-floor level to the central halls, staircases flowed elegantly either side, bringing anyone descending back to the centre of the room for the final six steps to the main hall. The hall rose a full three storeys high. The Rudolfinum didn't generally enforce a dress code, but this event demanded black tie, dinner jackets and ball gowns. Tonight's dinner was the place to be seen for the great and the good, a charity event that would cost five times more than it made.

Mac stood tall enough to see over most of the crowd, but not so tall he looked out of place. Unlike Demko. The man's six four frame stood out, almost as instantly recognisable as the mono-brow. And there, on the other side of the room, stood the beautiful Illyana. Not wanting to be noticed, Mac turned to Petr, and behind him, the four models he had brought along. With a beautiful young girl on each arm, Mac doubted anyone would be looking at him. They would assume him to be a sugar daddy. That was depressing.

The group followed Petr to their appointed table. Petr sat Mac where he could see Garin's table without being obvious to those sitting at it. Excellent food, interminable speeches, an auction for things 'money could not buy' sold for so much money it was clearly the only thing that could buy them, the usual for such events. Finally, subdued music played, guests started circulating, some couples moved to the dance floor.

He watched Demko move to the adjacent table and offer a hand to Illyana. Illyana spoke to the man at her side, kissed his cheek before she stood and took Demko's hand. Together they joined the dance and moved like practised partners, which they probably were. Subtle as the move was, he saw it. He watched so closely to ensure he did, Illyana slipped something into Demko's pocket. Whatever it was, Mac wanted it.

Mac moved to the edge of the hall. A black-dressed waitress with red hair in a tight bun approached, carrying a tray with only one full Champagne flute left. Absently he took it, sipped, and nearly choked as he focused on the woman carrying the tray.

Elaine smiled smugly and turned away as he struggled.

Gasping for breath, Mac followed her behind one of the wide square pillars that ringed the room, grasped her arm, forced her back behind the pillar.

"Don't," she warned under her breath.

"Don't what?"

"Lie to me."

He frowned. "What makes you think I was going to?"

"You were about to speak. You're a man. You're Jason's colleague." She shrugged. "Take your pick."

A suited man hurried to them, said something in rapid-fire German, which Elaine responded to, equally fluent, and Mac struggled to keep up. The general sense was that Elaine had work to do, and Mac was getting in the way. Elaine ducked under his arm and moved away. The way the other man looked at him, Mac knew it would be a mistake to go after her. He simply lifted the flute in mock salute and returned to the party.

As he did, he saw Demko heading out. The flute went to a table as Mac passed, following the bigger man. Demko headed to the gents. Mac waited a few heartbeats, then walked in.

* * *

Back in the kitchen, Elaine's hand shook too much to pour a glass of wine without spilling it.

"Did that guest upset you?"

Elaine turned to the man at her side, trying to translate his German. She blinked and tried to answer. She nodded, apologising.

The man, the maître d', said she was no use with such unsteady hands. He didn't blame her. Guests should know better. He told her to go. She didn't want to. She hadn't seen Lazlo yet. His expected presence was why she was there. She'd have to find another way to watch. Thanking the maître d', apologising again, she nodded and headed towards the exit, removing the apron from around her waist.

In the locker room, she retrieved her handbag and rucksack and moved away. She secured her handbag on her shoulder with the rucksack. Scrubbing her face with her hands, she moved into the public area. A concert was going on held in the main hall, the Dvorak Hall. And the foyer was busy during the interlude.

The house lights dimmed and brightened, signalling the end of the intermission and the audience filed back to their seats. The dress code was much more casual out here than the charity event, which turned Elaine's black dress into camouflage, but the rucksack was obviously out of place. She hid until the other patrons cleared out before she moved.

The quality of sound in the foyer changed as it emptied, and she reached into her bag as she heard the voice.

"I just don't have it."

Lazlo?

The only suitable shoes she had been able to buy at short notice were dancing shoes, so she moved silently over the highly polished floor. She propped her bag in the corner before creeping further out, scanning the area.

The sharp slap echoed through the space, drew her attention to the two men in front of the stairs to the upper tiers. Lazlo in casual chinos and what looked like a cashmere jumper. The other man wore full black tie. Heart beating hard, she dared to risk a head around the corner for a better view. The second she saw them, she ducked back behind the column. That man had been at table ten. She took a calming breath and slowed her heart as she moved back, she could see them through one eye.

"You had the locker number and the combination."

The man standing over Lazlo looked early fifties. Short grey-blonde hair, slim, healthy tan. He stood taller than Lazlo by a good few inches, so five eleven, possibly six foot. A big man, but lean. Lazlo, never muscular, looked unusually wimpy.

"It was empty."

He sounded like the frightened 10-year-old she had first met. Gut instinct to protect him, warred with the good sense not to get involved.

The word 'locker' told her they were referring to the locker in Berlin. With Madison's help she'd got there before Lazlo. But what had been their source? Jason? If so, why had she won that particular race?

"I want that data. You delayed too long, taking too much time with his wife. Now you find her, you bring her in."

"You can't use her against Jason," Lazlo argued. "He'd happily watch her tortured."

Her belly clenched; she'd have thrown up if she'd had anything in her stomach.

"Hell, he'd torture her for you."

She wasn't shocked. But one thing became clear: Jason was alive. *Bastard*.

"Get the book."

Even in the dark behind her eyelids, Elaine heard the implicit threat and saw Lazlo rush away as his footfalls echoed towards the front exit.

"Go with it."

Her eyes snapped wide open just in time to see Ladderman lean over her. Again, he pressed her against a pillar, placed his lips on hers. She wanted to push him away, but other footfalls were getting closer.

Go with it.

She softened her lips and kissed him properly. She felt his moment of surprise before he kissed her back. Her hands went to his waist, not expecting to find the jacket open, but since it was, she ran her hand up inside. His breath caught as she reached the middle of his ribs; her touch revealed swelling. She moved her hands to his shoulders. He pressed closer, deepening the kiss and for the first time in a long time, she found herself enjoying male contact.

She heard a tut, the footfalls moved away and disappeared; the man must have gone through a door. She pushed Ladderman away.

"What are you doing here?"

She had been about to ask him that. She swallowed and pointed upward. "Enjoying the Bohemian Rhapsody."

He rolled his eyes. "It's a Schubert Concerto."

He had hold of her hand now, pulling her along. His grip wasn't tight, so she jerked her hand away, rushed back and grabbed her rucksack. Tempted to keep running, she turned back, but froze. Ladderman was gone.

"Really?"

Typical, bloke. Runs out as soon as things get interesting.

She shouldered the rucksack and stepped away. Just in time to be out of the way before three men, all in dinner jackets, burst through the door.

"Where is he?" the burly man in front demanded.

"Who?" Elaine felt dumb just asking.

"From the dinner."

Elaine looked at them like they were dumb. "At the dinner?"

The man's expression suggested her total uselessness. The trio ran straight for the main entrance. She followed. Outside, it took a moment to adjust to the absolute cold. She knelt as the men looked fruitlessly around. From the rucksack, she pulled a puffer jacket, shaking it out to expand the padding, and putting it on. Taking each stone step, Elaine realised that she needed to change the dancing shoes—the lack of grip could prove dangerous as well as damn cold. Every bump and stone seemed exaggerated by the thin soles. Elaine kept her head down and kept going as the first drops of rain fell.

She glanced at the sky and asked God if He hated her. At the bottom of the steps, she felt every cobble. She walked across to Jan Palach Square, heading towards the metro station.

She stepped to the edge of the square as a blue Audi stopped sharply beside her. The door flew open.

"Get in."

Ladderman. She should run. A quick glance showed her the three men were still searching. If she cried out, he'd just drive off and she'd be left with freezing feet and no idea what was going on.

She got in the car.

CHAPTER THIRTEEN

"Elaine?"

She didn't want to wake up.

"Elaine?"

The voice grew more insistent and the cold bit harder. She blinked bleary eyes. Ladderman came into focus, the car door was open, and he stood outside, shivering. Automatically, she reached for her pack.

"Already inside."

Inside. Inside sounded good. He moved back, she swung her legs out, stood up, slipped and grabbed the top of the car for balance. His hand on her arm, he guided her, and she heard the car door shut, remote locking flashed the surrounding forest with orange. The stony path was painful to walk on, but Ladderman set a brisk pace, which was hardly surprising – it was freezing and the rain was that horrid misty kind that clung.

He led her into a log cabin. Once inside the welcome warmth, he quickly closed the front door. The open living area, roughly five metres by six, had two doors off. Two sofas sat either side of a fire, a few cabinets next to a stove. A sideboard held books, games, and crockery. There was a log fire, unlit, then she realised a gas fire was on, one of those propane affairs with the gas bottle at the back. The light came from candles.

"This is someone's holiday cottage," she realised.

"Yeah." Ladderman was already at the fireplace, stacking the fire as she moved towards it. She saw it was open back and front. It looked through to a bedroom. The other door must be a bathroom.

"What are you going to do now?" she asked.

"Light this fire."

"I meant with me."

He turned to look over his shoulder at her, brows raised, a strange expression she couldn't interpret on his face.

"There's no point trying to send me home," she said. "I won't go."

Without a word he returned to his task.

"Why should I trust you?" she asked.

"I never said you should."

And even though he hadn't turned this time, she knew he was right. She also knew she did trust him. Instinct or stupidity, she wasn't sure. It was odd how she had missed him since leaving Paris. Odder still how her bones wanted to melt when he kissed her. That had never happened before. And she shouldn't let it happen again. Ever. No matter how much she wanted to.

Without a name, she couldn't even ask Madison to investigate him.

The alternative of not trusting him right this minute was to run out into the cold. That frozen night in a tumbledown shack had taught her how bad sleeping rough was at this time of year.

Shivers trembled through her as she moved over to the sofa nearest the fire. She watched him work, his movements careful, controlled.

"Who did you fight?" she asked.

He stopped and looked up at her. "What makes you think I had a fight?"

"The way your breath caught when I touched the swelling on your ribs. The redness along your cheek. The marks on your right knuckles. Do you think me blind or stupid?"

His brows raised. He turned back to the fire, struck a match and put it to the balled-up tinder.

"Was it about that woman?"

He frowned, but kept his eyes on the tinder, lighting a different section. "Woman?"

"The stunner on table fourteen."

He threw the match into the mix before it burned his fingers but said nothing.

"I saw her looking your way. A lot."

He said nothing.

"She looked kind of familiar, but I couldn't place her. But there again, tall, slim, symmetrical. That kind all look alike to me. I'm pretty good with faces otherwise. I recognised you fairly quickly. Despite the makeup."

At least now he turned to her.

"In Paris. It only took a few moments to realise that you'd ditched the disguise you'd used searching my home. That was also when I realised I'd met you before. Bit risky, wasn't it? Pointing to yourself in a photo and asking if I knew you."

He shrugged and moved to the sofa opposite. "You didn't remember me."

"No," she admitted. "Not then. Still don't remember a name. You clearly didn't make much of an impression."

"I tried not to."

"Congrats, you succeeded." She stared into the fire. The kindling had caught. The dry logs started to char. "So, what it is?" She kept staring at the fire. "Your name? I can't keep calling you Ladderman."

"Letterman."

For a moment that didn't compute, so she frowned across at him.

"Cormac Letterman," he said.

"Real name or just the one you're choosing to use?"

"Real name."

"Okay – Oh! Macca. That's what Jace called you. Macca."

"He hated being called Jace."

"No, really? Think I care?"

"You've been trailing after him around Europe, so yeah."

She said nothing, just sat straight and turned to stare into the fire.

"I hate being called Macca," he said. "Prefer Mac."

Was he just filling the silence she was overly used to? Seemed odd that he'd crack first.

"What are you doing here, Elaine?"

She refocused on him. She owed no explanation. "I went to Paris on the misguided notion of helping Lazlo. But he lied to me. I went to Geneva because I discovered Jason had a bank account there. I figured I'd get as much as possible out of the bastard in his death since I got sweet FA in his life."

"How much did you get?"

She smiled. He made an oddly appealing picture sitting in the soft light of candles and fire, wearing a dinner jacket, even the perfect touch of an untied bowtie.

"Little wonder you reacted when I called you Ladderman. Did you think for a second that I'd used your real name?"

His face betrayed nothing, but she was sure she was right.

"You didn't answer my question," he said.

"Nor you mine, and you're too far away to try breaking my finger this time." Though he clearly remembered the incident in Paris when he'd tried, unsuccessfully to coerce her, he said nothing. "I'm here for the game," she said. "That's what this feels like. A game. Cat and mouse. You all want something you think I have. I just have to keep running, keep playing."

"You understand we often have to play this game to the death?"

Worryingly, that didn't bother her. "I do."

"Hmm." The sound of uncertainty. "Do you always sit like that?"

She glanced down, she sat straight, knees and ankles together, hands in her lap. "How else am I supposed to sit?"

"Hmm." With that inarticulate sound, he stood up. "It's late."

She checked her watch. "Two o'clock in the morning is early."

Narrowed eyes warned her to rein in the cheek.

"I'm going to bed. It's a big bed, you can join me or sleep out here, as you like."

"And they say chivalry is dead," she said as he walked around her sofa to the bedroom.

Her only answer was the click of the door closing. For a moment she just sat there, listening to him moving, undressing.

"What if I decide to just take the car?"

"I have the keys," the voice came back, mostly through the open fireplace. "And you don't know how to hot wire a car." Another movement. Stillness. "Do you?"

His uncertainty warmed her as much as the fire.

Exhaustion dragged at her. She still hadn't recovered from that night in a shed last week, but at least she hadn't fallen ill. No more sound of movement came from the bedroom. Nor snores. The bun pulled at her scalp, so she plucked the pins out. She wouldn't leave burning candles unattended.

Pushing herself to her feet, she stood, moving around the room to blow out the candles. She turned back to the sofa. A throw hung over the back she could use as a blanket, but it wouldn't be as warm.

Carefully, she opened the door into the dark bedroom and moved inside. The light of the fire showed her Mac slept on the left, the side nearest the door, so she moved around the bed and pushed off her shoes. It was a stylish, barely furnished room. Just enough though, if staying for a week or two for a holiday. The bed was a standard double, but the duvet seemed extra wide, extra thick.

Ladderma – Letterman clearly wasn't asleep, he'd turned on his side, away from her. She'd have to start thinking of him as Mac or she'd trip herself up. She undressed and slipped into the bed, put her back to him.

"Good God woman!" As he spoke, he twisted towards her in the bed. "You're freezing." His arm circled her waist pulled her against him. Much warmer. The fastest way to warm anyone up was to share body heat, and the moment he did, he stopped, very sudden, very still. "Annnd apparently you're totally naked."

A fact he would be hard pressed to miss given that he didn't appear to be wearing any clothes either.

"Really? I hadn't noticed."

"Ha."

For a moment she lay there and wondered. She put her hand on his arm, resting not holding, natural, welcome.

Warm and intimate. He wouldn't hurt her. Not tonight at any rate. She could trust him for now.

"Why did you come back for me?" she asked.

"I'll interrogate you in the morning."

"Really?"

"Yes." There seemed to be a smile in that. "Go to sleep."

She closed her eyes and tried.

"Why did you come to bed with me?" he asked.

Even with her eyes closed, she smiled. "After twenty-four years of marriage, I know how to share a bed with a man without having sex."

"Got the impression you two didn't share a bed."

"Not for the last year or so, but that doesn't alter the fact."

"True," he said. "Wasn't twenty-five years?"

"Twenty-five together, twenty-four married."

A subtle distinction.

Less subtle was the oddity of be discussing her marriage when in bed with another man. Odd but safe. He murmured something, burying his face in her hair and, judging by the steady rhythm of his breathing, was soon fast asleep.

The weight of his arm over her waist was a hot band across her skin. His hand being on her belly she wasn't sure about, but at least he hadn't made any unpleasant remarks about her fat.

She dozed, but she woke with a blink. The light had dwindled to nothing. When she picked up her head to see the fire, Mac moved his head to let her. The fire had died out. It must be four or five in the morning, pitch black outside and virtually inside too. As she put her head back down, she realised that at some point Mac's hand had moved up to cup her breast. She'd been in the same position for a while and tried to ease her back by shifting. That was when she noticed and stilled.

"It's not an actual choice."

His voice rumbled behind her head. She half-turned. "I understand how men don't always choose to get an erection, as long as you understand that what you do with it is entirely your choice."

"I was choosing to do nothing with it."

"Really?" she asked lightly. "And what about your hand on my breast? That not a choice? And I didn't say you should move it," she added when he shifted to do so.

A heartbeat of pause, then his hand moved back, thumb gently caressing across the swell of her breast. She shifted her bottom, moving the length of his erection more comfortably along the groove between her butt cheeks. Comfortable again, she relaxed and closed her eyes.

Her hand came up, her fingers ran along his forearm. With every run she enjoyed the sensation of his hair and skin; the hair was sprinkled lightly, but still there, quite different from her own smooth skin.

"Are you trying to drive me crazy?" Her hair muffled his voice.

"No."

"Really?"

That word was her habit, hearing it from him made her smile broaden. *Sod it.* Carefully, she moved, twisting to face him. His head lay on the edge of her pillow, and as she shifted, his other arm came from between them, to circle her shoulders, guiding her back to him. She smoothed her hands to his chest, stroking skin and hair there. A new and delightful sensation; Jason had been virtually hairless. She avoided the bruised area.

"Mrs Blake?"

"Mr Letterman?"

She moved her knee over his. His hand moved over her, drew her leg up, hitched it over his hip, putting them more intimately together. His nose ran up and down hers. He placed a light kiss on her lips, and she wanted so much more.

"Is this because he cheated on you?"

"No." She kissed him this time. "This is freedom of choice." But once she'd pressed her hips against his, choice, thought and conversation were lost to need and sensation.

* * *

"I know the Thames looks better at night," Neil said. "But would it be more help to tell me what the problem is, rather than staring out there?"

Madison stepped away from the windows and moved to sit with Neil. He was spending more and more time with her, and she liked that.

"Are you worried about your mum?"

She nodded. "I know it was only yesterday I spoke with her, but it was today that she was going to be seeing Lazlo, and I'm worried about how that meeting will go, or possibly went."

While she'd told Neil some of what was going on, she'd made it a family issue, not a criminal one, so he didn't really understand the depth of her concern.

"But how bad can it go?"

Oh, guns, knives, bullets, blood. Literal matter of life and death.

"Thing is this Lazlo fellow was her foster child too," Neil said. "From everything you've said, Elaine was a great mum, so why wouldn't he be glad to see her? Why wouldn't everything be fine?"

Because Lazlo is a little git, selling secrets to foreign powers and he'll do whatever makes him the most money?

She said none of that and smiled at Neil instead. "You're too good to me."

His arm moved around her and pulled her close. "Impossible."

Held against him, warm and comfortable, Madison made a suggestion that she'd been considering a while. "Why don't you move in with me?"

Neil shifted so he could see her better, and she tipped her head to him. "Is that what you want?"

She answered with a nod, more hope in her heart than expected. He looked especially serious behind those glasses.

"Well, if I do move in, that would save me a lot in rent. That would soon build up to be enough for a deposit on a house for us. Not to mention any kind of wedding you want."

Madison blinked. "Wedding?"

Now Neil nodded, looking less certain.

"Are you asking me to marry you?"

Definitely looked less certain now. "Erm, yeah." His voice squeaked. "That is, this isn't a big proposal or anything, I'd do better than this if I'd planned it. I didn't plan this. But I do mean it. If you want. I mean, I know it's still early days and all. Three months isn't long, but…"

"Four months," Madison said, warmth oozing like honey through her veins. "And yes."

CHAPTER FOURTEEN

Elaine woke. She lay in a warm bed, daylight softened by thick curtains. She smelled coffee. Her clothes lay on the floor where she'd left them, and her rucksack sat propped against the wall. She picked up yesterday's bra, found clean clothes from the sack and dressed. Thermals, jeans, long sleeved t-shirt, and a fleece pullover. She pulled thick socks on, but not shoes.

In the other room she found Mac sitting at the small table, a laptop before him, scowling at the screen. He also wore more weather-appropriate clothing. His own bag, a red North Face holdall, was easily the same capacity as her rucksack. It waited by the door, ready to go. She padded over to the stove where the coffee pot stood.

"You want a top-up?"

"Please."

He didn't move or glance up from his screen. She topped up the mug and returned the pot to the stove. She moved back to the sofa, wrapping her hand around her own mug before she sipped.

"Whose place is this?"

"No idea." He spoke absently, concentrated on the laptop.

That stopped her. "You broke in?"

"We."

"I didn't even know! You broke in all on your own."

"Picked the lock."

No breaking involved – a technicality.

"The car?"

"Stolen."

Oh, dear God! "What about ANPR?"

This time he looked at her, eyebrows raised.

"What?" she demanded. "This may be Eastern Europe, but it's possible they have automatic number plate recognition too. Technology doesn't have to stop at a border."

"It doesn't have to, but in this case, it largely does. Besides," he said turned back to the screen, "I changed the plates."

"Oh." For a moment she sat back. "How long are we staying?"

"Not long."

"Another night?"

"No."

She stood.

"Where are you going?"

"Change the sheets." She found clean ones in the ottoman his side of the bed and left the room the way she suspected he'd found it. With the used sheets bundled in her arms, she stepped out to study the kitchen, wondering how the owners did their washing.

"There's a deep sink in the bathroom. But no hot water."

In the bathroom, she had to pump the cold water, which made her need the toilet, which was, conveniently, at hand. At least the washing powder was biological, that should sort out most of the residue even in cold water. Her hands were frozen again, but the sheets were clean and hanging over the bath to drip dry when she came out.

Mac had put the laptop away, tidied up and her bag now stood beside his. The mugs and coffee pot were washed and away. He stood at the table glowering at her, his arms folded. He might not be the best-looking man she had ever met, but he had a wildness about him that was way too appealing.

"Done?"

She nodded.

"Sit down." He pulled out the chair he had been sitting in.

Like a naughty schoolgirl, she sat and looked up at him. He seemed awkward before he sat beside her.

"Why were you in Prague?"

"Why were you?"

He obviously didn't enjoy volleys of questions. Which made questions her best weapon and shield.

"Why did you think you had to hide from that man?" she asked.

"Why did you?"

Tit for tat, huh?

"I was embarrassed to be seen in that uniform."

"Liar."

She threw him a patently false smile. "Makes two of us."

"I haven't lied to you."

Before she answered, she rethought. "Only if I exclude lies by omission." She shrugged. "Okay then, you didn't lie. Now what?"

He scowled at her again. "Answer the question."

"Or what? Are you going to break my finger?" She wondered how far she could push him, but she held out her hand, little finger spread away from the others.

His eyes moved to the finger. His hand came up, wrapped around the finger, and lowered her hand to the table. His hands were boiling compared to hers.

"What did you hope to achieve last night?"

"Orgasm. And unless I'm very much mistaken, we both achieved that." Knowingly misinterpreting his question, she had clearly made him uncomfortable. "Thing is, Cormac—"

"I prefer Mac."

"Okay, Mac. Last night was not an attempt to trap you. It wasn't a revenge fuck or anything. My libido simply woke up ravenous. And you nudged it, so you got it. If you aren't comfortable talking about it, we won't. If you'd rather forget about it, we will. But last night was last night. Done. In the past."

He frowned. "Not sure how I'm supposed to feel about that speech."

"Relieved?" She shrugged. "I suspect most men would be. Though probably, in your shoes, I'd feel slightly used. If it helps, sex with you was fantastic. And much as I hate to pump any man's ego, it was probably the best I ever had. Though you're only number three, so it's not exactly a broad comparison. Still, it wasn't meant to be a noose around your neck. No offence Mac, but I can't even be sure which side you're on."

"I work for British Intelligence."

"So did Jason, and he's an untrustworthy shit."

"He's also dead."

"Not given what I heard yesterday."

"What did you hear?"

She'd paused and compressed her lips. She knew nothing about him for certain, except that he was a magnificent lover. If he killed her out here and no one would find her for months, years, possibly ever. "No." She pulled her hand from under his. "Now's the time that you have to decide: do you trust me? Why do you want the evidence Jason had?"

"You don't have sufficient clearance for that."

"Amateur night isn't over, Mr Letterman, and my chances of surviving it are slim at best. So screw clearance, do *you* trust *me*?"

He scrutinised her face for so long —

"No, right, well." She stood. "I need to get my boots on." She moved to her bag, retrieved her boots, and sat on the floor to put them on.

"You know what's happening with Russia and Ukraine, right?"

Elaine kept her eyes on her shoes, surprised how much his distrust cut. Just because he was only the third man she'd ever chosen to share her body with, didn't mean it mattered. Certainly not to him. *Keep it real.* "Putin sabre rattling for the last few years? The invasion of Ukraine in 2014?"

He moved to stand near her. She concentrated on her shoes, but she saw his; Salomon walking shoes, laces double knotted. She double knotted her own, but only because it was her habit.

"Yes," he sighed. "Around that time, we received some poor intelligence from one of our operatives. The same operative also indicated that a double agent had infiltrated our ranks. He died during that invasion."

Now she frowned up at him. "Sorry." Though she wasn't entirely sure what she was sorry for.

Mac shrugged. "I didn't know the guy."

She semi-turned her back on him to sort out the ties and buckles on her rucksack.

"So, Russia invaded, they're still there, and they're taking more. So what?"

She moved away from him to pick up her handbag, put it over her shoulder.

"It took a while, but other cracks started to show in the organisation. We had several agents working the possibilities, and one in particular pulling it all together. He'd been working on it for years. Seven months ago, we got an indication that that operative had all the evidence we needed, including who the link across the divide was."

"Divide?" she asked as she took up the rucksack. "You mean geographical or political?"

"Both. A few days later, that agent's body turned up, but the evidence didn't."

"So how did Jason get hold of it?" She couldn't face him, instead tying the back pack's waistband around her middle.

"We don't know, or at least I don't."

She nodded.

This time he sighed. "Are you really going to get all pissy because I took a minute to decide whether or not to tell you all that? Technically, I just committed treason for you."

"Yes. No. Apparently." She shook her head and finally frowned up at him. "What do you mean treason?"

* * *

Her eyes searched his face. Desperately searching for something to pin her hopes to.

"Well, it's not exactly treason. But you don't have clearance and I could lose my job for telling you."

She hung her head. "Sorry," she muttered. "I have a history of making terrible choices when it comes to men and trust."

"Jason was only one terrible choice."

The bitterness of the self-deprecating huff was obvious. "You say that because you don't know about Eric Kitchener." Her hand came up and pushed her hair back from her face. She took a deep breath and looked up at him, her eyes haunted. "I'm sorry. It's just…" She laughed at herself, short, bitter, and cold. "My melancholy blues."

He frowned. "Did you just quote a Queen song at me?"

She blinked up at him, clearly having to think about his question. "Err, yeah, I think I did. Sorry."

He shrugged. "It's oddly appropriate."

"Unlike me." She hung her head.

"That's what makes it appropriate."

Her head shook slightly. "I'm sorry. It's just that… I've been living with lies for so long, I'm not sure how to tell what's true and what's not anymore."

A feeling he was well acquainted with. "I get that, but this is true; if you build defences too high, you end up the one imprisoned." He made a mental note to find out all about Eric Kitchener. "You can tell me the rest of what you've been up to on the way." He picked up his bag and opened the door to an icy blast of wind. For a nanosecond, staying put seemed a good idea. But only for a nanosecond. "Time to play the game."

"Where are we going?" Elaine asked as she followed him out.

He looked down at her as he locked the door back up. "You could just trust me."

"And you could get a clip round the ear, young man."

He controlled his smile; she was back to being feisty and he was fairly sure that was a good sign. "I'm older than you."

Taking her by the backpack, he propelled her down the path to the car. Their luggage stowed on the back seats, they got in and he started the car, sliding the heaters to full before he pulled away.

"Isn't that going to look a bit odd?"

Carefully negotiating a 180-degree turn, Mac wasn't sure what she was talking about. "What'll look odd?"

"Luggage on the back seat, not in the boot."

"Maybe, but I'd rather have it where I can just grab it."

"Where are we going?"

"West. Back to Germany."

"Do you have a reason for that or is it just to keep moving?"

"To keep moving." That truth wasn't a problem to share.

"In which case, can I suggest south?"

"Why?" His hard stare didn't last because he had to concentrate on driving.

"You could just trust me."

CHAPTER FIFTEEN

He could just trust her, she thought, but she'd pretty much just proved she didn't exactly trust him, making his reluctance understandable.

"Yeah, okay, that is a bit of an ask at this point," she admitted.

"It's also moot. There are several miles before we intersect a decent southward road, you've got time to convince me to make that turn."

"Yeah." She sat back and stared out the window. "Where do I even start?"

"Start with this." Mac pulled something from the glove compartment his side and held it out for her.

She took it carefully.

"I'm not passing you poison," he grumbled.

"Really? It's hardly Brighton rock." Elaine frowned at the package in her hands. It was some kind of snack bar, but the Czech packaging was unintelligible. "Erm, what did you pass me?"

"An energy bar. You haven't eaten today."

True, and she was hungry, but nothing about this bar inspired her to eat. Still, she supposed she should, coffee and adrenalin alone were not a great survival plan. She tried to open the thing, but the foil defeated her. She put it between her teeth to tear, but it pulled clear and clacked her teeth.

"Apparently you really need to build up your strength."

The giggle bubbled over as Elaine reached into her handbag.

"What is with you and the two bags?"

She laughed again. "Essentials are in here." She tapped the big black handbag she had bought in Geneva, then pointed over her shoulder to the rucksack. "That is clothes and shoes and stuff that I can afford to dump if I have to."

"Oh."

Did that sound suggest he was impressed or disappointed?

"Makes sense."

She fished around and pulled out a small tin held together by a thick elastic band.

"What's that?" he asked.

"It's meant to be a baccy tin, but it's my stash tin. I keep useful stuff in it." Like the tiny sewing kit and the even tinier pair of scissors she retrieved and opened the wrapping with.

"Normal people tear them open."

"Good for normal people."

He glanced at her and smiled. "You don't take prisoners, do you?"

"Sorry." She smiled back. "My years of taking shit from others are over." She bit into the soft bar. The smile didn't last as she pulled the bar away, opened the window and spat the mouthful out. "Ew, you really are trying to poison me."

"What? I had one of those yesterday, they're fine."

"If you like blueberries."

"I love blueberries."

"I don't." She sat back as the window wound up and re-wrapped the bar. A glance around revealed nowhere to stash it.

"Chuck it out the window," Mac said.

She did. "Seems wasteful, but… Still, if not eating, I guess I can talk. You said you'd interrogate me today, so question away."

"Why did you go to Paris?"

"I told you that already. Okay, well I found a cypher and a key in the lagging, deciphered it – Keira was the keyword by the way. Not exactly flattering, but there you go, life with Jason." She shrugged. "That gave me watch tower, Godiva and North Gate Spell—"

"You only told me watch tower."

"Are you going to keep butting in?"

He glanced at her. "This is not a don't stop me now moment."

"Really? You're quoting Queen songs now?" She laughed as she looked at him.

"That was naming not quoting," he pointed out. "The cypher?"

"Okay. I didn't give you everything, I know, I lied. By omission. Just like you. Get over it. But I found the cypher, and you gave me something I wasn't expecting. Those pictures."

"Yeah, sorry about that."

"Selected, I suppose, to evoke an emotional response."

He shrugged. "You did throw your laptop across the room."

This time she gaped at him. "You set up cameras in my home?"

"No, Jason did. Some years ago, judging by the tech. I just used them."

"Aargh." She looked back out the window. "God, I've been so blind." She sighed, looked back at him, got back to the point and ran quickly through how she found the account, why she'd gone to Frankfurt, including her monobrow fears and how she got out of the conference. "But I had to go back for my rucksack. So, when I saw this homeless girl, a redhead, I told her if she helped me out, she'd get a new coat, a hat and twenty Euros. You, thankfully, fell for that and I got away. I called a contact—"

"Contact?" he interrupted.

"Yeah. Someone back in England I trust."

"Stop trusting them. Your calls will be monitored."

"Someone back in England I trust who showed me how to change the number of my phone, so I've never called from the same number or location twice." She hoped he didn't ask more, because she didn't want to get Madison in trouble. "Anyway, I asked that person to investigate Ohmnet because that was where the other guy seemed to be hanging out. My contact was also looking for signs of Lazlo and came back to me with news that Lazlo and Ohmnet's ultimate owner would meet last night in Prague. So, I went there. Blagged a waitressing job. Nearly had a heart attack when I saw you and the stalker, albeit at different tables, and thanked God I was working the far corner, away from the pair of you. When you started mingling, I failed to avoid you, served you champagne, which left me in quite a state. My hands wouldn't stop shaking and I couldn't hold a tray steady. The boss told me to go, so I did. That was when I heard Lazlo's voice. He was talking to the tall guy who later walked past us. Lazlo said he'd been in Berlin to get a code book, but it wasn't there. The guy blamed Lazlo, slapped him, sounded hard and painful, then he suggested grabbing and torturing me might make Jason talk. Lazlo said Jason would sooner do the torturing. Which I'd like to think was a bluff, but don't. And then you came along, so you know what came next."

"And that's why you think Jason is still alive?"

"It's a distinct possibility."

"Then why…?" His voice trailed off with a wave of his hand going between them.

"Really?" she asked, eyebrows raised. "Too squeamish to come out and ask why I had sex with you?"

He took a second to scowl in her direction.

"Why?"

She shrugged. "I told you. I wanted to. I thought you did too. Look, Jason may still be alive, but I'm not here for him. What I heard also suggested that Steve is still alive. I'm assuming here that you're as familiar with Steve Southgate as you are Jason?"

He nodded his confirmation.

"Well, I know Keira would take him back in a flash given the chance. But Jace and I, well we've not really been husband and wife for a lot of years, if ever. Besides, if anyone asks, he's dead and I have his death certificate to prove it. But beyond that, I don't feel anything for him, nothing. Well, maybe a hefty dose of contempt. I think that's why I didn't believe he was dead when first told, because it made no difference. He was already dead to me."

That was a depressing idea and she stared out at the rain, almost hypnotised by the swiping of the wiper blades.

"Elaine?"

"Hmm?" She turned her head to him

"In all that, how much did you omit this time?"

"A lot of details. But only details." Some pretty damn weighty ones, but now wasn't the time. She did trust Mac as much as she trusted anyone, but life had taught her she made terrible decisions about trust and men, especially about trusting men. Besides, she was pretty sure what he'd do if she told him the truth, and that would be counter-productive.

"Those are details I need."

"Really? Like what?"

"Like how the hell did you fly under the radar so easily this last couple of weeks."

She smiled at that. "Didn't seem easy to me, besides – paranoia, remember. I had to do something."

"Which was?" He didn't glance at her as he asked because he had to slow to avoid a minor flood stretching across their side of the road.

"Mostly hitching and cadging. I read this book once. *Broke Through Britain*. The writer wanted to find out if it was possible to survive money-free travelling across Britain. He basically walked from the south coast to, I think, Edinburgh. He said sleeping rough is pretty harsh, but he found that if he looked for people who had caravans on their drives, he would knock on their doors and ask to spend the night in their vans, it worked for him. For the most part it worked for me too, mostly. It helped that I'm a middle-aged woman not in crisis, well not visibly, and I speak fluent German, so I reassured people I'm not a total nutter. No money spent, no credit card trail, only a couple of nights in hotels when I needed a shower. I kept off the main roads, so little CCTV. Basically, I went back to basics. So, who did you fight with at the gala?"

"Ulrich Demko." He leaned to his left now, judging if it were possible to overtake the slow-moving goods vehicle in front of them. It wasn't, and she felt the car slow.

"Why?"

"He was passed something secretly and I wanted to know what."

"What was it?"

"A pen drive."

"Interesting." She sat straighter. "Where is it?"

He turned to her. "Why?"

She reached into her bag again, opened the middle zip compartment to bring out a ten-inch tablet, then fished inside again. "I wanna look."

"Tablets don't have USBs."

She returned a smug grin and held up the second thing she'd gone in for. "Converters do."

He glanced across, before returning his concentration to the road. The muscles in his jaw worked. "It's password-protected."

"Then I won't be able to get in and you've got nothing to lose by showing a little good faith and handing it over. Where is it?"

His lips pressed in a contemplative line. The rain was coming down harder now, so he slowed to put more distance between them and the lorry kicking up enough spray to distort visibility. As he eased off the accelerator, he shifted and awkwardly pulled the drive from his pocket. Threw it in her lap. As Elaine worked to put it all together, Mac concentrated on the driving.

"I would have found it," he said.

She stopped and looked at him. "Found what?"

"The cypher in the lagging."

"Really? You were looking in all the wrong places as far as I could tell."

"We hadn't got to the ripping up floorboards stage."

She frowned across at him. "What? Have your lot wrecked my home?"

"No. Once you left Cardiff, they assumed that you had the evidence and were taking the money to run."

Her jaw dropped as she stared at him. Stunned their assumption was so far from the truth.

"That's why they gave me the money." The penny finally dropped. "That's why you came after me. They want both the money and the evidence back."

"In fairness, I think they're slightly less concerned about the money."

"Good to know." Elaine nodded.

"Why did you change your hair?"

As the tab booted, she reached over the back of the seat and rummaged in the top of the rucksack. She brought the second passport out to show him.

"A fake passport?" He frowned. "How did you manage that?"

"Well for a start, it's not exactly fake." This time she put it in her handbag as she told him about bumping into the German woman on the Eiffel Tower, rushing to collect both their bags and their belongings.

"Nice move."

"Thanks, but I didn't do it intentionally."

"Why did you get off the Eurostar?"

"Technically, I never actually got on it."

He rolled his eyes and sighed. "Pedant."

"Okay." She chuckled. "Bloody-mindedness. Sheer bloody-mindedness. I'd had enough of people telling me what I could and couldn't do, so I decided I'd do what I wanted and at that moment what I wanted was to defy you. Besides, there was the whole Lazlo-evidence exchange thing to deal with." She shrugged. "Sorry, but also the didn't-know-you-from-Adam thing was ongoing at that point too. Interesting."

He turned to the tab.

"Eyes on the road, mister. It would be stupid to come this far only to die in a car crash."

"How the hell did you get into that so quickly?"

"Password."

"You figured it out?"

"Nope. None was set." She looked up and at him. "You know, for a bunch of spies, that's pretty lame security."

"Stumped me for two hours."

She chuckled at the grumble. "That's pretty lame too. To not even try a null. So, what you've taught me today, Mr Letterman, is that going back to basics completely undermines the intelligence services. You're like Sherlock, fooled because you're looking for the complicated answer when the answer is elementary. That's good to know."

"You still haven't told me why I should go south," he said.

"Berdyans'k is south of here. Well technically southeast. Mostly east."

"And where is Berdyans'k?"

"In Ukraine. It's a port on the Sea of Azov. That lump of water on the map above the Black Sea."

He shot her another disparaging glance; apparently he knew the Sea of Azov. She busied herself opening files from the stick. One opened revealing a picture of Mac, and a lot of information.

"I'd rather you didn't look at that." His dark tone bordered on the threatening.

"I bet. Wow, you have a really long list of aliases. Is Cormac Letterman really your real name?"

"It is, yes. If we need to get into the Ukraine, we should head east not south."

"Usually, but I need to go to Ankara first."

He paused; Elaine saved the file to the tablet.

"Why do you need to go to Ankara first?"

She chuckled again. "Don't speak to me like I'm some recalcitrant child." She told the system to eject the pen drive and pulled it out. "I don't entirely know why I have to go to Ankara, but my contact told me to." For a second, she chewed on her lip.

"What?"

She swallowed. "What do you mean, what?"

"You're dreadful at hiding what you're thinking, and you're definitely thinking something you're not telling me. What?"

She wasn't sure she wanted to tell him. "It's personal."

"Isn't all of this personal to you?"

"You, er, may have a point there." She slumped in the seat. Did she want to talk about this? "Another of the children I adopted is in Ankara. He's who I've been sent to see, but I still don't know why."

"That could be a security risk. Anyone looking for you, might look first for your foster children."

She felt herself slumping more. "Again, you may have a point there." Another chew on the lip. "But I'm going anyway. You just have to decide if you're coming with me."

He kept his gaze on the road and said nothing. She'd thought they'd got close after last night, then the issues this morning. And... and nothing. Elaine recognised that her emotions at the moment were less than stable, it wouldn't be unfair to hold that against Mac.

"Here, you can have this back." She held up the pen drive for a moment before reaching over to slip it into his trouser pocket.

His hand clapped over hers to stop her and do it himself.

CHAPTER SIXTEEN

"Really? Why are you so desperate to have me eat something?"

He had stopped in the first town they had come to and pulled her into the first café he saw. The day hung grey and damp, precipitation beaded in her hair after the run from the car. It dripped down and collected on her coat. The rain was more of a curtain than a veil now. Big drops crashed on the road outside, a white layer of splashes ten inches deep carpeted the tarmac. He wasn't worried about a seat by the window, visibility was too low.

"Because we've been together over twenty-four hours and you haven't eaten in all that time."

"Neither have you." She pushed the goulash around her still full bowl. He'd eaten his with relish. For a tiny place in the middle of nowhere it served one of the best beef stews he'd ever had.

"I had a three-course dinner at the Rudolfinum; you were working, so you didn't. I had a tin of soup I found in the cupboard for breakfast before you woke up. You didn't even look for food, just went straight to the coffee. I've now eaten a full bowl of goulash and a side order of dumplings, and you've hardly taken the top off that."

"It tastes good, too." She continued stirring it.

"Then why aren't you eating?"

And why wouldn't she look at him? In the car he'd thought they'd reached a new level of honesty, now she'd withdrawn again. But at least she picked up a spoonful and ate it. "Am," she said round the lump of beef. She swallowed. "The meat's so tender, it melts in the mouth."

"Yes, it's lovely," he agreed. "So why aren't you eating it?"

"Sorry, are we in a hurry?" She put the spoon down. "We can go if you want."

He grabbed her hand to stop her moving from the table. Her cold hand.

"Do you have carpal tunnel syndrome or something?"

"Nah, just poor circulation."

She relaxed back into the seat. At least she picked up the spoon, but she only stirred the stew again.

"Elaine—"

"Would you mind not calling me that?"

The request surprised him. "What would you prefer? Laney?"

She blinked up at him. "That wasn't what I was going to suggest, but I've never been called that before. Yeah. Okay. Call me Laney. I like that. Feels like there's a whole new me, coming soon."

The smile was genuine, but brief, and slid away as her eyes turned to the goulash again.

"Laney, since I came to your house, you've lost what? A stone? Two?"

Her eyes flashed up to his. "Then maybe I'll—" Her wide eyes switched from flaming to frozen in horrified shock. She pulled her hand away and covered her face with both.

For a moment all he could do was stare. Whatever she was experiencing, it hurt. She needed comforting, someone to tell her everything would be okay. But whatever she might say, deep down she was the all-or-nothing kind. She'd stuck out an empty marriage because that was what she believed people were meant to do. He couldn't offer her even that much.

"What were you going to say?"

She shook her head, it remained hanging, eyes averted as she picked up the spoon and took another bite.

"Laney?" the new name came easily to his lips. Possibly because it suited her better. He liked it, a new connection between them.

"It would have been entirely unfair to you."

Another spoonful. Eating as a cover? Comfort eating or avoiding speech? At least she was eating.

"Go on then, be unfair. I'm not easily offended." Especially when he saw how bad she felt. Besides, she'd put up with enough unfairness, he was strong enough to take some back.

She sighed, eyes down. "The last straw between Jason and I." The stirring continued as she tried to find ways to explain. "I tried to make things better, brought some fancy lingerie, put it on. All he said was I'd have to lose a stone or two before any man would want to see that. That I should be ashamed to be so fat and had to be crazy to think any man could possibly find me attractive."

Jesus. What a thing to say to any woman, let alone your own wife. "You've never been fat, though. You're curvy like a woman should be."

She shrugged and took another bite.

"Is that why you've stopped eating? What's the plan? You're going to starve yourself to death in retaliation?"

The spoon lowered, her eyes came up and glared at him. "If so, it would have been two years ago when he said those awful things. No. And I haven't 'stopped eating,' I eat when I'm hungry. Only, lately, I haven't felt hungry. No idea why, I just haven't. And right now, what's really bugging me is that I threw that in the face of…" She waved the spoon towards him, her cheeks glowing red.

He smiled. "Your bit on the side?"

She tried to glower, but a smile playing on her lips. "I could kick you under the table, you know."

"But you wouldn't." He moved his legs aside, just in case.

"Nah, probably not." She ate again.

"Wouldn't mind seeing the lingerie though," he mused.

"I threw it away." She'd stopped looking at him, but he saw the smile on her face. "I'm all plain t-shirt bras and briefs these days. Very boring. But you know that. You went through my drawers."

He wouldn't say boring after last night. "I would—"

"Can we change the subject please?"

"Okay." As long as she kept eating, he was happy to talk about anything. He'd imagine the lingerie later. "What do you want to talk about?"

Now she looked up at him. "That Demko bloke? What does he look like?"

"Why?"

"So I know who to avoid."

Made sense, two sets of eyes were better than one. "Six foot four, black hair, kind of blocky. Archetypal bad guy." As he spoke, she grew paler.

She swallowed. "Mono-brow?"

He nodded. The spoon slapped down. She slumped back in the chair.

"Laney?"

"That's the guy from the train. The one I saw in Frankfurt, that I hid from at the conference."

He reached out and took her hand. Still cold, but she turned her wrist and held him back. Clung to him. He shouldn't like that so much.

"It's okay. He's not here."

"Or he is." This time she pulled her big handbag onto her lap and opened it up, took out her sketch pad. She flicked through a few pages and placed it in front of him.

A photo couldn't be more like Ulrich Demko than this image.

"Is that him?"

Mac nodded. Elaine had captured the man's scowl perfectly. He felt a little intimidated by the paper. "He was at the dinner. Didn't you see him?"

She nodded. "That's how I managed to keep out of his eyeline."

"Well, I'm glad he didn't see you."

"No one notices waitresses, especially when they're waiting on other tables. Besides, once I noticed you and I was kinda busy balancing the waitressing, monitoring the pair of you, and keeping out of sight."

She'd done a damn good job of it too. Mac looked down at the sketch pad, and flicked back a few pages. He saw the couple she'd drawn on the metro in Paris when he'd been following her. An image of Madison looking happy. Other people and places he didn't know. He flicked forwards.

"No don't."

She reached for the pad, but he pulled it out of her reach. Looking at the image she didn't want him to see. The picture of him. Her hand pulled away. She had drawn him like Mr

Hyde lurking the shadows ready to pounce on some poor innocent.

"Turn the page again."

Dreading what he might find he turned the page. Another drawing of him. But not evil this time. Him. A flattering version of him. He was even smiling. "Different day? Feeling different about me?" Finally, he dared look at her as she reached out for the sketch pad, he let her take it.

"Same day. Trying to figure out how I felt about you."

"What did you decide?"

"That I didn't know enough, one way or the other." Her eyes clouded with worry. "Can we go now?"

She'd clearly lost what little appetite she had, but at least she'd eaten something. "Sure." He left money on the table and stood. He took her hand and she clung to him all the way to the car.

* * *

"Pull over."

Mac glanced at her.

"Please. I'm gonna throw up."

There was a layby shortly ahead, Mac swerved into it and stopped almost at the end, thankfully the rain had stopped and helped keep them safe. The car had barely stopped when Elaine released her seat belt, all but fell from the car, ran into the brush beyond the un-edged tarmac, bent over and threw up. Retching again, she fell to her knees and let more of the straining liquid pour from her mouth.

This was embarrassing, but unavoidable. Between the goulash, stress and what lay ahead, her stomach churned acid. An hour after eating, there wasn't anything in her belly to bring up, but the bile burned her throat. She had to explain it to Mac, but she wasn't sure how to face him, to tell him.

The weight of a hand burned on her shoulder.

"Laney? You okay?"

She sat back on her heels and stared into the scrubby looking bush. She nodded. "Sorry."

"You don't have to keep apologising," Mac said as he knelt beside her. "What's wrong? The goulash upset you?"

She took the water bottle he offered and swilled her mouth, spitting a long stream into the bush.

"Car sick?"

Turning to face him at last, the concern in his eyes was her undoing. With a shake of her head, she blinked back tears. "No. Guilt. There's something I need to show you. In the car."

Her knees failed on the first attempt to stand, but Mac was there. He held her up. "You sure you're okay?"

"Let's get back in the car, and I'll show you what's got me upset."

She remained unsteady as they sat and she told him what she'd found in the safe deposit box, admitted not knowing what she had. She needed someone with more background knowledge, and that was Mac. She passed him the book.

"I'm pretty sure it's a Russian Bible, but since I don't read Russian, I can't be sure. But the text is Cyrillic."

Mac took the black leather-bound book. The way he wasn't looking at her, and took a deep steadying breath, made her wonder how annoyed he was with her. He flipped the book open. She saw his eyes roaming the pages. In all fairness, she hadn't exactly held back, they'd only been together a day.

"It's a Bible alright."

Was this churning and uncertainty because the years had trained her this way, or because she feared his reaction. Because she didn't want to be sent home? Or because she valued his opinion of her? Too much confusion. She tried reason instead. "You speak Czech and read Russian. Take it you specialised in the Eastern Bloc languages?"

"While you studied German." He passed the Bible back.

As she took it, deliberately by the spine, the soft leather collapsed, and his eyes fell to the fore-page. As his brows knitted, he took the book back and fanned the pages to read the code.

"What's this?"

"Proof that Jason's a philistine."

He threw her a hard glare.

"Okay, I'm not actually convinced it's Jason's writing. But either way, it's also one of the details I omitted before. They're coordinates in Berlin, a locker number and the code for the locker." No more lies, but she still had to be careful with the truth. "It's empty—the locker. I'm guessing that's what Lazlo referred to last night."

"Any other 'detail' like this you should be telling me?" The hardness of eyes that wouldn't look at her, the tightness in his voice, scared her.

She pulled the crumpled medical letter from her bag. "There's this."

He took it and read it. "This was in the safe deposit box?"

"Yeah." She sighed. "Not sure why he'd want to keep something like that, I would have thrown it away, but I've given up trying to figure out how that man thought, cos apparently I didn't know him at all." She sighed and passed over the other documents. "Then there are these."

Mac took the documents, again in Cyrillic. Reading was a sedentary occupation, but he didn't seem to be reading them as much as staring at them.

For a moment Mac sat in silence and stared out at the damp road. She wondered what he thought but didn't dare ask. A few seconds later, he dragged in a deep breath.

"Who's your contact?"

"I'd rather not say."

"I'd rather not have this conversation." He turned to her, that blank emotionless gaze chilling. "Madison Turner, right?"

She swallowed as she looked back. "Why do you think that?"

"Because she's CIA."

"What?!"

He frowned. "You didn't know?"

"No! Oh God." Elaine hid her face in her hands. "I would never have gone to her if I'd known she worked for the American secret service. I am such an idiot."

He chuckled and she found herself hugged to his chest. "Technically, the CIA isn't *the* Secret Service, and at least they're a friendly agency."

"Is that like friendly fire?" she mumbled into his chest, heard his slight laugh.

"I know Madison, she's good at what she does, and she wouldn't see you hurt for the world. She's a good woman."

Hands still over her face, Elaine frowned. "If you've slept with her too, I'm going to shoot myself."

"Thankfully, we're safe there."

"Because we don't have a gun?" It wasn't as funny as she thought it would be.

"Because I'm not that much of a creep." His hands moved to push her to sit up, he pulled her hands from her face. "Stop beating yourself up over every little thing. This is good. I've been ordered to keep radio silence—"

"You guys still use radios?"

"Not often." He smiled. "And stop diverting with humour too. The point is, I can't get that level of data or analysis without back-up, and I don't have back-up, because I can't risk contacting my colleagues in case one of them is the double agent we're ultimately after and they derail my investigation. Had to make an exception with Tannek, because of you, and that was mostly to persuade him not to kill you. But, back to the point, Madison can call on the resources of the CIA if she has to and I'm the only one that knows for certain that you're contacting her, so it's the safest and surest path. If the lead to go to Ankara came from her, I trust it."

Elaine offered a small, uncertain smile, leaned forward and kissed his cheek. "Thank you."

"Oh no, you don't get away with that scrappy offering."

Pleasure and surprise warred when he pulled her forward and kissed her properly. Pleasure won.

CHAPTER SEVENTEEN

"What are we doing?" Elaine asked as Mac pulled into the Aupark, a shopping mall just south of Bratislava.

"There're things I need to do." Mac concentrated on manoeuvring into the parking bay, mostly because he didn't want to do what he was about to do. And his stomach sank. He had work that he couldn't do while she was with him. Mostly because the result could lead to uncertain actions. Somehow Laney seemed a different woman to the Elaine Blake he'd known, and he didn't want to lose Laney. Which was stupid, selfish, and potentially fatal. Whatever Tannek had reported Agent Smith's orders were, now was not the time to take Laney back to the UK.

Once parked, he shut the engine down, and turned to her. Damn it, leaving her shouldn't be this difficult. He had to treat her like any other agent. She wasn't his Laney, she was Elaine, he was just calling her Laney. Like a cover. Like any other agent. For all she wasn't even an agent. "Be out the front at the main entrance in two hours precisely," he said. "I'll pick you up from there." *Possibly*.

She checked her watch. "And what am I supposed to do for two hours?"

He frowned at her, confused. "It's a shopping mall, most women I know would think two hours too few."

"Really?"

She gave him that look again, the one that indicated his apparent deficiency. He felt deficient, certainly not good enough for her.

"Two hours in an altar to consumerism seven weeks before the world's biggest consumer-driven holiday," she said. "And it's late-night shopping as people begin the desperate trawl of tat because they've got to give something even if it is something they know the person they're giving it to will never use?" She raised her brows at him. "Two minutes of that would be enough for me."

He grinned. "You can't tell me you're not a fan of Christmas. I've seen the number of decorations in your loft. You have three Christmas trees."

"Actually, I have five."

The superior tone should freeze him out, but it warmed him.

"It's just that two of them don't look like trees until they're up."

Mac opened his mouth as if to say something but didn't know what.

"I love Christmas." She admitted. "It's shopping at Christmas time I hate."

If he didn't go soon, he'd never make it. He opened the door and got out.

Elaine seemed even more reluctant but did so too. He took his bag from the back. She took hers.

"Mac?" She stopped him as they moved away from the car.

Once they stood in front of the bonnet, the engine warmth radiated against one leg as the cold of the afternoon and the underground parking started to freeze the other.

"Are you ditching me?"

"No." The defence came automatically, but guilt hit him like a hammer. Because he might be. "I'll meet you out front in two hours."

"Take this, then." She held out a cheap phone.

"Why?" He took it all the same, a basic Nokia. She had a smart phone, so this came as a surprise.

"Because you haven't got one and I'm paranoid. It's just in case, okay?"

In case of what? In case I don't come back? Does she read me that easily? "Okay." He slipped the phone into a pocket. "Go shop. Don't lose your head, don't spend too much, and don't use that prepaid card, Mrs Hyde. If I found it, others may have."

He had to stride away, or there was a good chance he'd never leave her. Her expression bothered him. Elaine looked hurt and all he wanted was to hug her, reassure her, make everything right for her. *When did I get so damn soft?*

Now his irritation turned inwards. As he took the bus into the city he opened his laptop. Took time, but he found Eric Kitchener, well he found several, but figured the one of interest was the one who died twenty-seven years ago. The reference pages opened as he reached the city and had to get off the bus.

He found a coffee shop and ordered a double espresso, needing something strong to see him through. He found a table, sat and opened the laptop again.

Eric Kitchener. Died aged nineteen, accidental fall crossing a weir, head injuries, scrapes and bruises, nothing to indicate foul play, sufficient water in lungs to pronounce death by drowning and a conclusion of misadventure. Alcohol levels indicated drinking but not drunk. Eric had been cautioned a few times, four rape accusations that never moved forward. Nothing in the file suggested any involvement with Elaine Blake, sorry, Elaine Underwood as was, except that they lived in the same street. Elaine would have been fifteen at the time, so it didn't make sense that she considered Eric a terrible choice.

The boy's flat eyes stared from the photo, and Mac detected a vague familiarity, one he couldn't place it. A dog outside barked and pulled on its leash. Mac didn't know what upset it, but the big dog bared its teeth, barking. The owner yanked its chain and pulled it away. Mac looked back at the picture. Elongate the nose and—this was the face of the werewolf in Elaine's drawings.

Elaine knew Eric. Saw him as a figure of horror.

Mac finished his coffee as he closed the laptop, stowing it safely in his bag.

But why the horror? The proximity of their addresses made the acquaintance almost inevitable. She was bound to have heard about Eric's criminal activities. In all likelihood, the locals would know more than the police could record. What had happened to make Elaine draw Eric as an evil werewolf?

The question nagged at him as he left the shop, Elaine said that he was her third. Him, Jason, and who else? Eric? She would have been underage if so, but given the accusations that never stuck, that fit with Eric's profile. Lots of people lived to regret their first time, everyone made mistakes. Even if Eric had been her first, presumably her worst, it didn't matter now. Only it would matter to Elaine because that level of intimacy mattered to her. It had to, or there would be more than three of them. Given Eric's record and Elaine's own assessment of bad choices, Mac had to assume Eric hadn't been good to her. Nor had Jason. And if he left her now, Mac would be as bad as the both of them.

He had to do better. Show Elaine that she, his Laney, was worth more than that. A glance at the shop he walked towards gave him an idea.

What woman doesn't like presents?

* * *

Stupidly close to crying, Elaine stalked away, following large arrows that pointed in what she assumed to be the direction of the shops. She wanted to hear his footfalls chasing after her, but under the staccato stomp of her own pace, the heartbeat hammering in her ears, she heard nothing. She headed inside, blinking back idiot tears.

The wide-open spaces of the mall were just that. Wide and open. Not as many people as Elaine feared. It wasn't the shops at Christmas she hated, but the crowds and thankfully, there weren't many here yet. In the central hall, a tall gold tinsel tree with red outsized baubles both dominated and complimented the beige travertine. For a moment she stopped by a pillar and looked up at the towering tinsel construction.

Christmas was only seven weeks away. She thought about it, scratch seven, six weeks away. Normally by now she would have sent out invites, most of which would be declined. She could usually rely on Madison to come home for Christmas, Utku too, until recent years. Never guaranteed Jason would be there. Most years, Christmas cards would be ready to put in the post by now. Done but not to be posted before December 1st, didn't want to seem over-eager. She'd plan the colour scheme for the trees, trying to mix it up each year, hence the six boxes of decorations Mac referred to. The idea of sitting by a Christmas tree with him and a bunch of kids was way too appealing. She shook her head and moved on. No point dreaming.

The itchiness at the back of her neck started about three quarters of an hour later. There was a time limit on enjoying window shopping. Paranoia told her Mac had gone for good, and she was being watched. She stopped and looked around. Perhaps a store detective? Not going into shops would probably look weird and she had only set foot in one, which took ages and led to a bigger than expected payment. Add in the rucksack on her back, and her walking outfit, she probably stood out in all the wrong ways. Only no one seemed to be paying her any attention. She didn't even spot anyone who looked like a store detective. Thankfully, not a mono-brow in sight, it was just fear and paranoia had made her think of Demko.

The thought of him sent shivers through her.

Maybe a coffee would help, warm her up at least.

She walked on, and did a double take, stepped back, and hid in a doorway. Ulrich Demko walked straight past her. She looked at him walking away. Her throat dry and rough, heart trying to break out of her chest, she checked up and down the hall, desperate for a place to hide. Then she spotted stairs opposite. She ran across and up.

The food hall was stocked with ubiquitous brands; KFC, McDonalds, Starbucks. Elaine selected what appeared to be a more traditionally Slovakian coffee house. Traditional it might be, but everything seemed to be influenced globally these days. While Elaine did not know what to call Slovakian carrot cake, the thick slice was too tempting to ignore. For once, fear made her hungry.

The seating area was too open for comfort, but there was nowhere else to go, so she selected a seat near the back where she could watch the walkways and the people, plus it was behind a large group of big, overly made-up women who made an effective screen. She sipped the black coffee, which was way too hot and scalded her lip. She set it aside to cool and nibbled the cake, which turned out to be every bit as delicious as it looked, for all it sat like a lump of concrete in her stomach.

What was she going to do? Mac wasn't due back for – she checked her watch – over an hour. At this point she chose to believe he was coming back for her. The alternative was too painful. She seemed to have lost Demko. She took another bite of cake and looked up. He stood right outside!

She slumped down in her seat, covered her face with her hand. "Mein Gott." Apparently, she had become used to speaking German.

"Bist du unwohl?"

Head tilted, hand still raised, she looked up at the big orange lady who had spoken. "Mann Ärger."

The woman turned and looked out, a hushed exchange in a rapid-fire language Elaine couldn't identify but presumed to be Slovak. One of the other ladies looked to her.

"Exmanžel?"

She wasn't entirely sure what that meant but guessed ex-husband. "Ex-mann leibwächter." Ex-husband's bodyguard.

Knowing nods bobbed around the table, accompanying sympathetic 'ahhs'. These were women with a certain lifestyle who would want to be kept, but knew the realities of what that meant, and the likelihood of a newer, younger model coming along.

Elaine found her phone and texted the one she'd given Mac.

Demko here.

Conversation returned into the group and Elaine's attention turned to Demko. A man on the prowl, on the lookout, but she didn't think he'd seen her. The change of hair colour had been a help in central Europe, but here in Eastern Europe there were fewer redheads and she stood out; a red elf amongst the green in the grotto. She gathered her hair together, twisting and turning it into a self-holding bun. Suddenly an enormous hat appeared before her. The thick felt of the broad brim would cover all her hair and a lot of her face. The woman two to the right of the German-speaker.

"Danke," she offered, taking the hat she fixed it at an angle to shield her from the front of the shop and Ulrich's vision.

The women continued talking, then the first one leaned over, and pulled a chair towards their table, inviting Elaine by gesture to join them. Since being in a crowd was bound to be safer than being alone, Elaine dragged her rucksack under the table, and shifted across, removing her jacket. The black fleece beneath was cheap, but from a distance more in keeping with the crowd. As the women chatted, Elaine learned from her German-speaking companion that they were, as best as Elaine could describe it, a first wives club. All of them had been married and divorced, most more than once. Apparently, they were celebrating the latest freedom of one of their number, a particularly vivacious matriarch with a fearsome bosom, enough jewellery to rival Tiffany's, and false nails like talons. Under all the makeup she was naturally beautiful, no nip-tuck there. While Elaine didn't understand what they were saying, it was probably as well, the tone of their laughter was filthy in any language.

A check of the clock surprised Elaine with how little time had passed. Seconds dragged like hours, but a little over five minutes had passed. And Mac hadn't responded. She didn't even know if he'd actually received the text. The woman at her side asked her what was wrong. She explained she was due to meet someone, but not for a while and she was scared to get up and go just in case the man outside saw her.

"You need new clothes," the German-speaker said in German.

As she translated the statement, Elaine started to smile. She had other clothes in the bag. Then the smile dropped. The only outfit she had, she'd been wearing when Demko saw her on the train. Still, it might be enough. She agreed it was a good idea. Suddenly swept up they moved like a tide from the shop. She just about grabbed her rucksack and bag on the way. Hidden within the group of ladies they herded her away, her shortness effectively hidden by their high heels and big hats, fur coats, and more shopping bags than any group needed. These women were better than a battalion of bodyguards, and quite as effective.

Suddenly in the toilets, the women steered Elaine into a corner, almost ripping the clothes off her back.

Clearly these women wanted to help, and they were having fun.

Near nakedness wasn't fun for Elaine. The embarrassment flushed through more than her face as they looked at her old underwear. Some of the women spoke, but she forestalled them and crouched to her rucksack. She had made one purchase, and it seemed to meet with their approval. Apparently, the makeover had to start from the foundations.

Once the women stopped fussing again, Elaine looked down at herself, and didn't know what to think. She'd never normally wear a dress so tight, or so short. Heels weren't her thing, not over two inches anyway, but these were surprisingly comfortable. And she couldn't remember the last time she'd worn stockings. Was this how Laney would dress? Would Mac—Nope, stop right there, you can't make life about another man you barely know.

Now the women worked at her hair. One pulled out a hair piece, another painted her face. The foundation sat heavy on her skin, but only because she rarely wore any. She dreaded to think what she would look like when this was all done. The makeup woman stood straight, powdered Elaine's nose, then announced what Elaine assumed was a declaration of transformation. The hat returned to her head.

They guided her to a mirror.

Elaine had to blink to check she saw right.

Her hair looked blonde, figure full and on display, even her legs looked long for the first time in her life. Her own mother wouldn't recognise her – hell, she barely recognised her. The makeup might be plastered on, but it was extraordinarily well done. The expert contouring had changed the very shape of her face.

She turned to her interpreter and thanked her and her friends profusely in German. They passed her several expensive boutique bags, which contained her outdoor clothes and walking boots, all her belongings, she saw stuff even she had forgotten was in the rucksack. They had thought of everything.

Her phone bleeped.

Be there in 10.

The interpreter asked her how long. She checked her watch. "Zehn minuten."

A quick check of her handbag reassured her she had everything she needed, that went over her shoulder and the now empty rucksack got kicked into a cubicle. When they left as a group, the gossip seemed entirely normal. As she walked beside the woman who spoke German, she asked why they would do this.

"Our lives," she said in German, "are more boring than you could possibly imagine. This is fun, and we can pretend that we are helping a German spy escape the clutches of the KGB."

Elaine laughed. Too hard because it echoed and for a second, she looked up and straight at Ulrich Demko. Though he saw her, he looked straight away. The disguise worked perfectly.

They reached the front of the building. The gaggle paused and said their goodbyes, through hugs and kisses. Elaine kissed her interpreter last, thanked her again. When she straightened, she put on her best Roman accent and whispered in her new friend's ear, "Sicilian mafia."

The woman looked suitably aghast and incredibly pleased, taking the rightfully wrong impression that they were saving her from the Sicilian Mafia rather than the KGB. She waved and walked towards the road, desperately searching for the blue Audi Mac had been driving. No sign of it. She moved a little further along the road. No blue Audi, no Mac. She looked back. No women. No Demko.

She looked up and down the road again. Her grip on the shopping bags squeezed and moved. She stepped back as a large black car glided past her. She watched the car move away. Then she looked again, searching the traffic.

He said ten minutes. It's been ten minutes.

Oh lord, has he ditched me after all?

She saw the black car turn around. Her eyes went wide. That was odd. The hat tightening like a vice pressing her head. Was the person in the car working with Demko? The car moved towards her, and after blinking she focused on the driver.

Mac!

She lifted her arm; sure she had his attention, if for no other reason than he moved the car from that side of the road, only to screech to a halt a few feet later. She tottered to the passenger side, and got into the back, pushing her bags in before her. Mac stared at her, eyes wide and questioning.

"Later," she said. "Just drive."

CHAPTER EIGHTEEN

Mac pulled away to the resounding horn of the driver behind, who he'd forced to brake. As he joined the traffic flow, he glanced back at Elaine. Even knowing it was her, recognition was difficult with that new look. God, she looked good. She also looked worried.

"Are you okay?"

She dragged in a deep breath, and he tried not to notice what that did to her cleavage.

"I am now." She shifted in the seat and looked at him rather than out of the window. "I was terrified earlier. I saw Demko and tried to hide, but I think he spotted me. Then I managed to lose him in the crowds. I thought he left, then he turned up again and well… I changed my appearance, then I walked right past him. He looked straight at me but didn't recognise me."

"I can see why."

Her smile reflected in the rear-view mirror.

"How did you manage it?"

"With a little help."

"Money can do that," he muttered as he took an awkward left turn and moved onto quieter back roads.

"I only spent about forty quid."

He checked the mirror again. "On a fur coat?"

"I didn't buy the coat—like I said—I had help." She told him about the First Wives Club.

He laughed and shook his head as he moved into the car park of the next hotel he came to. "You are incredible. I can't believe you manage stuff like that."

She shifted in the seat. "We girls have got to stick together."

"That's sexist."

"Yes, it is." She bobbed forward and kissed his cheek. "We wouldn't be without you men though."

As he got out of the vehicle, Mac wondered how the mouse he'd seen all those years ago had turned into this lioness. Apparently, he, and everyone else, had been underestimating her for years. She smiled as she came to stand beside him. She had her shopping bags; he had his holdall, and the impression of being utterly underdressed. They didn't look like a couple. Her blond hair didn't trick up close.

"Think I prefer you as a brunette."

"Shame then, that you'll be stuck with a redhead once we're inside."

As she turned and headed towards the reception, he realised he'd unintentionally insulted her. He hadn't meant to, but it was probably just as well, he should try to maintain a professional distance. He looked down at his bag. He'd keep his shopping to himself; it seemed like a paltry offering now. As he stepped into the reception, Elaine was obviously getting on well enough booking the room without him, so he stood back and allowed her to get on with it. The receptionist glanced at him and Elaine turned to smile too. When she turned back, the exchange between them remained in German. The only word he recognised was 'husband'. Maybe he hadn't insulted her too much after all. Elaine took the offered key, led the way to the first floor and a room too small and chintzy for his taste. Still, it was for one night, not the rest of their lives.

Elaine moved to the far side of the room and put down her bags. When she slipped off the coat, he got the full impact of the dress and her figure. *This is what a woman looks like.* His own bag dropped on the end of the bed, and he unzipped it to retrieve his laptop. He had things to do and not another man's wife—much as he had to remind a certain part of his anatomy of that.

"What's that?"

He hefted the technology. "Laptop."

She gave him a sour look as she turned to him.

God, she looks too delectable.

"What's that?"

She pointed into his bag; he turned and placed the laptop on the limited surface of the dressing table shoved into the corner of the room. "Nothing."

Her sigh was deliberately audible. "In that case, I'm going to wash this gunk off my face."

The small room meant she had to squeeze past him. His lack of reaction was a lesson in self-restraint. As she entered the en suite, an inarticulate sound of revulsion said so much.

"How bad?" he asked.

"I'll wash in the sink, but I'm not touching that shower." Water started running. "Dear God, I paid too much for this."

"Welcome to life on the run." He opened the laptop before returning to his bag for the power lead.

He had logged on and was looking at the pen drive when she stepped out of the en suite. She'd removed the wig and the makeup, now she was a fresh and delectable redhead, his Laney again.

"What do you mean 'on the run'? I'm not on the run, I haven't done anything illegal."

He looked up from the computer. "You've travelled under an assumed name and on a stolen passport; the way you moved through Germany could be construed as begging; you worked illegally in Prague; you've travelled in a stolen vehicle—two stolen vehicles, and the roof over your head last night was secured by breaking and entering."

She took a moment to absorb all that. "You did the breaking. Not that you broke anything. And you stole the cars, not me."

He shrugged. "Accessory after the fact. Doesn't clear you of the rest."

"No." She looked away and her eyes caught on the box in his bag. "No, you're right. It doesn't." With a sigh, she slipped around him to the side of the bed where she sat on its edge and rooted through her bag.

Turning back to the computer, his throat dried at what he found. Details of several agents, all in deep cover across the European and Asian continents. With this knowledge, Demko, Illyana and Garin could do some serious damage to the UK's intelligence gathering.

"Mac?"

"Yeah?"

An absent-minded response as he stared at his small laptop.

"Can you tell me about that man Lazlo was talking to? At the Rudolfinum. The one you kissed me to hide from."

Hiding had only been half the reason. He'd really kissed her because he'd damn well wanted to. He closed the laptop and faced her. The shopping bags were all neatly folded into the bin and two thin-looking day sacks sat packed instead.

"Where did you get those?"

She glanced at the day sacks and back at him. "They're folding bags, I've had them years, always keep them in my handbags. They come in handy for shopping. And now this. So, the guy?"

Elaine sat curled on the bed, her handbag next to her, and she slipped the orange notebook back inside. She looked surprisingly vulnerable for a woman proving herself at every turn.

"Spartek Garin," he said. "You know all the terrible tales about the Russian Mafia? Garin is the real deal. A true-blue oligarch, well red I suppose."

"Great king rat? Or Tsar Rat?"

"Basically."

"What did he make his money in?

"What didn't he make his money in?" Mac saw Elaine wasn't that easily satisfied. "He started with his father's restaurants, his father was successful in his own right, owned a string of restaurants from Sochi to Rostov, to Odessa, to Volgograd. Spartek wanted more. He brought up a few clothing factories, a couple of bars, a pottery, a coachworks and, bizarrely, a few farms."

She frowned up at him. "So, he runs sweatshops, brothels and provides dishes and steaks for his dad?"

Her cynicism worked in his favour, saving him from explaining. "Well, yeah. He also found some mineral wealth in some of the land that helped. Still, the various legitimate businesses launder the money from alternative earnings, import-export. He also bought up land in Kazakhstan."

"Oil and gas?"

She impressed him, most people didn't even know where Kazakhstan was, let alone what its major industries were.

"And other mineral rights." Mac confirmed. "He is probably, but un-provably, running a number of protection rackets."

She smiled, almost laughed. "You make him sound like Al Capone."

"Al Capone was Snow White compared to Spartek Garin."

She went white.

"I'm sorry, I don't mean to scare you, but don't underestimate the evil that man can do."

"And he's got Jason. Possibly Steve too."

"What makes you think he's got Steve?"

"Well, Steve was supposed to have died with Jason. If Jason is still alive, which I'm pretty sure he is, there's every possibility that Steve is too. Possibly, the others. I was told it was a team of five. If Jace had the evidence, the others may have been used against him." She shrugged. "I don't know. I just don't like the idea of Steve being dead if Jason's alive."

Mac didn't want to consider the implications of that. "At least Garin hasn't got the evidence we're looking for."

She looked away again. "No." He watched her suck her bottom lip before she faced him again. "What will you do once you have the evidence?"

"Take it back to London and hand it over for the bosses."

She nodded, but she wasn't looking at him anymore. Her face was pale, her eyes hidden from him. Her hands were wringing in her lap.

"Laney?"

She looked up at the call. "Yeah?"

The frown deepened on his forehead. "Why wouldn't I?"

"Absolutely no reason at all. What do I do?"

That didn't make sense. "What do you mean?"

"Well, given what you say about Garin and Demko, if they find out I'm back in England, don't you think they're going to come after me? Want to know what I know?"

"It'll be too late by then."

"And you've not heard of revenge killings?"

Oh, he'd heard of them and a whole lot worse. She was right. If Garin found out where she was, he'd go after her. There was no way she could go home after this. What could he say?

"So what's in the box?"

It seemed she'd decided to change the subject. He looked at the box. God, it felt pathetic now. But he stood and pulled the box from his bag.

"It's a gift." He held it out to her.

She frowned. "You brought me a gift?" She knelt up on the bed, walking over on her knees to take the box. She held it in both hands and looked at it for what seemed like ages, then back up at him. "Why would you get me a gift?"

He shrugged, as gauche as an awkward teenager while she opened the box. When she peeled back the tissue paper, she revealed a black silk and lace bra and panty set. The walls and everything else were too close.

Eventually, she shifted, stepped off the bed and put the box on top of his laptop.

"You know I said I only spent a little?"

"Yeah?"

She turned to him. Her lips curved up in a smile and her eyes twinkled at him. "If you want to see what on, you'll have to help me out of this dress. Then you can judge quite how similar our taste in lingerie is."

CHAPTER NINETEEN

Typing away, researching, the light caught on Madison's engagement ring. It was a two-carat diamond that fitted perfectly. She'd been surprised when Neil presented it to her the day after his impromptu proposal. There had been red roses and Champagne and a lovely meal out. She'd even expressed surprise when he admitted he was in line for an earldom, something she'd found out before they started dating. It hadn't affected her interest in him, but she knew the company would run a background check if they got serious, so she'd run it first as she didn't want any nasty surprises down the line. Those checks were being officially undertaken now, and she hoped that she'd be able to go full disclosure shortly.

Neil meant more to her than she ever thought a man could. She was happy with him and whatever life threw at them, they'd withstand it together. Her only pang was not being able to share that joy with her mom.

Still, she had a job to do.

Searching keywords like Muslim, and attack, could bring up a lot of weird stuff from the internet, and often she saw things she would rather not. The search could trigger some very unsavoury links, especially to videos. Watching a beheading was not pleasant, and she had had to do that before now. Links to YouTube videos that suddenly rose to thousands of views however, that she had to see. Personal considerations pushed aside, she followed the link. What she saw surprised her.

This she had to pass on.

* * *

Waking up alone surprised Mac. He was more surprised to find Elaine sitting waiting for him. Fully dressed in travelling clothes, she was sitting stock still, the dead marionette, eyes downcast, bags packed and ready beside her. Her bottom lip was caught between her teeth again.

"Laney?"

She didn't answer immediately, and when she did, she still wasn't facing him. "Time to get up and go."

Her voice was dull, monotone. He rolled off the bed and stood. She still didn't face him. *Way to put a dampener on the morning.* He grabbed his clothes and headed to the en suite. Morning ablutions in the mouldy shower room didn't lead to any explanation of her odd behaviour. Last night, along with all that they had done together, he felt closer to her than he had ever felt to any other human being. Yet this morning she was a world away.

Dressed and ready, he moved back into the room. She hadn't moved. He grabbed up his bag, put his toiletries back in and was ready. "You okay?"

She nodded.

Didn't look that way to him. He stepped over and reached for her bags.

"Don't."

His hand stopped. This wasn't Elaine. He preferred his Laney, but she was AWOL too. He straightened and watched her.

"Do you know the lies that do the most damage?"

"I—" he floundered.

"It's the lies we tell ourselves."

He didn't understand. Time to listen. She kept her head bowed, her struggles with what she had to say reverberated in her tone. He didn't dare move in case of spooking her.

"I've been telling myself that this is right. That I'm doing the right thing. Only I'm not." She sighed as she stood. Finally, she looked at him. Her eyes were dry but didn't guarantee staying that way. Her lips compressed, she swallowed before continuing. "I tried to convince myself I wasn't lying because I never told you an untruth. But not telling you the whole truth is just as much of a lie. So, it's time I did. The reason Lazlo found that Berlin locker empty, was because I got there first." Her hand came up and in it was the orange notebook. "Take it."

He did.

"That," she said as he opened the book, "is the evidence that you want. It's a basic substitution cypher. In German."

He saw that. And she'd been working it out. For a moment, triumph flooded through him, closely followed by a wash of loss. He looked up at Elaine, took a breath—

"Don't say anything."

Good call. He didn't know what to say.

"You said that if you got the evidence, you'd take it back and use it. Well, now you have the evidence. Time to go. Go get in the car. This path I'm on is probably insane, but I can't get off. I can't go home, not yet. Maybe never. I have to carry on. I need to know what it all means. I want to find out why Lazlo turned against me. I need to know definitively if Jason is alive or dead. I can't have another man's ghost haunting me for the next twenty-five years."

He didn't understand what she meant, but she wasn't going to give him the chance to ask.

"You're going to leave now." The tone of clear and decided authority. "I'm going to wait ten minutes. If what you are going to do is take that to the UK, don't be outside when I leave."

She was deadly serious, meant every word. She'd known what she was going to do last night. That was why she'd been so—he struggled to find the right word. Magnificent. Desperate? No. Generous. Giving. There was so much he wanted to say, but not a single word formed.

He slipped the notebook into his pocket. Bag in hand, he turned around. Carefully opened and closed the door. The bill was paid; nothing more to do here. The reception door opened with an icy blast, but inside he was colder. He counted twenty-seven steps to the car. The car was cold. He scraped ice off the windscreen. The gusting wind buffeted him.

He had the evidence. It was his duty to get it back to the UK. The bosses wanted it. Needed it. They had to stop the double agent. Agents—as proved by what little he had read of what Elaine had decoded and translated.

He got in the car, inserted the key into the ignition.

He started the car.

I have to do this.

Turned up the heating.

It's my duty.

He pulled slowly and carefully from the parking space, crawled. Stopped, in front of the foyer, watching the road, the traffic. There wasn't much.

The passenger door opened. Two stuffed day-sacks landed on the back seat. The door closed. The front door opened. She got in.

"That was the longest ten minutes of my life," Mac said as he pulled away from where he'd waited for her.

"No more lies."

He nodded. "No more omissions."

"Can you do that with your past?"

He couldn't even lie to himself about that one. "No."

"Then don't give me piecrust."

Mac had to stop at the intersection. He used the pause to ask. "Piecrust?"

She turned to face him. "Easily made, easily broken." She smiled. "That kind of promise I don't need."

* * *

Elaine watched the road, the motorway from Bratislava to Budapest was much the same as every other motorway she had ever been on. She battled nausea again. Which made little sense given how grateful she was Mac had stuck around. Her phone beeped and she pulled it out of her bag.

"What is it?"

She frowned at the phone. "It's a link. Message from Madison. A YouTube link." She glanced up at Mac, his eyes on the road again. "Mac, you're not sorry you stuck with me, are you?"

He frowned, but he needed to concentrate on driving, the traffic was heavy, with some very slow-moving vehicles causing the rest of the traffic to bunch up around them and drive far too close.

"No."

She wasn't convinced and luckily the beep of her phone called her attention again.

"Another message?"

"Yes, a photo downloading." The picture slowly de-pixilated and she realised she was looking at a picture of Madison's hand, which made no sense until she saw the ring and the title —Neil. "Oh my God!"

Mac's frown deepened as she literally bounced in the only celebration she could manage.

"What?" he demanded as he checked the mirrors and moved into the next lane.

"It's from Madison. Obviously." Madison was the only one who had her number. "She's engaged!" She couldn't help squealing with delight. Then she realised that all the things she should do but couldn't. Not even sending flowers or congratulations. There wouldn't be any dress shopping or wedding arrangements. She put the phone away and looked out of the window. Good to know that Madison was happy though. Neil had seemed like a good man. She closed her eyes and forced herself not to be upset.

"Congratulations." Mac was turning off the motorway and towards what looked like a large petrol station.

Unsure how to take that gruff remark, Elaine bit her lip and waited for Mac to pull into the petrol station, only he went straight past and headed instead for the McDonalds behind it, moving into the slanted parking space beyond. Once the engine was off and the handbrake on, he turned in his seat and looked at her.

"I'm happy if Madison is happy. So should you be."

"I am," she felt quite defensive about that.

"Good," he nodded.

His expression was so serious, and she feared what he might say next.

"And to be clear, no, I am not sorry I stayed. Why would you even ask that?"

Elaine pressed her lips together. Not sure exactly how to say this, but she needed to know. "It's just that since we left the hotel, you've barely said a word and you've been frowning a lot."

Mac shook his head as he faced her. "I was thinking." He reached out and put his hand on her head, bringing her to him to place a heavy kiss on her lips. "I've been thinking about the best way to get to Ankara." His stomach rumbled, and hers growled in response. "I've also been thinking about getting breakfast." He moved back into his seat and opened the door. "You coming?"

Inside they sat down to McMuffins and coffee. As she chomped on hers, Mac opened up the small laptop he'd brought with him and signed into the free Wi-Fi.

She swallowed hard as she looked at him. "Is that a good idea? Aren't these public access systems open to hacking?"

"Yeah, but I've got good anti-spyware. Have you got that URL?"

She pulled her phone from her pocket and called up the message as he started his breakfast and typed in the link. While it buffered, they both dug into their food. Mac frowned with curiosity, and Elaine found the food stopped halfway to her mouth as an image of the London Underground came on screen. Her first solo trip to London since her teens. On her way to see Madison at the very start of all this.

Stunned, she watched the men abusing the young Muslim woman. She also saw herself looking around to see if anyone was going to do anything about it. She hadn't realised how many people had turned away. Then she stood and got between the bullies and the woman. The view changed to show her from the back, and she realised that someone had edited together the two recordings, one from the front, one from behind. She finally understood just how rude and aggressive the men had been, something she hadn't really taken in at the time.

"Oh my God!" she gasped. The muffin went down as the video continued.

"You didn't tell me about this," Mac grinned.

"I don't remember doing that."

Mac chuckled. "You flipped him the finger. I'm so proud."

He offered her a quick hug. She had given the man a one-finger hand signal and left it in view by holding the middle finger of her right hand up against the upright pole. They both watched to the end of the edited video, right to the end block where the same young woman in a different hijab, held an A4 pad in front of her that just said, "Thank you."

"That gobby one could have really given me a kicking." Even though the video had finished, Elaine stared at the screen.

"He was the loser in the end," Mac pointed out as he disconnected the internet and closed the laptop.

"Wonder why Madison sent me the link," Elaine wondered aloud as she started pushing her muffin away.

"Eat it."

She glanced up at Mac, surprised when he indicated the food while eating his own.

"Perhaps," he answered as she ate, "Madison sent it because she wanted you to see you the way the rest of us see you."

Elaine didn't understand and asked what he meant with an eyebrow raise.

"You're a hero."

Mouth full she still scoffed clearly enough.

"You are," he insisted. "Look how you stood up to that bully, protected that girl, a stranger. No one else in that carriage was prepared to do anything until you did. Look what you've done since."

Uncomfortable under the praise, she shrugged and looked away. "I did nothing special."

"You did! You did what most wouldn't. You could have just stayed at home and lived quietly. But you chose to go out into the world and do something."

"To take care of my son."

"But he's not your son, is he?"

She looked away. Mac's hand smoothed her hair; his grip gentle but enough to make her turn to him.

"Come on, hero. Let's get moving."

They gathered up their belongings and dumped the rubbish in the bin before returning to the car. Mac put the key in the ignition, but he didn't start the engine. Instead, he turned to her.

"I know you're upset at seeing Madison's engaged. You want to be with her and can't. You can't be there to make everything perfect for her as any mother of the bride would want to be. That's the biggest sacrifice this journey has asked for you yet. Laney, you have the most incredible capacity to love. You love Madison. Not being there for her is going to hurt you. But it's the best motivation of all. You love where others can't."

She wasn't looking at him, instead studying the hands she was wringing in her lap. He reached out and covered her hand—her cold hands—in his and she finally looked at him.

"Plus, you came all this way to take care of your son, but he's not your flesh and blood, and he was playing you. You know that, but you haven't stopped. Haven't given up on him. Or Jason. Or Steve. That's what makes you a hero."

Offering a weak smile, she swallowed the lump in her throat. "You would have done more."

He shook his head. "I couldn't. I tried but failed. You found the evidence I was looking for. You found that cypher and the key, figured out what it all meant, and given that you're pretty much the only person in the world who could have got past Coutts, it's likely I'd never have found it. Even if the British authorities don't have that information yet, you and I, we know it's safe. You've saved a lot of agents, the lives of a lot of people you'll never know. This isn't over yet, and you're willing to carry on. You are an incredible woman. And you found what I needed."

Elaine looked away, embarrassed by how close she came to telling him she'd found what she needed too—him. "But I've stopped you doing anything with that evidence."

Mac smiled at her uncertainty. "Hmmm, I've been thinking about that."

CHAPTER TWENTY

What Madison found was interesting. Definitely impressive. And something Elaine would doubtless want to know.

The woman from the underground and YouTube was Panina Binici. A Doctor of Marine Biology. Her specialism was The Effect of Climate Change and Industrialisation on the Diversity of Marine Life in The Black Sea and Sea of Azov.

Panina was renowned in her field and clearly well thought of. She was working and acting as a visiting lecturer all over the world. Quite recently she had been working with the Natural History Museum in London.

It didn't take long to discover that Panina was 29, originally from Samsun, where she had located her research base. Though she officially worked at the University of Ankara.

And if Panina was prepared to create a video to thank Elaine, Madison was pretty sure that Panina would love a phone call.

Finding a mobile number was simplicity itself.

* * *

Elaine worried as they sat on the bus from Ankara airport to Central Ankara. She'd received another text while she'd popped to the ladies earlier, and she hadn't told Mac as yet.

She wasn't sure what to do about it. Besides, right now other things had precedence in her head. She knew Utku worked in Ankara, but that was all she knew. A surprising warmth circled her wrist and pulled her hand, she had been chewing her thumbnail.

"What's wrong?"

She turned from staring unseeing out of the window, to looking up at Mac. She offered a smile. "Nothing's wrong, exactly. It's just that I haven't seen Utku in three years. Last time, when he came home for Christmas, there was, well…" How to describe it? "Tension."

"Tension?"

"Arguments." She bowed her head and remembered. Jason had been home and whenever they were alone, he'd dragged her spirit to hell. His constant private criticism had stretched her nerves; she could do no right. After dinner on Christmas Day, they were all full and drinking. All Jason had said was not to spill any of the wine. She'd snapped back something about being the one who had to clean up the mess when he brought rubbish into the house, and Utku had taken it wrong, as if she meant him and the other kids. "Well, one argument. One terrible argument. We haven't spoken since. I'm not sure how to break the ice now."

"The guy's a doctor, right?"

She nodded. "*Médecins Sans Frontières*."

He frowned a little. "They don't have an office in Ankara."

"No, but they work everywhere." She shrugged. "Or maybe he's changed jobs. I don't know. Madison said he was working here and to get in touch with him."

"Well, generally speaking, doctors aren't stupid people. He probably already knows that whatever was said wasn't meant. Perhaps he wants to make up too but doesn't know how to break the ice either."

She smiled and rested her head on his shoulder, as much as anything so he wouldn't see her doubt. There had been opportunities. She'd written, sent invitations, got no response. She told herself that Utku was busy. He didn't always get mail, couldn't always answer it. But even she didn't entirely believe that.

Mac kissed her hair. "Listen, if he's anything like your other kids, he loves you enough to forgive you."

"Really? Like Lazlo?" she asked. "Who basically stabbed me in the back?" It was unfair to throw that at Mac when he was trying to cheer her up. "Sorry." She sat up and looked at him. "I will find Utku. I'm just worried about what kind of reception I'll get when I do."

"You're probably worrying over nothing."

"Probably," she agreed. "Hopefully. But that won't stop me worrying."

He offered a supportive smile. Not having children of his own, or anyone else's, he didn't fully understand.

"I'm also not entirely sure how I go about finding him. It's kind of odd that Madison didn't say."

"She probably thought you knew. Don't worry, we'll figure it out." He squeezed her hand.

"Even if we have to go to every hospital and ask?"

He smiled again. "Even if we have to go to every hospital and ask twice."

"Do you speak Turkish?"

This time he shook his head. "No, but I have been here before and you can mostly get by in English."

"Something to be grateful for from imperialism, I guess."

Mac shrugged. "These days I think it has more to do with the internet and the Americanisation of the globe."

She smiled up at him, the urge to laugh was momentary. "Oh, where's your patriotism now? God Save the Queen, you know."

Three hours and another dull hotel room later, they stood outside the first hospital on their list. The receptionist didn't speak English or any of the other languages they tried between them. It was frustrating. Back outside the hospital, Mac looked around. The November air was chill, the wind picking up with dark clouds building above them.

"Let's see if we can get a taxi," Mac said.

Elaine had to look away, biting her lip to control herself.

"Okay, what was that look for?"

She shook her head, but he wasn't so easily distracted, and took her by the arm, giving a gentle shake until she looked up at him. The smile stayed on.

"I'm glad you're not planning on stealing another car."

He returned the smile. "Not right now. Depends how long getting a taxi takes."

He looked over her head, raised an arm and hailed an approaching cab. It stopped.

Two hospitals, and more frustration later, they took another taxi to another hospital.

"One more, then break for food?" he said.

"And rest?"

"You tired?"

The sound of his concern warmed her as she nodded. He leaned forward and gave the driver the address of their hotel, they changed direction with stomach churning rapidity.

"What about looking for Utku?"

"Looking after you is more important right now. Food first, then you rest and I'll research. Maybe I can cut down the footwork."

* * *

She couldn't eat much and Mac insisted they go to their room. Elaine really wanted to continue searching for Utku, but she was exhausted. She took off her coat, sat on the bed to kick off her trainers, groaned as she wriggled her toes.

"You might as well take your socks off too. Let your feet breathe awhile."

She followed that good advice. "What are you planning to do?"

"A little more research." He smiled as she failed to control a yawn. "Lay down and relax, nothing you can do right now."

Even as she scooted back on the bed she smiled. "You're bossy." Yet somehow the slight tap-tap of the keyboard became comforting as she closed her eyes.

She blinked gummy eyes, her mouth inexplicably dry. She sat up sharply, quickly realised that she'd been asleep. Mac was no longer in the room. He had propped a note up on the table. Elaine jumped off the bed. Apparently, he'd gone out for 'cloak and dagger stuff' she shouldn't ask or worry about. She sighed. In his absence she couldn't ask, but of course she would worry.

A check of her phone told her no new messages, but there was still the one from Madison to consider. It was sent as a cypher, thankfully a simple substitution one, Rot13. Elaine could figure that one out in her head. She made the call.

One other thing she had learned was how walking calmed her. She pulled on socks and shoes and headed out. She had regained the fabulous sense of direction she'd had in her youth, and she trusted she wouldn't get lost. She hadn't walked far when she found the edge of a park which looked calm and peaceful—exactly what she was looking for. Even as she wandered, she worried about Utku, about how to find him. How would Utku react? What would she say?

A long pool with the pipework down the middle for a fountain reminded her of the Trocadero and the start of all this. She pushed the past away and focused on the now. The fountain had been drained not to freeze in winter. Yet the café at its edge remained open. There again, November here was a lot milder than back home. Elaine figured a cup of coffee would warm her.

Two problems stood between her and liquid warmth; she didn't speak Turkish and she carried Euros, not Lira. Not to mention that she was on the opposite side of the pond from the café. Good eyesight was always a bonus, and she saw prices in Euros.

Coffee time.

She heard an exclamation in Turkish, and while she had no idea what the shout meant she looked up. A woman rushed towards her, leaving her male companion behind as she approached Elaine.

Icy fear swept through her. Was she being targeted? Rooted her to the spot.

"Elaine!" the younger woman called.

The relief threatened to jellify her knees even as she welcomed and returned the other woman's hug. They were both grinning when they stood apart. "Hello, Panina, I'm so glad to meet you again. Glad you didn't have any more trouble in London. But what are you doing in Ankara?"

Her broad smile didn't waiver as the woman twisted slightly to acknowledge the man she had been walking with, before turning back to Elaine. "That was going to be my first question to you." She turned to the man who had caught up to her. "This is Goker. Hope you don't mind me bringing him along. Are you still okay for a coffee?"

"Fine on both counts." She smiled as she greeted the younger man.

Panina led them to the café, ordering for the three of them. They picked a table under the canopy, Elaine wincing as the wicker chair groaned under her weight.

"Goker, this is the lady who called as we were leaving the university."

"Yes." Unlike Panina, Goker had a strong accent. "The lady from the London Underground. I have seen YouTube, I thank you."

Elaine felt her cheeks redden. "There's no need. I did what anyone would."

"No, you didn't." Panina reached across the table and squeezed her hand. "No one did or said anything before you, and those men were frightening."

"I suspect they're nothing more than frightened little boys in men's clothing. Still…"

They leaned back as the server slipped their coffees to the table.

"Let us talk of better things," Elaine said.

"Like how you got my phone number?" Panina asked.

"Ah, yes. Sorry I didn't have time to explain on the phone, but once you said you were in Ankara, I figured meeting would be easier. Actually, it was my eldest who traced your number. My foster daughter saw the thank you video you posted, and somehow managed to identify you from that. She sent me your details. So, why are you in Ankara? Do you live here?"

"Used to," Panina explained. "I came here for university, but I live in Samsun."

Elaine frowned. "And here I thought that was a tech manufacturer."

Panina laughed, a light joyful sound. "Not Samsung, Samsun. It's a city on the north coast. We work out of there. We're here for a series of lectures with the University of Ankara's Ecology and Environmental Sciences department."

"Giving or taking?" When Panina frowned, Elaine mentally slapped herself. "Sorry. Are you attending the lectures or presenting?"

She could imagine Goker as a lecturer, the ragged hair and thin beard, the oversized glasses and something about the 'not-quite scruffy' dress sense fitting such a role, where Panina with her more modern, neat styling looked more like a model than a lecturer.

"Both actually."

"You're environmental scientists?"

"Marine Biologists."

Elaine's brows rose. "I'm impressed. So that's why you live on the north coast?"

Panina made a sound of agreement as she sipped.

"We're monitoring salinity and temperature across the Black Sea," Goker explained. "And checking microbial levels to determine if global warming and the industrialisation of the sea are impacting the most delicate of ecosystems. You see, there's only a relatively thin layer of the Black Sea that can support life and the way we're abusing—"

Panina's hand moved to Goker's forearm to forestall him. "You must excuse Goker, he can spend hours boring the world on our favourite topic."

Elaine smiled. "It's fine. It's wonderful to see people passionate about what they believe in. And it's important. So, I take it you spend a lot of time out on the water?"

"Oh yes." Panina smiled.

"Bet that's lovely."

"It is, especially when we get to dive. At night, when the surface traffic is less, it can be absolutely breath-taking down there."

"You dive?" Elaine was impressed. "In that case I am envious, always wanted to dive."

"Then why haven't you?" Goker asked.

A cold like the waters of the Bristol Channel washed over her. The scuba lesson had been great – or it would have been, had Jason not grumbled the whole way through, making her so nervous she became useless. So nervous the instructor noticed and told her to come back again alone. She shouldn't let Jason's inabilities curb her natural abilities. She'd smiled, thanked him, and never gone back. "No opportunity." Now she considered new opportunities.

"You should give it a go. Though, it can be quite cold at this time of year."

"Cold? You should spend some time in the UK. This is positively balmy," Elaine said, just in time for a light rain to start spotting on the overhead canopy. "Ah rain, now I feel at home."

She looked at Panina again. "So why were you in London? Don't tell me you were holidaying there in October?"

"No. More work, I'm afraid. I was visiting the Natural History Museum, working with one of the curators on a revamp of displays."

"Wow, you are a talented lady."

Panina offered a small agreeable laugh. "So why are you in Turkey?"

Elaine didn't want to lie, but full disclosure was impossible. "Actually, I'm looking for my son." Both Turks paled and Elaine suddenly realised they must think the worst. "No, no, it's nothing terrible," she assured them with a smile. "No, actually he's my foster son, my husband and I didn't have children, so we used to foster, not all of the kids were English. Some of them I haven't been in constant contact with, and the Turkish one, Utku, I haven't heard from for a few years, but I believe he's working here in Ankara, so I'm here to find him."

"Are there not professionals who can search for people like that?"

"Doubtless." Elaine smiled at Goker's question. "But Utku isn't hiding. We just lost touch. He's busy. You see, my husband died a short while ago, and it's not news I want to put in the first letter he gets to re-establish contact. Also, I figured travelling to see him would be... well, different."

"Different?"

"My late husband wasn't much into foreign holidays. I haven't been abroad since I was 16. So, this is an adventure with purpose."

"And are you enjoying the adventure?"

Elaine smiled. All things considered, she shouldn't be. "Yes. Yes, I am." She looked at Panina and Goker and wondered. It was an odd idea, but odd ideas seemed to be getting her through of late… "So, when do you return to Samsun?"

"This evening actually, why?"

"Out of interest, how much does a day's research out on a boat cost you?"

The two scientists exchanged a questioning look. "Why do you ask?" Goker asked.

"Well, I'm just wondering how much a night on the water would cost you. I'm thinking I might need to do some research in the next few days…"

* * *

"Where the hell have you been?" Mac demanded, shooting to his feet the second Elaine stepped into the hotel room. She reared back, a hard look replacing the smile she had been wearing. He mentally kicked himself for that, but had she no consideration for how worried he'd been? Carefully she closed the door behind her.

"Out for a walk. Like I said in the note."

"For two hours?"

"Yes!" she snapped back, striding over, nearly knocking him out of the way to grab the note he'd left that she'd written on the back of. "Like I said. I also said I'd be back by five." She checked her watch. "It's only 4:36, so what's your problem?"

She wouldn't take the wind from his sails that easily.

"Anything could have happened to you. How would I have known?" He'd been sitting here imagining worst case scenarios.

"Well in twenty-five minutes, you'd have known there was a problem. Unlike waking up to a note that just said, 'be back later.' How late is later? How long should I have waited for you?"

He got as far as opening his mouth before realising he'd just lost this argument. He turned, sighed, and scraped his hair back. His gut had been churning from the moment he got back.

"Anyway," she said. "I had a surprising and pleasant afternoon and I'd be more than happy to tell you about it over dinner. After I've freshened up."

Mac turned to see she was already looking through her bag. Watching her, he marvelled that she managed go from righteous anger one second to complete calm the next. But seeing her safe he let the tension wash out of him, and a smile spread across his face. "How did you get so reconciliatory?"

She froze and looked up at him. "I'd require a lot of alcohol before answering that."

As she disappeared into the en suite, he guessed the real answer was 'the unpleasantness of Jason.' He waited while she changed and wondered how bad her marriage had been. He'd always known Jason to be a selfish bastard but apparently the man was an idiot as well. To keep a good woman so chained was pure cruelty. Keep her happy, and she'd do anything for him. Jason could have had the best of both worlds were he less of an arse. As Elaine stepped from the bathroom and stood before him in that tight dress, Mac realised the hunger in his belly wasn't just for food. An hour later they sat in a lovely local restaurant with great steak and an impressive house red. She'd told him with genuine pleasure of her meeting with Panina.

"It's good. Makes it more personal having a name, knowing the real person. So, what did you get up to while I slept?"

"Went around to several more hospitals: no luck I'm afraid. Managed to charm one doctor into checking and found five Dr Solaks but none with the initial U."

"Ah."

Mac frowned. "What's 'ah' mean?"

"I didn't think to mention it because I thought we'd be searching together. His first name is actually Reiji, but he prefers to be called Utku, because of what Reiji means."

"Why? What does it mean?"

"Well-mannered baby. He was a headstrong boy when he came to us." She offered a small laugh. "He's still headstrong, that's how he got through med school. But the first time I met him, I call him Reiji, he pulled himself up to his full height, which at twelve was all of four foot ten, and announced that he was to be called Utku instead."

"Presumably, he prefers that meaning?"

She nodded. "It means victory. It's also his middle name, so not exactly a huge jump, and since it made him more comfortable, I didn't see a problem with complying. Did you get any results for an R Solak?"

"No, but I did get a list of the five possible hospitals. Then I came back to get you, but you were out gallivanting."

Her smile broadened. "Gallivanting? Oh, I see. And the doctor you charmed – male or female?"

Mirroring.

Flirting technique. She drank, so he drank, which meant his lips were covered when he mumbled an answer. Elaine nearly laughed. "Really? So, it was a woman?"

He put the wine glass down. "Yes."

"And the charm? Hard, was it? Flirting with an intelligent woman?"

He'd been trained to withstand various interrogation techniques, but not this. Not big hazel eyes that pierced his soul and had the ability to break his heart. There was no resisting her. She looked away.

"Don't worry." Emotion thickened her voice. "I'm not concerned if the flirting was hard, but I'd be somewhat disappointed if you could classify it as penetrating."

This time he reached across the table and took her hand. "You've no reason to be disappointed." This time. Though, looking back there had been times when she would have been. He hoped tomorrow wouldn't be disappointing either. Any of their tomorrows.

Her hand shifted under his, and she twined her fingers with his. Her smile rose like the dawn.

"I don't know what the hell Jason's malfunction was," he said. "But you make me want to be a better man."

"You are the better man."

"I mean—"

"I know what you mean, but I don't want you to be anything other than who you are."

CHAPTER TWENTY-ONE

"Just who is Utku?" Mac sighed as they turned from yet another hospital reception the next afternoon. "The invisible man?"

"He's more a Doctor Dreamy, actually," Elaine shrugged.

"Doktor Dreamy?"

The Turkish accent pulled their attention back to the woman at the desk.

"Evet." Yes, was one of the few words of Turkish that she had picked up. "Doctor Dreamy. Doctor Solak. My son." Seeing the woman didn't understand, Elaine held up her arms as if holding a baby. "Bambino?"

The woman looked at her like she was crazy, not understanding what she meant. Mac figured she thought Elaine claimed that she was carrying Utku's baby, which said a lot about how Elaine didn't look her age, which even if she did wasn't exactly old enough to be Utku's mother. The receptionist frowned and said something rapid-fire and moved away. The glance they exchanged showed Elaine didn't understand any better than he did.

They were running out of options; they were reaching for straws. Then Elaine pulled out her phone and opened the gallery, scrolling down quite a way before she picked out a photograph of a young man. Tall and strong, wearing a white doctor's coat and taking a selfie along with two ebony skinned kids with various bandaging and on a makeshift bed in war-torn-Lord-knew-where. All grinned at the camera. Mac saw image and annoyingly, understood why the guy would be called Doctor Dreamy.

She showed the picture to the woman behind the desk, who stepped back to look more closely. "Doctor Reiji Utku Solak."

The receptionist looked at the photo and Mac had to look away from the expression that came onto her face. The woman was old enough to know better.

She said something ending with Utku's name. Elaine glanced at him, but he couldn't help with translation. With a shrug, Elaine nodded to the woman.

The woman held up two fingers and pointed to the floor.

"Looks like she wants us to wait." Mac guessed.

The woman moved to talk to another at a computer on the far side of the reception area. The second woman took earphones out and they exchanged words, not that Mac understood any of the conversation. They did something on the computer. More words, the second woman wrote something. The receptionist looked at the paper, then back at them before turning to her colleague again. While Mac didn't understand the words, the tone and expression suggested the woman was impressed. She returned to the desk and spoke rapidly. Mac didn't have the foggiest what was said. The receptionist passed over the paper, pointing out of the front door, she said. "Taksi." Then she tapped the paper. "Vermek. Taksi."

Elaine glanced at the note, clearly an address, Mac looked over her shoulder, the only word he recognised was 'Memorial.'

She smiled as she started to step backward. "Thank you. Danke. Grazie."

"Teşekkür ederim," the other woman supplied.

"If you say so." Swivelling on the ball of her foot, Elaine joined Mac as they stepped out of the building. "What did that mean?"

"No idea on translation, but hopefully it means we now know where Utku is working." At the edge of the pavement Mac raised a hand, hailing an approaching yellow cab.

They both got into the rear and Mac held the note for the driver, who nodded and sped off. Inertia forced Mac back. Both of them scrambled to get seatbelts on as the driver wove like Lewis Hamilton going after the Driver's Cup through traffic the Circuit de Monaco would never allow. Elaine grabbed Mac's hand. If this was for her fear or his, he wasn't sure. Some of the gaps the taxi went for couldn't be big enough. The worst kind of white-knuckle ride.

Suddenly they had parked in front of another building. Disengaging his hand, Mac paid the fare, Elaine got out on shaky legs.

"You okay?"

"Divine intervention."

For a moment Mac frowned at her, then broke out in a smile. "Surviving that ride? Yeah probably, but that's normal over here. Not all countries are safe and sedate like you drive in the UK."

"You've clearly not seen the M4 at rush hour." She said then turned to the building. It was impossible to miss the massive red letters stating Memorial over the entrance. The building was tall, modern and welcoming. As they stepped inside, they took a moment.

"Is this a hospital or sci-fi set?"

Mac moved her out of the way to avoid her getting caught in the revolving door. They looked around. The cream floors were patterned with large, rounded beige triangles, the walls looked like sage green glass, the energy efficient lights reminded him of honeycomb, and the two strips of yellow recessed lights poured down the length of the entrance foyer like golden honey. The big 'i' on the white frontage of the information desk looked like something out of a quiz show, but the LED information guide above the desk and the massive screen behind were reminiscent of a ticketing station.

"Kinda funky, isn't it?"

A few people waited at the desk, so they joined the queue. Finally, they got to the front of the line, but the language barrier seemed insurmountable.

The woman must have been older than them both, looked older for dressing younger and caking on so much makeup it sat like a mask over her skin. Botox was the only plausible explanation for that unwrinkled forehead.

Mac tried a charm offensive, it didn't work. Elaine tapped him on the shoulder.

"Have you still got that piece of paper?"

He pulled it from his pocket, passed it across and turned back to the woman, trying again as Elaine turned away.

Mac wasn't getting anywhere, and the receptionist was trying to get rid of him. Elaine reappeared and took his hand.

"Come on."

Confused, he didn't resist as he was pulled around the corner towards the elevators. They were in luck. The elevator arrived immediately, the doors parted, and three people got out before they stepped in. Elaine pressed the button, they rose gracefully.

"What happened?" Mac asked.

"I read one of the screens." She pointed to the top line of the address. "This phrase came up, with a number that I am guessing is the floor we need."

Mac frowned at the paper, he hadn't actually read it, just assumed it was an address. Maybe he was getting slack, or too old for the job. *Pediyatrik sağlık merkezi.* He could only guess at the first word. "Utku is a paediatrician?"

"Yeah."

"I thought you said he was a surgeon."

She nodded. "Paediatric surgeon."

"But you said he worked with *Médecins Sans Frontières.*"

"What, you don't think kids break bones regardless of borders?" As soon as she said it, she clearly regretted it. She closed her eyes and sighed before looking back to him. "I'm sorry, of course you don't think that. I just get a bit protective. I know how hard Utku worked to become a doctor, to help kids. To just be allowed to do what he wanted to do in the place he wanted to do it. Which was Africa, with *Médecins Sans Frontières.* But as I also said, we lost touch, so I'm not sure what's going on with him now."

"Always assuming we've got the right Doctor Dreamy," Mac said.

"Oh god, don't. I can't cope with much more if not."

He took and squeezed her hand. Being here for her was all he could do.

The wide lift doors pinged and swept open.

"What's wrong?" Mac put his hand against the edge of the lift door to keep it open when Elaine didn't step out.

"Awful orange."

Mac turned to where she looked straight ahead. He saw a rather nice warm orange, but that colour wasn't the problem here. Her colour was more problematic. She was white. Fear gripped her for what she was about to face.

"We don't have to…"

Her grip tightened around his hand, almost painfully, like she needed the lifebuoy. Perhaps she did. "We do." Her smile wavered, but she moved and together they stepped out of the lift.

A child's giggle shimmied around a corner. The giggle extended to a chorus of many giggles and joined with a baritone chuckle.

Without a word, she led off in that direction. As they turned the corner, Mac saw a dozen kids with various bandages, one in a wheelchair and two with drip stands, seven parents, three nurses and one very large male in a white coat. He was sitting on the floor among the children, one on his lap, clearly telling them funny stories. One nurse noticed them and the man spotted the change of gaze and turned. All chiselled features and lean good looks.

Of course. Mac just about controlled the eye roll.

When he turned the doctor's eyes lit up; recognition and delight. He put the child from his lap to the floor and stood. The attention of everyone in that open space focused on Elaine and the doctor. The grip on Mac's hand faded away in the light of the wide, white-toothed smile. Elaine stepped forward, swept up into the big man's arms and turned around, her feet flying off the floor.

Mac could see that they spoke privately. Clearly whatever had happened was now forgiven. No two people held one another like that without a strong bond. Funny old thing, love.

One of the children called out. Utku stopped facing the group, keeping her close with an arm around her shoulder.

It looked cosy and intimate. Unexpectedly Mac felt like an intruder.

Utku gave some kind of introduction. The adult women relaxed, the child said something that was probably hello. Elaine offered an awkward wave and looked up at Utku.

"I told them you're my mother."

The little boy who had been on Utku's lap got to his feet and toddled up to Elaine, arms up in what even childless Mac recognised as the universal demand for 'pick me up.' Elaine did.

The boy put his two little hands either side of her face and screwed up his eyes, giving her a real hard stare. She smiled so naturally it twisted Mac's heart.

"Superanne."

The others laughed, Utku's a deep rumble. Elaine looked at the boy, in every way but words asking what he meant. This time the boy pointed to Utku.

"Superman."

Utku stepped back and held open the white coat. Underneath his t-shirt bore the Superman S logo. This time Mac did roll his eyes.

"Superanne."

"He's calling you 'Supermum.'"

"Ahh, that's so sweet." Elaine hugged the boy and kissed his head. He blushed red and squirmed, so she put him down and he returned to the others. With a lot of words that Mac didn't understand, Utku said goodbye to the group and turned to Elaine.

"We're not dragging you away from a shift, are we?" she asked.

"No, I'm not actually on shift today. A patient had some difficulties last night, I was called in, but it's all good now."

They were back at the lift, and as they waited, Utku picked Elaine up and hugged her again. "I'm so sorry about what happened."

She hugged him back. "Me too, but it wasn't our fault, not really."

The lift doors pinged and opened, Utku put her down and the three of them entered.

"Utku, this is Mac. Mac, Utku."

The men shook hands.

CHAPTER TWENTY-TWO

Elaine had no idea why she had been so nervous about seeing Utku again, as she introduced him to Mac.

Since they had checked out of the hotel that morning, they collected their bags and Utku drove them to his apartment. A very spacious one-bed apartment, all open plan and surprisingly similar to Madison's without a river view. Elaine smiled. Utku and Madison had always had similar tastes and got on so very well that she had harboured hopes they would become a couple. Son and daughter to husband and wife. A silly little dream because she wanted them happy, and they both were happy with their own choices.

She'd had to bite her lip to hold back the laugh when Utku turned out to be an excellent cook and Mac rolled his eyes, muttering a question of whether there was anything Utku couldn't do. Actually, now she came to think about it, Utku was a total overachiever. Compensation for losing his parents or what he'd had to go through in her household? She daren't ponder that too long or closely.

"So," Utku sighed as he came back from the kitchen, "Madison's given me the gist of what you've been doing, and she's passed on a load of information I'm to give you and not ask questions about. But I am going to ask anyway."

Elaine smiled. "Wouldn't expect anything less. What information?"

"Two tickets in Sochi."

"Sochi?" Mac asked.

"Where were you expecting?"

Utku's question was fair enough, but couldn't be answered.

"She definitely said 'in' not 'for'?" Elaine asked.

"That's what she said. Two tickets in Sochi." Utku frowned, concern in every line. "What does it mean?"

Elaine wiped her hands over her face. What did it mean? "I don't know. I've heard the city's name recently, but I don't remember where or why."

"From me," Mac said. "I told you the person we believe to be at the head of this has links there."

"Of course. It's just…" She licked her lips.

"Laney?" Mac frowned at her.

She reached over to her bag, unzipped the middle pocket.

"I found this." She handed the picture to Mac, but Utku leaned around the small circular table to see. Mac held it out so they could both see.

"Looks kind of sea front-ish," Utku suggested. "But then, it would. That's probably Berdyans'k, in Ukraine. It's on the sea."

"I think one of those boys is Jason."

"Are you sure?" Utku asked.

Elaine shrugged. "No, not really. It looks like I think he would have at that age. But I'm not sure when the photo was taken. I don't know enough about Ukrainian fashion history to judge the clothes they're wearing, besides all the clothes look rather well-loved, possibly pre-owned. I'd guess they were 1950s styles, but they could have been worn into the

1970s or 80s if well cared for. There's nothing I see to date the photo."

Mac looked more closely. "It's not Jason."

"If that is Jason—" said Elaine.

"It's not," Mac repeated.

"But if it was, then he'd be four or five, which would put the year around 1980, give or take."

Mac shook his head. "It can't be. When any of us join the service, extensive background checks are done. If Jason was related to Ukrainians, we'd know about it."

"Would you?" Utku asked. "Isn't keeping secrets what you lot are all about?"

Mac glanced at him. Not a hard look, no censure or annoyance. "If he had known Ukrainian connections, it's unlikely he would have been used in Eastern Europe without his contacts knowing about it, as that can present a compromise risk. Jason didn't come this far east often, but when he did, I was his contact. Until six years ago anyway. I would have been informed. Or at least I should have been."

He added the last quietly as he refocused on the picture.

"Where did you find this?"

Elaine hesitated, he had asked for her honesty, and she hadn't given it. Time to do so. "In Jason's safe deposit box, with the bible."

Elaine found Mac's expression unreadable, hiding his disappointment. She couldn't blame him. She was still keeping secrets.

"Was there anything else there?" Utku asked.

Elaine refocused on the younger man. "Yes." She took a careful breath. "A letter from the NHS confirming Jason's successful vasectomy."

Utku's face slackened. "When?"

"Before our wedding."

This time his jaw actually dropped. "But…" When he recovered, he couldn't seem to find the words. "He said…"

"Yeah. He blamed me while robbing me of the chance of being a mum."

"You'd have been a great mum," Mac assured her.

"You were." Utku reached out and grasped her hand across the tabletop. "You are."

Something dry and unswallowable lodged in her throat. She knew Utku was in earnest and that meant a great deal to her. Without words, she covered his hand with hers, squeezed lightly and offered a wobbly smile. Then she blinked away the cloying emotion.

"Well, whatever," Elaine sniffed and moved on. "I'd figured I'd need to go to Berdyans'k, so Sochi is a surprise. But if that's where we have to go, then we will. The question is, how do we get there? And what are we looking for once we do?"

"Well, the message isn't all she sent." Utku fetched a pad from the side. He put a sheet in front of Elaine.

"Killer Sudoku?" Mac glanced up long enough to say. "Hate those things."

"I love 'em." Elaine smiled.

"And I love these." Utku held up another grid. This one with letters instead of numbers.

"Another cypher?" Mac asked.

"You and Madison were always swapping those when you lived with us," Elaine remembered.

Utku nodded. "Our way of communicating privately."

"Yeah, and making the other kids paranoid. I told them you were sending love notes. I'm guessing it was the only way the two of you could communicate about what Jason was doing to you both."

"Yeah, well." Utku looked uncomfortable. "How did you find out?"

Elaine indicated Mac. "He found photographic evidence, and I talked to Madison."

Utku looked to Mac, who shrugged. "Abuse is never the child's fault."

Elaine reached out and covered Utku's hand again. "I'm so sorry."

This time Utku offered the trembling smile. "It wasn't your fault either." He cleared his throat. "Anyway, I took a copy of the Sudoku and completed it, that gave me the key to the cypher, which in turn took me back to the killer sudoku and gave me this." He turned his notebook around.

Mac and Elaine looked.

"You shouldn't have solved it," Elaine said. "This isn't safe."

"Mum, how safe do you think the places I went with MSF were?"

"Not overly," she admitted. "They wouldn't have needed MSF otherwise. And that was your choice. Following this is mine, and I don't want to drag you in too deep." Again, she squeezed Utku's hand. "What you do every day, is incredible. Joining MSF and going into dangerous areas of the world to help kids, that's so brave, and changing to come back and work in a hospital is no less auspicious. You're a hero to so many of those kids and it has nothing to do with your t-shirts. I am immensely proud of you. Just so you know." She ended with a smile and pulled back, aware the men looked uncomfortable.

"And twenty-one of us think you and what you do is pretty damn special too." Utku sniffed and blinked. "But, erm, to get back to these numbers…"

"Lat and long," Mac said. "I'd guess that's where we need to go."

"Sochi. The Grand Marina to be precise," Utku confirmed. "You're probably best flying direct and—"

"No."

Mac's pronouncement surprised Elaine because she was about to say the same thing.

"No offence, Utku, but we'll make our own way forward from here, and in a way you don't know about and won't be able to tell anyone about."

"I wouldn't!"

"Utku, he's not questioning your integrity. He's protecting you. It's best for all concerned you don't know. You're already too involved. So is Madison. You can also tell her I really appreciate the help. She's been brilliant through all this."

CHAPTER TWENTY-THREE

"He seems a good bloke."

Elaine smiled at Mac's less than enthusiastic assessment of Utku as they waved him goodbye at the train station. A night on his sofa bed during which she'd barely dared move because it squeaked so much had left her stiff and uncomfortable. Mac being at her side had allowed them to talk, but cuddling proved noisy and therefore dangerous, sex had been out of the question. Despite years of abstinence, not being able to act with a lover who drove her crazy had been surprisingly difficult.

He can look out tonight.

That idea also made her smile. "Utku is a good bloke. Really good. Eventually I hope he'll be a good husband and great dad, when the time comes. But right now, he's the best son I have."

He looked at her with eyebrows raised. "You're not supposed to have favourites. What about the other twenty-one?"

"Technically, it would be the other twenty, though if we're talking sons rather than daughters, it's only eight." Elaine adjusted the pack on her back. "And you're right, mothers shouldn't have favourites, but I'm only a foster mum and Utku is the boy who came to us first and stayed longest, and the one I grew closest too. So, he's my favourite. Right or wrong. Besides, I reckon all parents have their favourites, they simply don't admit it." She took Mac's hand as they moved toward the taxi rank. "Did your parents have a favourite?"

"I'm an only child."

"Oh."

"And they had me late in life. It was as if I—" He cut himself off, as they joined the line. "I grew up thinking my dad's favourite was Leo."

"Leo?"

"Leonardo Fitzgerald Coventry."

She frowned at him. "Lady Godiva's son?"

He tipped his head to her. "I'm impressed you got the reference. My dad was a history teacher."

"Yeah, well, I've had reason to research Godiva recently. But who was Leo to you?"

"Our dog."

She laughed. "You're joking." He wasn't laughing. "You are joking, aren't you?"

He tightened his chin and shook his head.

She gripped his hand and leaned into him, kissed his cheek. "Well, I love you."

The statement surprised them both. She stood straight and looked at him, searching for anything other than surprise. The slightest hint of pleasure would have been enough.

The man behind them coughed loudly, drawing their attention. She didn't understand his words, but the way he pointed showed that the taxi queue had moved on so they took the four steps to catch up. They stood side by side, still holding hands, but Mac seemed a million miles away now. She shouldn't have said it, she hadn't meant to drop the L-bomb, it just slipped out. Chewing on her bottom lip, she shifted, wondering how long they were going to have to wait.

What the hell is wrong with me? Why did I say that?

The wait of six minutes felt like six months.

They had to part hands to get into the cab, Mac sitting forward to speak to the driver. Elaine wasn't in the least surprised when he sat back and didn't reach for her hand. She stared at the traffic through the front window, and mentally kicked herself. Had she even meant it?

Yes. Absolutely.

Which was a problem. Mac clearly didn't want her love. She couldn't take back the declaration, didn't want to. She looked at the threatening grey sky. Like the seasons, everything passes. They had. For a second, she glanced at Mac. A winter's tale. That was all.

Besides, they had other things to worry about.

At the airport, Mac requested the tickets, but didn't have enough cash, so Elaine paid. They were in the departure lounge when she looked through her purse and took out about half of the notes she had there. He frowned when she offered it to him.

"Well, you're out of Lira and I have plenty, no point in losing any more in exchange rates." She sighed and tutted when he didn't respond. "Oh Jesus! You can pay me back some time if you're that bothered about it." They sat side by side, so she dumped the notes in his lap and turned away, crossed her arms, stared unseeing at the runways.

His shifting suggested that he'd taken the money and put it in the wallet he kept in his back pocket. "How am I supposed to respond?"

Turning just her head, a scowl grew as she faced him. "When someone gives you money for nothing, a thank you is usually appropriate."

"I meant to you saying you love me."

The magically appearing lump in her throat was hard to swallow, but she managed. "Your response already said everything."

"Hardly."

With a sigh, she gave him her attention again. "Look, it wasn't intentional. I didn't mean to say it. I didn't even know I meant it, felt it, until I said it. But I've said it, I meant it, and you don't reciprocate." She shrugged and looked away. "It is what it is."

The flight was called to boarding. She stood, aware of Mac at her side. She half wished he wasn't. These next few days would be all she'd ever get with him, so she had to make the most of their time together. She had to put this hurt and resentment aside.

The aeroplane seats were cramped, or maybe Mac just felt too close. As they rattled down the runway, forced back in the plane, the inertia did nothing to ease Elaine's racing mind. With nothing else to tap her fingers against, Elaine tapped them against each other and tried to figure out timing. Could she do this all in one evening? Would timing work? It was a big ask, would she even get agreement? If she did, would it work? Was it survivable?

Elbows on the armrests, she brought her hands up to her lips, lips she was sucking on. If her middle fingers hadn't been tapping together, she might have looked to be in prayer. Her hands were freezing again. She blew on them to warm them. The rising aircraft seemed to be air-conditioned, which at this stage of the flight wasn't exactly helpful, and she was glad she had kept her coat on.

The plane jolted in turbulence.

"Ouch!"

Mac turned to her. He had had his eyes closed, head back. She so envied his ability to sleep anywhere. "What?"

Her cheeks burned at the answer. "I wasn't ready for that jolt and accidentally rammed my finger painfully up my nose."

His eyes crinkled with the smile. "Nice. You going to tell me what the engrossed contemplation was all about?"

"Are you going to tell me why you were so curious about the picture I found? Or why you haven't passed it back?"

"Ah." He leaned closer to speak more quietly. "I didn't think you'd noticed."

"I notice lots of things; don't necessarily comment."

"I'm learning that." Their heads leant close together, and for a second, she hoped he might kiss her. Turbulence dropped the plane, they butted heads.

Someone screamed and Elaine laughed even as she rubbed her aching forehead.

"Good Lord," she said, looking out of the small window. "What?"

She pointed. "I'm assuming that's the Black Sea?" It had been a surprisingly short flight, not even an hour.

"It's a big body of water, so probably."

She looked at Mac, he wasn't even looking out the window.

"Bloody big body of water. I didn't think…"

"What?" Mac asked as she fell silent. "What didn't you think?"

She shrugged. "Dunno. Just never really thought about, the size of the sea. I mean I think of the Black Sea as inland, so like a big lake."

"An extremely big lake," Mac told her. "Seven hundred-ish miles east-west, three fifty north-south. It's a sea. Perhaps not as violent as the Atlantic, but it can still swallow ships whole if it wants."

"Hmm." She kept her attention on the view.

"What are you thinking about?"

"Nothing."

"Liar," Mac said gently. "Men sit and think about nothing, but the female mind is always on the go. You lot are always plotting."

She faced him. "That's sexist."

He rolled his eyes. "Okay then, let's get you-ist. You chewing your bottom lip is a sure sign your brain is busy. So, what were you thinking?"

"I was thinking about taking a dive into the Black Sea."

"I'd advise against it, it's about 5 degrees C this time of year, you'll be hyperthermic in seconds, dead in minutes."

"Oh, I'll have a bullet in the brain before I get wet."

His jaw dropped.

"Anyway, meant to ask, why—"

"Oh no, no, no. You don't get to drop a line like that then casually change the subject. What do you mean you'll have a bullet in the brain before you get wet?"

She shrugged. "Sochi is coastal. If our opponents gets to us before we get what we're after and get out, the best way to dispose of us would be a bullet in the brain and dump our bodies at sea. Sick and twisted, as I often am, but you did ask."

"I didn't expect something that sick and twisted."

"Really?" She shrugged again. "Guess you really don't know me very well after all. Oh, you know I met Panina?" He indicated he did. "She's invited me to visit her and her mother in Samsun. I kind of demurred, but..."

"Go."

She looked up at him. "That was a bit quick."

"Sorry." His smile did weird things to her belly as ever.

"It's okay, I can see being rid of me for a while would work for you." *Especially after my* faux pas *earlier.* "Erm, but if that's okay with you, a night of relative normality would be really good. And I'm guessing you don't want to come, it's likely to be a girly night, so you'd not enjoy it anyway."

"Probably not, no."

She'd like to think that dull tone meant he didn't want to spend time without her, but his silence on a topic so literally close to her heart, told her he probably couldn't wait to be rid of her. The silence stretched, and it hurt. Well, if Jason had taught her anything, it was how to sound normal when she really wanted to cry. With a deep breath, she dived in. "Anyway, to get back to my question, what's with you and that picture?"

He held silent, watching her.

"Oh, stop trying to be all inscrutable and tell me."

"Why do you think it's a picture of Jason?" he asked instead.

Another shrug, she needed a new way of expressing herself, only after expressing herself way too freely, she had to rein back. "Kind of looks like him. I've never seen a picture of him as a kid. He told me they were all destroyed in the fire that killed his parents when he was a teenager… Why are you looking at me like I'm a moron?"

"Well, erm…" He shifted in his seat. "Jason's parents are alive and well, living in Devon. He drops in on them every two or three months."

Her jaw dropped. She deflated into a slump and turned her eyes back to the window.

"It's not your fault he—"

"It's my fault I married him."

"You didn't know what he was."

"I didn't know he was a liar. I knew what the marriage would be like. Well, what I thought it would be like. I fully expected life with him to be dull, quiet, steady. It was at first. Then the criticism started, and I... well it doesn't matter now."

"We all make mistakes, and Jason has a knack of engendering trust. It's one of the reasons that he's good at the job."

"Yeah, but my mistake wasn't trusting Jason. Even when I lied to myself about wanting a quiet life, part of my brain screamed 'Don't do it!' My mistake was not trusting me."

"I trust you."

She looked across and up at him. "I figured. We wouldn't be on this plane otherwise." And that was true. He might not love her, but he trusted her, and that was more than she'd ever had before.

* * *

Elaine was smiling as she walked from Panina's home to the hotel where she and Mac were staying.

The street was busy despite the cold and the hour. She spotted an alley, realised it offered a shortcut. It smelled, as far too many alleys do, of the waste humans leave behind. She committed to travelling those shadows, the chicanes of big industrial waste bins and various detritus.

Footfalls echoed.

Not only hers.

Fear mounting, she pulled her big handbag forwards, reaching to unzip even as the footfalls neared. The zip stuck as the blow thumped into her back, sending her skidding forward. She only just kept her footing as she twisted and slammed spine first into the wall.

At least she now faced her opponent. She saw the next move. Wasn't fast enough to avoid it.

Icy gun metal pressed into her neck. She froze. Memory was a cruel companion. It reminded her of watching medical shows where a gunshot under the mandible didn't kill. She didn't know what medical care was like here. Nor if she'd survive this alley to find out. She didn't want to end up in a vegetative state alone in some foreign hospital.

Swallowing her fear, she raised her open hands. Her desperation to stay calm was as strong as the fear screaming through every cell of her body. "What do you want?"

The gunman was taller than her, but thin.

"You know what we want." The accent was less distinct now in a whisper.

Elaine realised it wasn't a gunman, in the dark features were indistinguishable, but she looked at the woman. What hope was there against a trained and capable assassin? "Illyana."

"Elaine." The tone was as icy as the gun. "Where is it?"

"Where's what?"

"Da book." Illyana pushed the gun up, tipping Elaine's head. "I know you have it."

"Do you?" A pointless delaying tactic.

Breath whooshed out of Elaine. The pain in her diaphragm was sharp. She hadn't seen the blow coming and Illyana struck with practiced precision.

"You are an irritation," Illyana said.

Elaine didn't have breath to answer.

"I see why Jason lost interest in you."

She sucked in air. "Yeah well, his only interesting feature was a big dick, which got boring real fast."

"Not for me." Illyana smiled. "But I satisfy him."

"You and any woman he can get it up," Elaine agreed. "Not to mention as many young men—" A second blow stole her breath and her words.

"You lie," Illyana sneered. "Like you fake those photographs."

Unable to speak for the searing pain, Elaine could only blink away the tears and marvel at the level of self-delusion.

"Lazlo tell me it all a lie," Illyana said. "He spoke da truth. They don't lie in pillow talk. Their brains are too fried by de time I'm done."

Wow. More self-delusion.

"Where is book?"

Elaine met that stony gaze. "Alice has it."

Those eyes tried to bore into her. "Alice who?"

A bore with a cutting edge more coal than diamond. "Alice Liddell."

Illyana frowned. "Where did she take it?"

Elaine couldn't hold back the grin. "Down the rabbit hole."

A quick jab. Sharp and hard, the repeat of locale making it sting.

"Where's evidence?"

Elaine glared at Illyana. "Up the cuckoo tree."

Another jab. Years with Jason had hardened Elaine to pain.

"Where's evidence?" Illyana asked again.

"With a gnu in Timbuktu."

Another jab.

"I set fire to it."

Jab.

This time, Elaine clenched her jaw and eyes as a wave of pain washed through her. She looked back to Illyana.

"I wrapped it like a Christmas present and—"

Illyana punched her again. "Lie again, I will hurt you."

"Good luck with tha—" The jab of the gun smacked the back of her head into the brick wall. It hurt. "Ow!"

"If you won't tell me, you will tell my colleague. Ulrich will enjoy taking you apart. Piece by piece." Illyana stepped back, the gun still on Elaine. "We' are going for a ride."

"Great," Elaine managed. "Which way?"

Illyana pointed with the gun. Back the way they had come. Elaine took a painful breath. Hands still up, she shifted her weight forward, moving carefully, not to spook Illyana. She started back towards the entrance to the alley.

"You' are being surprisingly cooperative."

"You've got a gun," she pointed out. "If I fought you, I'd lose; then you'll kill me. In a struggle, there's a risk of the gun going off; fifty-fifty it'd kill me. If I try to run, you're a crack shot; I'll die. Cooperation seems my only choice."

"For now," Illyana agreed. "If you give us what we want, I make it easier."

Hands still up, Elaine twisted to look at Illyana. "Kill me quicker, you mean?" What to do? Maybe she'd —

She went flying, only just got her hands forward in time to avoid a face plant. A full body weight crashed onto her, driving breath away. The shot cracked loud as thunder. Fear burned. Wherever Elaine was shot it was too much pain to register. She reared to throw Illyana off, her feet abnormally restricted. A leg wound?

No. Illyana was struggling back. Blood pumped from her left shoulder. The gun had skittered about four feet down the alley. The two women were crawling away from each other. Pain had pulled Illyana's snarl into a grimace. Hate washed the beauty away. Her eyes darted to the gun.

Elaine couldn't let the other woman get it. In desperation, she flung herself forward, kicking free of the plastic packaging tape around her ankles.

She expected wrestling, but Illyana just fell back, lay panting on the stinking ground. Looking down, Elaine saw sweat on the other woman's brow. Flecks of blooded spital foamed at the edges of Illyana's mouth. Elaine reared back, kneeling now.

Unfamiliar with guns and gunshots, unsure even how the accidental firing had hit Illyana and not her, Elaine watched as Illyana drowned in her own blood. It didn't take long.

A last gasp rattled from the body. Elaine didn't know what to do. Should she run? She should run.

On her feet, she looked to the end of the alley. The night was dark. Little light penetrated the alley. No one to see them. But tomorrow, someone would find the body. They'd raise the alarm. Things would happen. Elaine didn't know what, but the police would be involved. She and Mac were leaving in the morning, but this was a risk too far. She had to hide the body.

CHAPTER TWENTY-FOUR

Mac paced the small hotel room. This was driving him crazy. Elaine drove him nuts. He checked his watch again. Five to nine. Three minutes after the last check.

Not responding to her declaration of love had been an act of self-preservation. Not to mention, utter shock. He hadn't known what to say, then he had but he dare not let himself say it. They'd been here a day, and he hadn't found a way to bring up the topic. Last night had more than made up for z-bed enforced abstinence, but even during that intimacy, he hadn't been able to say it. Love and sex were different things, and the first admission of affection shouldn't be mid-coitus, not if he wanted her to take him seriously.

Cold sweat bathed him as he returned to the window to stare pointlessly at the solid darkness. Would she remember where they were staying?

Why wouldn't she? She's not a five-year-old. If he trusted her, he had to trust her.

But she had been five hours…

Demko might be out there…

He grabbed his coat and yanked the door open—only just stopping before walking into Elaine as she stood there wide-eyed and hunting through that overlarge handbag.

With one quick, slightly haunted, glance over her shoulder she put her hand on his chest and pushed him back into the room, allowing the door to slam as she moved past him to the windows and quickly closed the curtains. She threw her handbag to the bed, twisted on her heel, and headed straight for him, tightening her arms round his waist, and resting her head on his shoulder. She released a huge sigh.

"You okay?" Tentatively, he wrapped his arms around her.

Her head nodded, but her obvious anxiety suggested otherwise.

"Laney?"

She tutted and pulled back enough that to look up at him. "I felt very alone. And not..."

"I'm here now. Well, technically, you're here now. But we're together." He stroked her hair. "You're not on your own anymore." He frowned. "What do you mean, 'and not'?"

"It doesn't matter." This time she reached back and moved his arms from around her, stepping away to take off her coat.

"Laney?"

"I thought I saw…" She shook her head and reached for her bag again now. "It doesn't matter."

"It seems to be freaking you out. It matters."

She shook her head, offered him a weak smile. "I took enough diversions that I would have known if I was followed. Though in fairness not all of them were planned. That's why I'm so late." The bag open, she looked inside, then up at him. "Have you eaten?"

The prospect of eating while worrying himself sick hadn't mixed. "No. We can order room service."

"No, I'm stuffed, but you might like these." She pulled a plastic box from her bag and passed it over. "Panina's mother pretty much forced them on me. She decided I don't eat enough."

Mac opened the box. The smell of freshly cooked samosas and falafel was gorgeous.

"Panina couldn't have been happier to let me take the heat for that one. Apparently, it makes a change from her being told to eat up. Which just goes to show none of you have seen me on a normal day." She pulled two bottles of water from the bag and put them on side as she sat on the chair. "Go on. Eat up. They taste as wonderful as they smell. Trust me. I'm so full of them, I could burst."

"How was your evening?" he asked.

"Great, actually. Really great."

"Aside from food, what did you talk about?"

"Nothing much."

"I could torture it out of you."

She looked at him with her brows raised. "After two decades with Jason, torture might be a relief. Besides, I told you, it was a girls' night."

Sometimes some things had to be allowed to pass. His stomach suddenly reminded him that his throat hadn't been cut. He tried a samosa—every bit as good as promised. Crisp pastry and rich savoury filling, including lamb. Whatever, it was gone in two bites. The first falafel lasted no longer.

As he ate, he considered the chances of her having seen Ulrich Demko. Possible, but highly unlikely. He also worried by the way she was sitting. She hadn't sat like that for a while. Was she stressed? "How do you do that?"

She blinked and looked at him. "Do what?"

"Sit like that, so still. Like at switched off robot."

"Fear."

The word concerned him. "Fear of?"

"Fear of doing something wrong. Of making a mess. Of making a sound. Fear of Jason's opinion that women should be cleaning, cooking, satisfying their men, or silent."

"So that was when he'd hit you?"

"Sometimes, but Jason was a master manipulator. Often it wasn't a physical punishment, but he'd say something or arrange something that would hurt, cause problems."

"So, what are you afraid of now?"

Her lips parted, but no sound came out. He got the distinct feeling she was hiding more than a girls' night out. Another smile. More genuine this time.

"Right now, I'm not afraid of anything." She brought the two bottles of water with her, passing him one as she came to sit on the bed beside him. "I'm safe with you."

He was glad to hear it as he reached for the next item, but there was neither samosa nor falafel left. He'd hoovered up half a dozen of each. Now his stomach was happily full.

"Wow." He leaned back on the bed. "They were marvellous."

She chuckled. "Yep." Now she bit her thumbnail.

"Laney? What's wrong?"

"Nothing."

"Elaine."

She looked at him. "If you're using my full name, you must be pissed off with me."

"I'm worried about you. What's wrong? Laney."

She smiled at that last, but it sank as quickly as it rose.

"Nothing. Really. I'm probably freaking myself out."

He put the lid on the box and placed it out of the way on the floor. "Demko being here is possible."

"Demko? Possible, I suppose, but unlikely. Besides, I'm pretty sure it was nothing."

"Yeah, I can tell that from the way you came in."

Her eyes briefly lowered when she turned to him, her expression scorched him with the scorn. "Well parading in front of the windows with the light on and the curtains open wasn't overly smart of you, either."

"You saw that from the street?" He was impressed. They were on the fifth floor.

"Yes, which means anyone else could have."

He smiled. He shouldn't be surprised; she had taken to this life like a duck to water. But she held something back still. "Is that really all?"

Her head bowed. "When I was a kid, my parents called me Annie."

"It's your middle name."

Not looking up she nodded. "If you knew that, why call me Laney?"

He shrugged. "I think it suits you."

"Does it?"

"You don't like it?"

"I don't know who she is."

Mac blinked as he looked at her hung head. "What do you mean?"

"Annie was a kid. Elaine was a mouse. I don't know who or what Laney is."

"Laney's the phoenix." The answer didn't make her smile as he'd hoped.

"I don't like keeping secrets from you."

What did that mean? It didn't matter. The answer was a simple. "Then don't."

She looked at him. That look again, searching his face for something he wasn't sure she found. Whatever she wasn't telling, it wasn't about a girls' night out. But Elaine had needed the change of pace. She was good at this, but such a big change meant stress, and a night off should have done her good. It probably had, but something had spooked her.

She sighed. "I've been thinking about after."

He had too, and his realism offered little hope. There was a chance that they wouldn't have an after, but he couldn't say that, she needed hope. So, he found, did he. They sat side by side on the bed, legs out, ankles crossed. It was comfortable and… new. He couldn't let that disappear, so he put his arm around her, held her close. Not being able to say how he felt, didn't mean he didn't feel.

"You…" she swallowed.

"Me?" he prompted when she paused.

"You're good at what you do."

The huff of a laugh came automatically. "And you're a natural."

"Because right now, I have to be. Don't get me wrong, I've loved the last couple of months. I've never felt so alive. But I don't want to live like this. With Jason, if he left, I always kind of hoped he wouldn't come back, which makes me a horrible person, and I don't want to be like that anymore, either."

"Seems to me Jason deserved that."

Her head rested gently on his shoulder. He'd never been the hearth and home type, but she made him want to be. Still, he couldn't make promises he doubted he could keep.

"You never answered my question."

He searched his memory. "You asked if I'd eaten and—"

"I asked what you saw in the photograph. Back on the plane. I mean that's where I asked, not where you looked at the photo. If that's not Jason, who is it?"

Should he tell her? Every protocol he had worked to his entire career said no, but protocol went out of the window when he had to deal with Elaine. "I think it was Garin."

"Garin?" She frowned at him now. "The guy in the Rudolfinum? The Capone guy?"

He nodded.

"Why would Jason have a photo of Garin? Especially as a child? They're hardly dear friends."

"Why would he keep a vasectomy letter?"

"No idea. A trophy? Maybe he planned to throw it in my face one day. I don't know. Probably just because he's a total bastard." She shrugged. "But I still can't see why he'd have a photo of Garin. Are you even sure it's Garin?"

"95 percent. But if it is Garin, why would Jason have it?" he asked. "Why would he keep it?"

"Why would he keep the bible?" she asked. "I mean it's beautiful. And a rare work of art, that fore painting is exquisite. Well, it was before some philistine wrote on it." She sighed. "That's Jason all over though. Wants something beautiful but doesn't understand the value of what he has."

"He certainly didn't with you."

She turned away, apparently uncomfortable with the compliment. Had he totally ruined everything? He didn't know how to make this right, so he kept to business. "Was there anything about Garin in the book?"

"Not that I decoded. But I didn't finish all of it." She sighed. "What about the other documents? The ones I showed you in the car?"

"One was a death certificate, the other a letter from a solicitor transferring ownership of a parcel of land to Ivana Moroz."

"Who?"

"I'm not sure. But Garin's mother was Draga Moroz. There may be a relationship."

"Okay." She frowned. "But why would Jason have those?"

"I don't know," he admitted. "But I suspect it has something to do with proving that Garin has control of the land, but without knowing exactly where that land is, Ukraine being a big place, I can't guess what that means."

"So it's just more stuff we don't know."

The truth of that dragged over the pair of them with a painful pause.

"So, what do we know?" Mac asked rhetorically, mostly to break the tension. "We know Garin has business connections in Ukraine generally and Berdyans'k specifically. We know he has a thriving import-export business."

She gave a short-snorted giggle.

"What was that for?"

When she turned to him, grinning broadly. "'A thriving import-export business.' Sounds like something out of a bad 1970s TV police show."

"Yeah, well, in this case, it's a fact. From Berdyans'k, he works mostly in precision engineering. Parts come out of Ukraine. He imports electronics. He owns a lot of properties across Europe, everything from warehousing to social housing and private dwellings. All of which he uses to move drugs and people around the world.

"Has Jason worked a case involving Garin?"

"Several, same as I have, but there's no direct link between the two."

"Wrong."

Mac sat back, not sure if the ice water in his veins was irritation or shock. "Pardon?"

"Well, there is an obvious and direct link."

His teeth clenched. Irritation was winning. She looked up at him confused.

"Lazlo," she said.

Mac closed his eyes, hung his head. Of course. Lazlo. Jason's foster son. The man who had been working for Garin for who knew how long. The obvious link that had been staring him in the face for so long he hadn't seen it. "I must be slowing down in my old age."

"Yeah, right, it's senility."

He opened his eyes in time to see her serious face split into a wide grin.

"Or possibly you've just been too distracting." He shifted to prove what a distraction she was.

CHAPTER TWENTY-FIVE

"Am I the last person in the world to still have a standard double bed?" Elaine asked as she put her bags on yet another hotel bed. Another three-pillow wide piece with perfect white clean sheets. It was good she'd managed to sleep on the planes, direct flights had been unavailable, two connections had been exhausting. She almost wished they'd driven the coast road, it couldn't have taken much more time.

"You don't need bigger when you sleep alone," Mac said from the other side of the bed.

She sighed. "Thanks for the reminder." Turning from the furniture and Mac, she paced over to the wide windows. This uncertainty, the distance she'd put between them was like Chinese torture, she needed to find a way back. No, she needed to find a way forward to a new place with fewer spikes. She'd start with releasing her own anxiety over the relationship, it wasn't as if she didn't have enough to be otherwise anxious about. She took a deep breath, released it, relaxed.

The room looked out over the Sochi marina. The moored boats barely seemed to move on the sparkling sapphire water. The boats were luxury, some of them huge.

Mac stepped up beside her.

"Is that where Garin's going to moor up?" She asked before he could say anything. She was afraid of what he might say. They had hardly spoken since leaving Samsun, and she wasn't at all sure where they were on a personal level. Or even if there was a personal level. She probably deserved that, she'd certainly not done anything to deserve a good man in her life. Be professional. Mac is, she reminded herself. Release the angst.

"It is," Mac agreed.

"How the other half live, huh?"

"Do you want to go down there tonight? We could have a meal in the marina. They have some fantastic restaurants down there."

"Guess they'd have to be good if they serve the likes as can afford those yacht."

"Oh yeah. And they charge accordingly."

"Can we afford the time, or should we be working to find Garin?"

"Madison's information was that Garin won't be here until tomorrow, so we can afford a night off."

"Really? Have a bit of a blow out?"

"Why not?"

She agreed. "Shall I wear the red dress?"

Now he grinned at her. "If you do, you'll look great, but you might freeze."

"And if you wear that tux you can pretend to be James Bond for the night. Though I guess for you that's not such a stretch."

"I'll be 007 if you'll be my Bond girl."

"Definitely the red dress, then. Though for a Bond girl I'll be under dressed without a Beretta."

His laugh was light. "They didn't all use Berettas."

"No," she agreed. "They did all pretty much end up dead though." That rather soured her mood, she turned back to the window. "Yeah, one last blow out would be good. Before I lose it all."

"What do you mean?"

"Mac, I've lost everyone." Including you, she added internally. "I haven't spoken to my parents or siblings since I left for Uni. I lost Jason years ago, if indeed, I ever had him. Lazlo, alive or dead, I lost in Paris when he betrayed me. Madison might still be helping, but the truth is, I'll never be able to see her again, because I can never go home again. Same with Utku and the rest of the children. Even Keira and Jessica are 'gone on sabbatical,' which I suspect is code for 'never to be seen again' anyway."

"Only in part," he assured her. "It probably means they've been relocated with new identities. You know, like witness protection. There's a good chance no one they've known before will ever see them again, but it doesn't mean anything especially bad."

She closed her eyes and hung her head. "Good to know."

"So, what was the rest of the losing about?" he pressed.

She shrugged at this point. There was no real point in lying or even covering up. "I've been a loser all my life, and I just don't want to lose anymore." She didn't want to lose Mac either, but that seemed inevitable. Besides, truth be told, she'd never had him to lose.

"You're not a loser," Mac said. There was an odd tone in his voice that she couldn't define. "If Jason's alive, do you want him back?"

"God no." The passion in that answer surprised even her. "Do you still not understand? I'm not here to rescue Jason; I'm here to make sure he's dead. Happy to rescue Steve, if possible. Even Lazlo, but Jason can go whistle. Preferably via a nose ventilated by a bullet through the brain."

His surprise quickly turned into a headshake and a wry smile. "You never cease to surprise me."

"Really?" She huffed. "Most people think I'm completely predictable."

"Would 'most people' expect you to do everything you've done this last two months?"

She looked at him. "No."

He smiled. "There you go then."

"But where do I go? The grave?"

He pulled her into a hug. "Not all the Bond girls die you know."

"Erm, pretty sure they do," she said, holding him back. "Anyway, I have to. In this case death is freedom. No more guilt, no facing retribution."

He held her tight. It seemed neither of them knew what to say.

Eventually, she heaved a regretful sigh. "It's all in the lap of the gods now, anyway."

He pushed her away, so he could look at her. "It's... I..." He cursed. "I have no idea what to say. Do you have any hard currency left?"

She frowned. "Cash, you mean? Some euros. Some lira. About seven grand sterling. A couple of grand still on that prepaid card. Why?"

"I need to get some supplies and cash talks in this country."

"Supplies?" she asked. "No. Actually I don't want to know." She moved to her bags and started pulling out various bundles of cash. "Take what you need. I'm going to have a bath."

* * *

Mac's contact was still active, and he had what Mac needed and at a bargain price. The only downside was where to collect.

Not the best part of town? Even the worst part of town would disown this area. The car he had hotwired wouldn't be missed quickly. The mechanics it was waiting outside of wouldn't be happy, but he couldn't worry about everything.

What worried him was Laney. When she'd said she loved him every sense had screamed at him to run. Only he hadn't wanted to. He wanted to say the same right back at her. Turned out he was emotionally constipated as his dog loving father. Oh, the joy of an English upbringing.

Since then, he'd got the distinct feeling he'd built a wall between them. Despite trying to show her how he felt, he hadn't found her way to tell her what she needed to hear.

The slap on the car window made him jump. He smacked his knee on the bottom of the dash. The window slid down.

"Cash?"

"Three grand." He held up the envelope but pulled it out of reach when the pockmarked man moved to snatch it. "The goods?"

The man swung the day sack off his back, opened the top and showed Mac. Everything Mac needed. He grabbed the bag as he passed out the envelope. Then his contact was gone with the money, and he had the bag in the car and was pulling away.

Good, that was one thing sorted. He felt better in possession of firearms. But he needed to ditch the car. He found a side street and left the vehicle, striding away. He knew the city well enough that he was soon somewhere he dare to make a phone call without worrying about being mugged.

He might be on radio silence, but the world wasn't, and things were coming to a head now. He couldn't contact anyone in MI6, but there again, he didn't intend to.

* * *

"Do you come here often?"

Mac looked up at Elaine's broad grin and wondered why she would use such a corny line. The meal had been spectacular, their conversation light and easy, relaxed. It was the kind of evening he'd love to have more often. "Not at these prices."

"One last blow out, remember?" she said. "But I didn't mean this restaurant. I meant Sochi generally. Well, I think I meant Russia generally, but given your skills with the language, I'm guessing that would be a no-brainer."

"I've spent a fair amount of time in the country, yes. I've also been to Sochi before – 2014 and 2018."

"You say those years like they should mean something to me."

He had hoped. "You're not a sports fan then?"

Her frown was slight, her eyes narrowed in calculation. "I'm vaguely aware that there was a Sochi Olympics. And given those dates I'm guessing it was a Winter Olympics. But those are never held in the same place twice in a row, so no idea what the other event would have been."

"FIFA World Cup, 2018." It was odd to relax and tell the truth while trusting she wouldn't ask the wrong questions.

"Did you get to see any of the games?"

He smiled and shook his head slightly. "Only on TV."

Noise from the marina caught their attention, another yacht coming in.

"Such a range of boats out there. Some look like fun playthings, others are… well… very big."

He smiled. "The marina can take anything up to 140 metres in length."

Her draw dropped. "140 metres? That's huge."

"You should see them inside." With an eye roll and a grin, he returned his attention her. "Plush is not a good enough word for it."

"Is his boat out there?"

"Yes. It's right on the far edge. Silver-grey and huge. Probably is 140 metres. Several decks visible. And even though you can't see it from this angle, it has a helipad. You can just about see the name however, *Nevermore*."

To actually see it, she had to lean back a little. "Wow." She sat straight again. "That's less a yacht, more a mobile island. What kind of crew would he have on that?"

"Minimum ten, could be up to forty."

Her expression was all surprise, but she said nothing. That was a lot of people, they would be seriously outnumbered. Not something to dwell on in this particular moment. She nodded and took a sip of the wine. "You know, even though I've only seen this tiny bit of the country, I think it's lovely. Not at all what I was expecting. This is more like I'd expect from the Riviera then Russia."

"Well, the comparison isn't unfair, Sochi and Nice are on roughly the same latitude. And they are both rich men's playgrounds. The West doesn't show much of the diversity of Russia. Mostly just negative views of the politics, they make the country seemed depressed and full of hardship. Which, to be fair, much of it is. But what you rarely get to

227

see is the real beauty of the country. The variety of locations. The talent and artistry. The innovation here. All are just as good as the rest of world. It's just the rest of world doesn't get to see it."

She was curious. "Would you live here, if you could?"

It was an interesting question, and a few months ago he wouldn't have had to think about it. "I could, but these days I'd rather live with you." It wasn't exactly the declaration either of them wanted.

A cheeky grin spread across her face. "I could live with that. Though I'm not sure how much of this fine dining and champagne I could take. I mean this is lovely, but so rich."

"Well, you're worth it."

She laughed. "Just as well, since I'm paying for it." Her hand was cold when she placed it over his. "I want you to know that I've enjoyed the last two months, probably more than any other period of my life. And a lot of that has been down to you. Even running away from you was fun."

"Well, you've certainly made the last two months of my life interesting."

The smile left her lips in her eyes turn serious. "In that case, let's face one brief dark prospect. There's a chance that you and I could get separated at some point—"

"Laney—"

"No, Mac, listen. I can hope it doesn't happen, but I would rather make provision. To give things a chance. So, if we do get separated, remember this. St David's Day, Ladderman Hertz in London International Airport."

"Laney—"

Her hand squeezed his. "St David's Day, Ladderman Hertz in London International Airport. Say it."

"St David's Day, Ladderman hurts in London International Airport." It seems so silly.

The way she smiled did foolhardy things to him.

"Promise me you'll remember that?"

Turning his wrist, he took her hand to his lips leaning forward he said, "St David's Day, Ladderman hurts in London International Airport. I promise." Then he kissed her knuckles and the sparkle returned to her eyes. "Are you ready to head back? Our night off isn't over yet."

The promise was obvious and welcome. She nodded.

"I'll nip in and pay."

CHAPTER TWENTY-SIX

Elaine decided Mac was just too gorgeous as she watched him walk into the restaurant. She closed her eyes and sipped the champagne, enjoying the cold liquid on her tongue, she savoured the moment. Mac didn't need to go inside to pay, a waiter would have sorted that at the table, so there was only one reason he'd go in.

Cold metal touched her nape beneath her hair. Her eyes snapped open.

"No sudden movements, Mrs Blake."

Elaine carefully placed her glass on the table. "Why would that be, Mr Demko?" Who else could it be?

He leant down, his voice low not to carry. "Because all I'd have to do is squeeze the trigger."

"Thereby ensuring your boss never gets what he wants. And all I have to do is scream."

He hunkered down now, his face close to hers, his breath on her cheek was surprisingly fresh, minty. "Then I'll start shooting your fellow diners. How many deaths would you like on your conscience?"

In truth, less than she already had. She swallowed and offered a tight smile. "If you'd just move back."

He stood, the gun discreetly under his jacket, but still too ready for use.

Carefully she rose as he eased back her chair. As she twisted, reached for her coat, Demko questioned with a look.

"Leaving it would look odd," she spoke quietly. "I assume you want this to look as normal as possible?"

The nod was slight. Careful to reach her fingers under the strap of her shoulder bag she picked up it and the coat together. With luck she could keep it hidden from him. As she left with Demko, her heart was hammering, but she managed to slip her arm into the strap of the bag as well as the coat. All it took then was to hold the coat closed to keep the small bag hidden.

* * *

It had been the perfect evening, Mac reflected as he settled the bill. The future prospect of more such evenings was temptation indeed. He left a tip more reflective of his mood than their service and stepped back outside.

His heart stopped. The table was empty.

Movement caught his eye. The fur coat, and a tall, black-haired man standing too close.

Demko.

He ran, hurdling over the restaurant barrier to follow. He skidded towards the car park in time to see her slip into a limousine, he was catching up as it pulled away and he lost all hope of keeping up.

* * *

Demko led Elaine to the kind of stretch limousine that belonged in a Bond film, not in her life. She slid inside, feeling anything but comfortable.

Her captor's silence gave her time to take stock as they moved away. She was still alive, and the fact that Demko had threatened strangers rather than her or Mac proved he needed to keep her that way. She wasn't sure what it meant regarding Mac. She could assume that coming for her when she was alone was easier and it suggested that Demko was alone. Except for the driver, obviously. Had he come ahead of Garin for some reason?

Numbers wise, she might be okay. If it were just Demko and the chauffeur, the gun in her coat pocket was something of a field leveller. It all depended on where they were going.

The bag contained those things she hadn't been prepared to leave behind. Two passports, cards for her bank accounts, the rest of the cash, and most importantly, her phone. In her head she started composing the message she would send Mac as soon as she could.

* * *

Mac had rarely felt so frantic.

Calm down and think.

Breathing deeply, he set his emotions aside. He'd never found that act harder, but he did it.

Demko had Elaine.

To stay standing in a car park was dumb, stealing a car from here with security and passers-by would be a mistake, besides, in this city limousines were ubiquitous. There were three others in this one car park alone. He couldn't be sure of catching up with the right one. Mac turned around and sauntered back to the marina. Sliding his hands into his trousers, he presented a relaxed façade, thinking the issue through. Demko was unlikely to kill Elaine. Garin would want her alive. He wanted the evidence. Evidence she no longer had although neither Demko nor Garin knew that. Elaine was smart enough to outthink the pair of them and delay long enough for him to get to her.

He'd phoned Madison that morning, a useful call. If her information was right, Garin would be sailing on the *Nevermore* tomorrow toward Georgia. If he could get the *Nevermore* into the southern part of the Black Sea, to Turkish waters, Madison could have the ship boarded and he and Elaine would be safe. It wasn't a great plan, getting the crew of the *Nevermore* to agree to it would not be easy. In fact, depending on the size of the crew it could be virtually impossible. Even with a gun in his hand he would be heavily outnumbered. That, of course, didn't mean he wasn't going to try.

* * *

The limousine hadn't travelled far, but this was a very different part of the city. Glitz and glamour had given way to dark and dirt of working warehousing. The chauffeur pulled into a warehouse. Demko stepped out and opened Elaine's door. The muzzle of the gun indicated that she should step out.

Standing again, she allowed her eyes to adjust and looked around. Crates, packed goods, and a shipping container. That was the biggest worry. Could be anything in there. There were two things she didn't see – one good, one bad. There were no other men around, which was good on numbers, but there was nowhere to hide. The crates were stacked far too efficiently to give her routes between or behind. Her hand slid down to feel the reassuring weight of the small gun in her coat pocket.

Then she felt the weight of Demko's firearm in her side. Pushing her forward. The stumble was unavoidable, but she only went a few steps before she stopped. Demko's gun nudged her, but this time she didn't move.

"Go on then," she said. "Shoot me. See what your boss has to say then."

"A shot doesn't have to kill."

"True. And I don't have t—"

Before she could say another word, he simply picked her up from behind. Obstinance chilled to fear. As he started forward, she instinctively struggled.

SING.

Side. She tried to elbow him in the side but couldn't get sufficient room to make a decent impact.

Instep. She tried to stamp on his instep, but he held her too high. She aimed for his shins instead. Ineffective.

Nose. She couldn't move her arms for a punch or her head for a butt to get to his face.

Groin. Again, the way he pinned her, she just couldn't reach.

He was carrying her into the dark belly of the warehouse, Elaine squirmed harder. Her arm came free, she swung blindly, connected with something, then found herself flying through the air towards a wall of packing crates with no way to stop herself.

She got her hands in front of her face just in time, they scraped painfully against the rough wood, splinters dug into her skin. Worse than the alley floor.

Pulled up by her hair, the blow to her kidney forced air from her lungs, strength from her knees, and thoughts from her head. This time when she was picked up, she didn't have the energy to fight. The blow to her kidney had aggravated the bruising on her ribs from Illyana. The simple truth was that Demko could outfight her in every way. There wasn't any point in screaming, there was no one to hear or help.

Metal groaned as the container doors opened. Elaine was slammed onto some kind of seat, pain reverberating around her chest and along her spine, numbing her legs, threatening to crack her skull. She couldn't hold back the yelp.

"Wha—?"

The groan surprised her, but her eyes adjusted to the dark. She had to blink away the starburst of pain from her vision. She realised the voice came from the man shaped silhouette in the chair opposite.

She jumped at the clang of the door, the sudden total dark.

"Hello?" Her voice didn't echo, the sound was dead. That matched her impression of foam spikes on the walls. Sound proofing. No one wants to hear you scream.

"Who are you?"

The words were slow, slurred. Not the drunken slur she'd heard before, this was a man in pain, lacking energy, struggling to think. "Steve?"

"Elaine?"

She almost laughed with relief. "Oh, thank God you're still alive. Hold on." With relief she pulled the undamaged phone from her purse. She typed quickly.

"Elaine?" The voice cracked in the dark. "What's going on?"

UD. Gun to head. Phone silent. SS here. Call you soon as.

She hit send, but didn't expect the message to go until she was out of the container. Right. Deal with the here and now.

Nothing more than a voice in the dark, but it was enough. The lack of echo gave Elaine a fairly good idea of direction. Carefully she stood from the seat. Her legs trembled, but she stepped towards Steve's voice. Her one cold hand pressed the plaster under her arm, before both hands outstretched wary of obstacles.

"Talk to me Steve, help me find you."

"Why you even looking?"

Two steps. She stretched forward and her fingers touched cold flesh that flinched away.

"It's okay Steve, it's me." Carefully she reached forward again and found a shoulder. Gently she ran her hand down his arm as she knelt beside him. Once on her knees, she reached around him, hugged him. "Oh God, Steve. Keira will be so glad you're alive."

His head leaned against her, the rough fabric of the bag over his head became obvious.

"Keira's here?"

"No." She pulled back, running hands down his arms to find out how he was bound. "She's safe. Not sure where." Scooting around behind the chair, she started working blind on knots she couldn't see.

"Why are you here?"

Her fingers struggled on the hemp.

"Long story." She eased the first loop. "Tell you later. Right now, there's something else I want to say. Do you remember my thirtieth birthday?" It had been a hell of a night. Jason away, the kids all gone, Madison and Utku to uni, and no new arrivals. Steve arrived with a birthday card to find her alone and miserable. Since Keira and Jess had been away—she couldn't remember where or why—Steve took her out to dinner. They'd picked up bottles of wine on the way home and relaxed in the house, drinking, talking, laughing. When he'd leaned in to kiss her it had been so natural, so easy. The kiss. It had felt like the most perfect kiss ever. She'd kissed him back. Hell, she'd have done a whole lot more than just kiss him had a wrong number not interrupted.

"I'll never forget."

"I wish we had."

"Hmph."

His hands now free she let him flex as she shuffled back to his side. "Better?"

"Much." Suddenly his arms were around her, pulling her to him and holding her unbelievably tight. It hurt like hell after the blows to her torso, but she could still breathe. She reached up and removed the hood from Steve's head, then the blindfold beneath.

"Elaine, I regret not being with you. You take my breath away. Always did."

Good to know, even if now wasn't the time. "Steve?"

"Mmm?"

"Have you got any clothes on at all?"

"No. Standard dehumanising tactic." Now he'd pushed her away, hands on her shoulders. She suspected she'd be getting a stern glare, though it was meaningless in the dark. "You shouldn't be here. If you get the chance to run. Run. And don't look back."

"Really?" The sardonic tone said more than the word. "You don't know me at all if you think I'd do that. There again, these last few weeks, I don't much know who—"

Elaine cut off as the container door opened and a bare bulb above their heads switched on. Steve flinched and shielded his eyes. Though she had to blink to adjust, she saw Steve was not only naked, but covered in bruises, old beneath new. His nose was broken, pushed to the right. There were cuts and dried blood all over.

She turned back to the door, to the man standing there.

Ulrich Demko.

He dragged another man in.

Elaine's stomach flip-flopped thinking he'd caught Mac, but the blonde hair told her otherwise.

Jason.

Unlike Steve, Jason was fully clothed in a ratty old boiler suit, but better that than nothing. He fell to the floor, curled up in a foetal position. Her total lack of concern surprised Elaine as she faced the hulking Demko.

The big man stepped close, leaned down and grabbed the back of Jason's boiler suit. He dragged him further, dumping him at her feet. Jason was close enough to kick, but he wasn't worth the effort. Instead, she concentrated on Demko.

"Did you think that would help?" He nodded toward Steve.

I'm going to die.

She shrugged. "Gives him a little relief."

Demko stepped forward, slapped her, her chilled cheek caught fire. The inside of her mouth swelled but there was no taste of blood. She turned back to Demko.

"Ouch."

The sarcasm earned her another slap. That one took a little longer to recover from.

"Where is he?"

"Who?"

His hand rose, she closed her eyes, tensed, but the slap didn't come. Opening one eye, she saw Demko grinning at her, his hand at his side. Only when she had both eyes open did he strike, kicking Jason in the gut. Jason cried out; Elaine winced.

His eyes narrowed. "Where's your friend?"

She tipped her head, pointed to Steve.

Another kick. Another cry of genuine pain.

"Stop it!"

"Do you care about your husband?"

She swallowed. "Love of my life."

Perhaps Demko didn't believe her. Perhaps sarcasm didn't translate. He kicked Jason.

"Okay, okay! I'll tell you whatever you want, but I'm not sure what you want."

"Where is Cormac Letterman?"

"Mac's here?"

She turned her head slightly towards Steve. "Yes. Well, not right here, no." She looked back to Demko.

Another kick.

"Oomph!" Jason let out a sound of real pain.

Serves you right, you bastard. "Demko, I was having dinner with Mac when you put a gun to my head and told me to leave with you. I've no better idea than you where he is right now."

She looked up at Demko, putting all the fear she had for her, Steve, and Mac into her eyes. He kicked Jason again, the high-pitched howl suggested he'd caught something sensitive.

"Where would he go?"

"I don't know."

"Where were you staying?"

She said nothing. He kicked Jason again. She wondered how long she could keep that going.

"Where were you staying?" Demko demanded.

"Why should I tell you?"

He kicked Jason again. She thought she heard something snap. She hoped it was painful.

"Enough!" she cried. "In..." she paused to make her voice wobble, deliberately hitched her breath to continue. "In the Pullman." *And the Oscar goes to....*

CHAPTER TWENTY-SEVEN

Mac couldn't get close to the *Nevermore* tonight. The marina had 24-hour security and there weren't enough people around for him to get lost in the crowd. Still, he was close enough to lean on the safety rail at the edge of the marina and see what he needed to see. Superyacht was about the only description that would suit the massive construction. It had six decks, the top two for the luxurious accommodation of the owner, the wheelhouse was at the front of deck 4 along with the captain's office. There were two helicopter pads. Neither currently holding a helicopter.

Four more decks had flexible accommodation, and the bottom two decks were for storage, plant and crew accommodation. From what he could make out, stores could be loaded on the deck 1, but passengers would board at deck 2. He could make out sun loungers on deck 1 so that must be the lowest passenger point and almost definitely his best bet for incursion. Shaded glass throughout meant he had no hope of seeing crew numbers.

Maybe he needed to make another phone call.

Phone.

How had he missed that?

He stood. Long strides took him back to the restaurant table. Elaine had left nothing behind, so she had her handbag and, therefore, her phone. He raced back to their hotel.

* * *

Demko turned on his heel, striding away. The doors on the container closed again.

Darkness.

"Elaine?"

It was Steve's voice. She reached down, felt the coldness of his shoulder, then took his hand. "Still here."

"When did you get so ballsy?" There was a tone of admiration in Steve's voice that warmed Elaine.

"Well, every mouse has to roar sometime."

"Do you have to do it when it could get us all killed?"

That grump was Jason's. The temptation to kick and hopefully strike him in the balls was great, but Elaine worried she might miss.

"Who wants to live forever?"

"Why couldn't you just give them the evidence they wanted?"

In the total darkness, the rustling of clothes told Elaine that Jason was moving, sitting up.

"I'd advise against going anywhere," Elaine said. "When he gets back, he's going to expect us to be where he left us."

"And if we're not, he'll shoot first."

The way Steve said it suggested no later for questions. Jason stopped moving.

"Jason?" Elaine said into the darkness. "Really? Why didn't you just a hand it over? The evidence? It would have saved a lot of time and effort."

His silence stretched in the darkness. "I didn't have it." It was his 'poor me' voice, the one she'd stopped caring about years ago. "Boguslav only gave me that bible and some papers."

"Boguslav?" Elaine asked

"Boguslav Wozniak," Steve supplied when Jason didn't. "He worked the Russian border. It was him we came to Prague to meet. Jason couldn't hand the evidence over, it would have cost too many lives, weakened British, world security."

"But you were captured before you could met Boguslav?" Elaine asked.

"Oh, we met him," Steve admitted. "But he was long since dead."

"What happened to the other three?"

Their silence spoke volumes.

Something else was wrong here. Timing. "Jason, when did he give you the bible?"

There was a pause.

"You know they're probably listening to us?"

"Unlikely," Elaine said. "Won't do them any good even if they are. Seems I'm the only one who knows where that evidence is, and I'm not dumb enough to say. So, Jason, when did you get the bible?"

"Fifteen months ago."

Roughly the same time the water hammer started in the house. That explained so much. The water hammer sounded worse than it was because one of the belts holding the lagging on the tank was loose, the metal crimp on the top belt sometimes rattled against the pipe making the hammering louder. It was in changing that lagging that Elaine had found the cypher and the key and all this adventure had started. "So, what was with the cypher? Why bother? Why not just hide a statement?"

"Didn't want it to be too easy."

"Who for?"

Silence again.

Elaine wanted to scream. She wanted to kick out. She wanted to kill. But now wasn't the time. "Jason, who did you leave the cypher for?"

"Keira."

"What?" Steve demanded. "Why would you leave it for my wife?"

"Because she was the only one I could trust!"

"And that tells you everything you need to know about our marriage," Elaine said. "You told her the answers." Elaine surmised. "That's why the key to the cypher was her name. You left it all as prompts to remind her, never expecting that someone else, that I, would work it out instead. Steve, please release your grip on my hand, it's getting painful." She waited for the vice to reduce. "The truth, Steve, is that Jason has something to control Keira with. She's terrified it will be revealed. And she's terrified because, Steve, she loves you and she wants you back. Thinking that you're dead is literally killing her. She was never a big eater, but she's eating less than a sparrow now. I worry about her, and Jess."

"I miss them."

This time she squeezed his hand lightly.

"We'll get you back to them," she offered the promise she couldn't guarantee.

"No, we won't," Jason said. "None of us will survive this. Not even your friend out there. Letterman's not that good."

He was a damn sight better than Jason, but again, now wasn't the time for that either. "Well thank you for that cheery thought," she said instead.

"He thought you were nothing." Jason sneered the word.

"He was right." It surprised Elaine how little Jason could hurt her anymore. "At least, he was right back then. Did Keira know about the picture too?"

"What picture?" Steve asked.

"There was a picture of our wedding anniversary party," Elaine explained. "Our fifteenth wedding anniversary. Everyone was there. You and Kiera. Jessica and LaTrice. Madison and Utku. Even, I recently discovered, Cormac Letterman."

"I remember the day," Steve admitted.

"The picture was doctored. Or retouched. Not entirely sure what the difference is, whatever. But hidden in a tiny corner of the picture, was a code. An IBAN number."

Jason swore under his breath.

"Was Keira supposed to find that too?"

Jason huffed. "No."

"Just as well," Elaine said.

"Whose account was it?" Steve asked.

"Mine," Jason answered.

"Was being the operative word." Elaine pointed out.

The container door swung open.

* * *

The Mercure was quiet when Mac returned, the room even more so. He pulled his laptop out and as it booted, he changed into more practical clothing.

This shouldn't take long. As long as Elaine's phone was on, he could trace it.

Only he wasn't getting a signal.

He was right to suspect that, now they knew about Another presence, the two lovers would set them to them. How long do we wait, sir?'

'What indicates the weapon?'

'He is very... Weapon's the Teacher armoured weapons done suggested 'Out himself, Weldon, almost as his line was home, he didn't save Peter, and I know that would not if the Tenth from some such armoured.'

"Between a wolf to hunt,
Take solace in search to find itself,
So, I am hunting Shall,
That as well, I have said,
Where do mountain or snow peaks?
What, I say, answered
Was it the the mother's error, I think of intact or,
They could not close with a spur.

The moment was calm when Max rescued the common soul. So, the moment his hidden out, and as it moved, he changed into the dazzled of sitting.

'This should not feel free. As long as Peter's place was one for either will.'

'Only he was restrained again.

CHAPTER TWENTY-EIGHT

The sudden light of the container opening again made the three captives blink. Elaine knew she had no back up. Neither Steve nor Jason was in any condition to get away under their own steam. She'd need a small army to get them away unless she could manage to shoot both Demko and his driver. Which was a million to one chance. Which as Terry Pratchett said, succeeded nine times out of ten.

Her vision cleared when the Demko's hand became a vice, pulling her forward. Good, she'd shoot him once they were out of the contain...

Ah.

A group of men in dark clothing waited. And two crates. She didn't have time to count the men as Demko moved her forward, but there were at least six. Not good odds.

"What are they doing here?"

"Goods to package and transport," Demko said without pausing his march. They were heading for the limousine again. The chauffeur waiting.

"Goods?" Elaine asked as she was bundled inside, sliding over to let Demko join her. The crates were roughly the size of a dog cage. "You're going to shove Steve and Jason into crates to move them?"

"Yes."

Demko got himself comfortable as the chauffeur started the car.

"Barbaric, but at least you acknowledge that Steve and Jason are the good guys."

His scowl glanced off her. The deluxe vehicle was at such odds with the warehouse, Elaine felt she was yoyoing between worlds. Nothing felt like right.

"Where are we going?"

"Wherever I want."

He clearly wasn't in a chatty mood. But she was. She was nervous and she wanted sound to hide inside.

"Are we there yet?"

Again, he glared. She smiled. And counted to ten.

"Are we there yet?"

It was on the fourth repeat that he pulled the gun on her. "Do you want me to shoot you?"

"No, I want you to talk to me," she said. "Look, Mr Demko, or should I call you Ulrich now? Whatever, we both know this isn't your choice. You're just Garin's gun dog. The only reason you left me with Steve and Jason was so you could make a call." She hoped her message had got through now. "You called Garin to tell him what I told you, and get updated orders. Was he pleased with you for capturing me?"

"Yes."

"Ahh," she grinned. "And the good little gun doggy got a pat on the head?"

The way he looked at her suggested he would do more than pat her on the head.

"I think all that champagne is finally getting to me," she muttered. "So where did he tell you to take me?"

"You'll find out when we get there."

The eye roll was instinctive. "Then what? You going to hurt me like you did Steve and Jason?"

"Interesting." He watched her now.

In the intermittent light of the city streets, it was clear that that monobrow had led her to a mistake. Demko might look like a neanderthal, but he didn't think like one. She had been underestimating him.

"What's interesting?"

"You. You keep putting a friend before your husband."

"I've got paperwork that says my husband's dead."

"You don't seem a very grieving widow."

"When I heard he was dead," she said conspiratorially, "I celebrated. Lovely bottle of wine it was. Couple of days later, over another bottle of wine, our eldest and I were actually laughing about him. I really don't understand why people think I came for Jason. I don't suppose you know what time it is?"

He checked his watch. "Twelve forty."

"Already? Explains why I'm so tired." A glance out of the window led to a glimpse of something familiar. "Are we going back to the marina?"

"Do you always talk so much?"

"Only when I've got something to say." She grinned. "Or someone to annoy."

"Childish."

That made her laugh. "Effective."

This time the gun came up to her head. Mirth died. "Dangerous."

She swallowed and nodded.

"Will you say where the evidence is?"

"Nope."

"Then you have nothing to say that I want to hear."

That was clear and sufficient warning. Her thoughts turned to Mac. Emotionally she felt they were closer, but the physical distance was a concern. And a blessing. He wasn't captive so maybe he could rescue her.

* * *

The bleep of his phone made Mac jump.

Automatically he picked it up. From Elaine.

UD. Gun to head. Phone silent. SS here. Call you soon as.

Relief washed through him. Elaine was okay. For now, at least.

UD was of course Ulrich Demko. But SS? Steve Southgate? Was that possible?

As he stared at the message, movement in the corner of his eye caught his attention. The tracer on her phone had registered, and was on the move.

* * *

"What's in all this for him?" Demko asked as they travelled.

Confused Elaine turned her head to face him. "For who?"

"Cormac Letterman."

"Oh," she said, then considered the answer. "Erm, actually I'm not sure."

Demko look up to her up and down. "I assume he's fucking you."

She shrugged. "Really? Maybe Mac's a good old-fashioned lover boy and we're waiting."

"Don't expect me to believe you're innocent in all of this do you? I don't for one second believe that you would stay faithful to a husband you claim is dead."

"Well in fairness, it is only this evening that I have discovered Jason isn't dead. But I suppose, no you have to be an idiot to think I wouldn't fancy Mac, and you're not. An idiot that is. What do you think is in it for him?"

It was Demko's turn to stop and consider. "He was sent for the same information I was. I'm not sure why he is still with you, however."

She met Demko's eyes as he considered her. And tried not to give anything away.

"If he had the notebook," Demko reasoned. "He would have gone home taking it with him."

"But he hasn't gone home," Elaine pointed out.

"No," Demko agreed.

When he didn't go on Elaine smiled. "So maybe he's here to stop you."

Demko laughed. "Then he's doing a very poor job of it. And it won't get any easier."

"Easy is boring," she said. "I made life easy for Jason, he made my life boring." With a shrug as she turned back to stare out of the window.

* * *

Mac shifted like a shadow through the streets. It was nearly one in the morning now and he was on foot. The way the blip on his silenced screen moved told him that Elaine was in a car. He considered stealing a car and following, but he quickly became obvious that their direction of travel was back towards the marina. He only had to wait.

In the cold and the shade, he waited, eyes and attention split between the screen on the approaching marker, and the car park. There was a Porsche parked on the edge of the marina which hadn't been closed up properly. If he had to chase the tracker, he could.

A glace between the screen and the road told him the precaution was unnecessary. Mac snapped the laptop shut and slipped it into the backpack he had with him.

The black limousine crept into the car park. Elaine was first out. She held her arms around her, but he reasoned that was to keep her coat closed, to hide her bag.

Demko was out behind her. Closer than Mac was comfortable with, and clearly in control of Elaine. The big Russian said something to the driver and then he and Elaine were walking. It was obvious where they were headed.

Demko guided her to the marina, used the keypad to open the gateway. They headed to the extreme end of the marina. When the gang plank of the *Nevermore* was extended, crewmen in livery saluted Demko and his guest on board.

* * *

Elaine could only stare at the luxury around her. This was more than she'd ever expected on any kind of sailing vessel. The height of luxury. Though she didn't approve of decorating everything in white. What a colour to choose. She felt sorry for whoever had to clean the place.

"Glad to see you're impressed." Demko said as he moved to the wet bar.

"I should think this would be heaven for everyone." She considered her words. "Well, next to no one really. It has to remain exclusive, or it loses its value. You wouldn't want any old riffraff in here, would you? I'm honoured to be allowed on board."

Demko laughed as he poured a generous measure of whisky in a cut glass tumbler. The way he tipped the decanter suggested an offer to her.

"Thank you, but no," she said. "I'm not a lover of spirits. Is Garin on board? Will I see him tonight?"

Demko took his time to savour the oaky flavour. "He'll be here in the morning."

"Then is there any chance I can get some sleep?" Elaine asked. "I'd like to be at my best when I see him."

Demko laughed. "You amuse me, Mrs Blake. I don't think Jason had the vaguest idea who he married."

"I think that's true on both sides."

Demko took another gulp, placed the tumbler on the bar and moved, raising a hand to indicate she should precede him.

* * *

On Nevermore. Gate code is 75Y39.

Elaine's message came through as Mac headed for the small boat he had secured. Getting the dinghy into the marina was questionable at best. But the code meant he could simply walk in. He turned around.

The code was perfect, he was through. On the pontoon, Mac walked past the various moorings, checking each. Finally, he saw what he was looking for. An inflatable left on the deck of an empty yacht. In moments, he was on the water manoeuvring the small craft between the other boats.

The hour and the temperature meant most were asleep, and those awake and still partying were doing so inside closed yachts, all locked up tight against the cold. There was no one to see, unless someone in security was watching, in which case he was stuffed, but he couldn't think about that.

He paddled out and soon the *Nevermore* was looming above him. The beach deck wasn't as low in the water as he'd hoped, but it was doable. He paddled up, the rubber dinghy making only a minor squeak as it encountered the sleek hull of the massive superyacht. A gnat on an elephant. Mac stood, rolled his shoulders to shift his backpack to a more comfortable position. He stabbed the inflatable to sink it.

Years of press ups and pull ups got him on board without wet feet.

The beach deck was open and he could see the main staircase. He could also hear some of the crew in their quarters. Seeing a door moving from the galley, he hid behind a jet ski. The chef didn't look back, just disappeared into the crew quarters.

Mac still didn't have a plan. Find Elaine, yes, but then what? How were they to get away? He looked at the machines in front of him. He'd never ridden a jet ski. Had heard they were a bit like riding a motorbike. Not that that helped, he couldn't ride one of those either. Besides, part of the point of being in Sochi was to find Lazlo, the other being to confront Garin. Here was the very place they needed to be. Though he wished it was more on their terms than Garin's.

First things first, he needed to know that Elaine was safe and well.

There seemed no more movement from the crew quarters, so on soft footed steps, he moved out from behind the machines, jogged the length of the deck to the circular main stair. Light, lithe movements took him up the stairs without movement from the crew quarters. He was on the next deck when the sound to his right caught his attention.

He turned just in time to see the fist come out of the shadows and knock him on his arse.

CHAPTER TWENTY-NINE

Elaine felt dreadful. She'd messaged Mac, hoping that he got the message, got the code, but had received no answer. The bed was big and comfortable, and with nothing better to do, she lay down. She must have dropped straight to sleep.

She woke with dribble down her chin and a desperate need to pee. The en suite was better appointed than her bathroom at home. She could tell the boat was on the move now, she had her sea legs.

In the bathroom, there was a brush and comb set, not to mention some pricy cosmetics left for a guest's convenience. She was happy to take advantage of the offering. If she was facing her final day, she wanted to do so with a fresh face on.

The thwup-thwup-thwup was soft and distant, but she recognised it as she pulled the brush through her hair. A helicopter approaching. Garin was due today, and if they were on the move, this was likely the way he was arriving.

Definitely needed her best face today.

Once done, she checked her phone. No messages. She sent one instead.

* * *

Mac had the grandmother of all headaches.

It wasn't exactly a surprise, though Demko's punch hadn't knocked him unconscious, had hurt like hell. He hadn't fought back. There was little point. He'd allowed the big man to drag him to one of the rooms, and lock him in. Demko had swiped his backpack and his gun.

The headache was from dehydration. Not a hangover, he hadn't drunk enough. Elaine had drunk the bottle of champagne and barely been affected. She had told him that she enjoyed the odd glass of an evening, then she admitted that it was more like the odd bottle, and on bad days, two. She hadn't drunk that much in the time he'd known her, but clearly, she was used to drinking, and given her messages, she hadn't been very affected last night.

Right now, he needed a drink. Preferable a coffee, but water would do.

Though this was one of the smaller cabins, it was still better than some of the hotels he and Elaine had suffered since joining forces. He moved over to the tiny bathroom and made use of the facilities. The gash across his right ear had scabbed, a few hairs had caught in the matted blood. His head had hit the banister when Demko's punch floored him. His left cheek was red, and the left eye marked with bruising. All in all, he'd come off lightly. He sorted himself out, using the tumbler to drink two glasses of water in quick succession. It would take time to get into his system, but this would help.

He felt the phone in his trouser pocket vibrate. Demko had taken the pack and gun without checking for more.

A message from Elaine. *All at sea. Heard Chopper.*

He messaged back. *Me Too.*

* * *

Elaine pulled her bag strap across her torso, and the fur coat over that. She sat on the bed to await her fate.

A key turned in the lock. Her phone vibrated.

She didn't dare move, just sat quietly and waited while the door was opened and Demko, recently shaved judging by the rash on his neck, appeared.

"Do you need a coat?" he asked.

"Well, it is December, and sailing can be cold."

He grinned and chuckled. "So much for the mouse." He pushed the door wider and indicated she was to come out. "You're expected for breakfast."

She stood and moved towards him. "Am I to eat or be eaten?"

He didn't answer as he led the way back to the saloon he'd taken her to the previous evening. From there she saw a smartly dressed man sitting out on the open deck beside a table that held coffee and breakfast. His blond hair was stylishly cut, and she could see the grey threads in it. He wasn't alone out there either. The open part of the deck was easily five metres deep. At the edge, away from Garin and to the side, two men flanked Jason, still in that orange jumpsuit. Steve was now wearing a similar suit, but he clearly couldn't stand, and was slumped against the rails, shivering.

"Glad I kept my coat on now," Elaine muttered as she stepped through into the cooler air. She turned directly to the suited man. He was lean in build, and hard in expression.

"Hello, Mr—erm, Garin?"

He dipped his head to acknowledge the name. "We meet at last, Mrs Blake."

Elaine had to bite her cheek and try not to think of megalomaniacs stroking fluffy white cats. Her grip on sanity felt increasingly tenuous. "I might have put it off a while longer if I'd had a choice, to be honest."

Garin's eyes narrowed.

"Still, here we are."

"Take a seat, Mrs Blake." He indicated the second place at the table.

She stepped towards it. But paused before sitting down. "Would you mind if I moved Steve over to the bench there?" she pointed to the moulded seat at the edge of the deck. Close to her offered place. "He doesn't appear to be in a good way."

"Does it matter?" Garin asked.

"It does to me."

He considered her for a moment, then shrugged.

"Thank you." She moved over to Steve and let him lean heavily on her as she helped him first to his feet then over to side bench, where he audibly gasped and sighed in both pain and relief to sit supported. Once she was sure he was safe and as comfortable as possible, she straightened, glad to note they weren't the only ship on the waters. Then, she took the indicated chair. She looked at Garin and tried really hard to forget every thriller movie or book she had ever watched or read. "Beautiful morning, isn't it?"

"We're heading towards a rainstorm, but that shouldn't be a problem for the *Nevermore*. Do help yourself to coffee. Would you like a cooked breakfast?"

"I can't imagine much being a problem to the *Nevermore*. I will have coffee, thank you." She reached to pour it. "And no breakfast for me. I'm still full after a wonderful meal last night, but, again, thank you."

"The marina restaurants are extremely good."

She sipped her coffee and relaxed back. "Indeed, and so they should be, the kind of clients they serve."

"Only the best for the best."

She grinned and agreed. "This is certainly the best coffee I've had in a while."

"My own blend." Garin watched her. His expression gave nothing away. "Your friend isn't in too good a condition."

She turned to look at Steve.

"Not that one." Garin raised his hand and another man stumbled into view from the saloon.

* * *

Whatever Mac had expected of this morning, it wasn't to be pushed around and then find Elaine calmly taking breakfast with Garin. He noted the rest of the scene. Jason flanked by two bruisers, he named them Tweedledum and Tweedledee. The only thing that told them apart was the hair. Tweedledee had some. Jason looked tired with signs of beating. Steve sat to the side, beaten. It seemed to take all the strength he had to stay sitting up right. Garin and Elaine shared the centrally placed table. The wrought iron and glass top had an Italianate styling. Demko waited by the entrance to the saloon, blocking the way. There was nowhere to go but over the side.

Elaine stilled for a moment on seeing him. He almost felt her gaze roving over his injuries. "Must have been one hell of a punch," she observed. Then her eyes slid up to Demko. "Your handywork?"

The big man confirmed it.

"Naughty puppy." Elaine shifted her attention to Garin. "Does he always leave his playthings in such bad condition?"

Garin regarded her without emotion. "From what I hear, your marriage is in worse condition still."

She grinned. "My marriage? Well, I'd say that was dead in the water, but given who's standing over there, it might be a little early for that proclamation."

"A little," Garin noted. "But you did come looking for him, after all."

"She is my wife," Jason muttered.

"And he's got four million reasons for saying that," Elaine said. "Well, actually, I have four million reasons for him to say that, but that's beside the point."

Garin was clearly uncertain how to take what she said.

"Anyway, you're wrong. I came looking for my son. I did all this for Lazlo."

Mac gave her credit for how cool she sounded. He had no idea how this would play out, but as far as he could tell, they were still heading southwest, which was what he needed if they were going to reach Turkish waters.

Garin displayed no emotion as he watched Elaine. "You are no threat to me, Mrs Blake."

"Then why am I here?"

"You are going to tell me everything I want to know."

"Seems unlikely," Elaine said. "What do you want to know?"

"Where's the evidence?"

"I can't tell you that." Elaine finished her coffee and returned the cup carefully to its saucer. "That is a good coffee. Would you like a top up?"

Garin shook his head. In truth his own cup was still full. Elaine folded her hands in her lap and smiled at Garin.

"You are too happy for your current situation, Mrs Blake."

She shrugged. "Well, I've lived miserably for a long while, I may as well die happy."

His left eye twitched. "You, Mrs Blake, will die screaming."

"Well, they say pain is so close to pleasure, maybe you'll tip me over the edge. So, there's something to look forward too, then huh?"

Mac wasn't quite sure where this nihilistic humour was coming from, but it seemed Elaine wasn't about to stop it.

"Where's the book, Mrs Blake?"

"What book?"

Garin smiled. "I don't believe you're stupid, Mrs Blake. Don't treat me as if I am."

"I'm not. You're asking about a book, there are many, many books in the world. I merely need you to be a little more specific, so that I can be equally specific in my response."

If playing for time she was doing a reasonable job of it, but Garin wasn't the man to annoy. Mac tried to figure the best way forward.

"The notebook," Garin said. "The orange notebook of code which your darling husband kept in that Berlin locker. The one you retrieved. Where is it?"

"So, you're still looking for that marvellous, mysterious evidence everyone seems to be after. And you want me to offer it to you?"

"You can't offer that in exchange for your life, Mrs Blake. But, if you give it to me, I'll make your death quick, painless."

She met his gaze easily enough. "You're right, I can't offer that." She shook her head. "Mostly because, as it turns out, I wouldn't even if I could. Anyway, I can't. I don't have it."

Garin's face darkened. "But you had the cypher. You gave us a fake."

"What makes you think it was faked?"

"Because I'm not stupid, Mrs Blake. We decoded the cypher. At least the first word. Watchtower. The rest was gibberish. The locker key was the wrong sort and the pen drive… What was the point of giving us those images? Did you think it would hurt?"

Again, she shrugged. "Not really. I just had to give something over and that was what I had. I figured if Lazlo came with me, he'd be safe and if he didn't, he'd have to look out for himself."

Garin looked her up and down. "So much for motherly love."

"Oh, I still love him," Elaine said. "Nothing's going to change that. But if fostering twenty-one children taught me anything, it's that some people just can't be helped, no matter how hard you try."

Garin appeared entirely relaxed as he stood, pulled the gun from beneath his jacket and pointed it directly at Elaine.

"But I know where the evidence is," she said. "And if you kill me, you'll never find out."

His grin broadened. The gun moved. Towards Jason. "Maybe I'll kill your husband instead."

Elaine didn't turn a hair. "According to the paperwork he's already dead. But before you fire. Perhaps you could do me one teensy little favour?"

Garin finally looked confused, and while he didn't move the gun, he did look back to her.

"Ask him what he knows about Eric Kitchener. Would you mind if I have another coffee?"

When Garin didn't respond, she simply poured herself another cup, and added a dash of cream. No one had moved and all eyes were on her. She surveyed her audience before focusing on Garin. "Oh Spartek, dear fellow, do indulge me. Ask him about Eric."

Garin put the gun back away and nodded to the guards.

"I don't know anything!" Jason said.

It was possibly the worst thing he could have said. Tweedledee punched him in the stomach.

"That's what I thought," Elaine said.

"Then why the question?" Garin asked.

"Personal satisfaction. I want Jason to know about Eric Kitchener before he dies. It explains so much, you see."

Mac knew about Eric Kitchener, and it didn't explain much to him.

"Mac, dear," she said conversationally. "Did you ever research Eric?"

"I did."

"Then do tell. Jason is likely dying to know."

This made no more sense to Mac than Jason, but he trusted Elaine more than he trusted anyone. "Eric Kitchener died aged 21. You would have been what? 16?"

"Not quite, I was still 15 then. Do go on."

"Eric was found in a river near his home, the death certificate said misadventure. Pathologist concluded that he'd fallen headfirst from the top of a weir into the water, smashed his head on the rocks beneath, the damage to his skull rendering him dazed and confused and unable to help himself. He drowned. Toxicology report suggested alcohol had been consumed, but not sufficient to fully intoxicate."

"Hmm, sounds plausible." Elaine looked squarely at Garin now. "Guy gets tipsy, crosses a weir, misses his footing, falls, knocks himself out, drowns. Very plausible, wouldn't you say?"

"Very," Garin agreed. "But much about you seems one way, when reality is another thing. What really happened?"

Elaine smiled at him. "I think I'll take that a compliment, Mr Garin, thank you." The smile soon faded. "But you're right. It's not what happened. You see Eric was a neighbour. I was having a tough time. He was around. So when he moved to comfort me, I let him."

Mac schooled his features not to react, but inside he was screaming. Comfort would mean something hugely different to the likes of Eric than it would have to Elaine back then.

"Only he wanted more, he tried..." She took a breath. "Well, no point in beating about the bush. That bastard raped me. When he was done and off me, I saw this large stone. I didn't even think about it. I just picked it up and smashed it into his head. I ran. Across a weir. Dropping the stone in. Eric yelled and followed me. At the other side, I turned, grabbed a handful of water, and threw it in his face. He tried to dodge and..." She had to swallow at the memory. "There was that frozen moment, like in a cartoon, when he was suspended in the air. Blood flowed down his face where I'd smashed it in. His eyes were wide with surprise. We both knew he was going to fall, there was no stopping it." She took a breath. "He did fall, but as far as I could see, he didn't hit his head again. The water wasn't that deep, and he tried to stand, but..." She shrugged. "I don't really know, but he just couldn't seem to stand or walk. I stood there and watched. He screamed for help. I could have too; I could have helped. The life ring was right there. I did nothing. I just stood there and watched him drown. I watched him die." She let that sink in for a moment. "Then I walked home."

There, that made more sense. Unnecessary guilt. She had struck in retaliation for her attack. There were a million ways that Eric could have reacted to the situation that would mean he would still be alive today. But Eric had chosen to follow her across the weir. That choice led to his slipping and his drowning. His choice, not her action. Given the likely size and comparative strength of the two, there was a damn good chance that, had she tried to help him, Eric would have pulled her in, drowned her. She was blaming herself unnecessarily. Besides from the reports he'd read, the world was better off without Eric Kitchener.

"The Police never even asked. The coroner declared it an accident. So, you see, really, I've already got away with murder once. Well, twice, but I'll tell you about the other one later. So, there you are. That's the story of Eric Kitchener."

"And what, exactly, does it explain?"

Elaine looked at Garin as if surprised he didn't understand. Suddenly Mac did. The first night he'd watched her in her home. She'd said it to herself, and his bugs had picked it up, carried it to his ears. Now it made sense. Marriage wasn't a word. It was a sentence.

"I suspect that you and I have very different views on murder. I've never forgiven myself for killing Eric. And I was never the same after. I married Jason because I thought it would be safe, boring. I didn't realise it would be a life sentence. But twenty-four years is more than most sentences last. So, if you want to kill Jason, go ahead. I won't stop you. In fact, if you'd like, I'll shoot him."

"Elaine!" No one paid Jason any heed.

Garin grinned and placed his gun down on the table. An open invitation. Elaine's eyes moved between the gun and the man. She stood, but instead of reaching for the gun, she slipped the fur coat from her shoulders. The red dress and the push-up effect of her lingerie drew attention. The assembled men didn't say as word as she casually moved around to push her coat at Mac. "Here, hold this for me."

He did. Not because he was some sort of check girl, but because the way she had oh so casually swung it meant that the pocket had swung into his knee. Reminding him that that was where she had stowed the Berretta. She also still had her bag slung across her torso. So, cash, cards, passports and her phone.

Casually, she reached for the gun. Garin enclosed her wrist with his hand. "Don't try anything stupid, Mrs Blake."

"Wouldn't dream of it, Mr Garin, and please, call me Elaine."

Garin let go, she took up the gun and faced the three men at the open rail. She raised the gun. Then lowered it. "Gentlemen, I'm not a great shot."

Tweedledum and Tweedledee stepped away from Jason.

She levelled the gun. Mac's heart was in his mouth. Would she really kill in cold blood?

"Elaine, please," Jason begged.

The gun went down. Elaine turned back to Garin. "Oh, he's just too pathetic. Distinctly not worth the effort." She changed the position of the gun, taking it by the muzzle to hand it back to Garin. When he moved to take it, she held on for a moment. "We're none of us stupid, Spartek. We all know we're the ones who'll die here."

He glanced to Tweedledee, signalled with a look. Tweedledee went below deck. Garin returned his attention to Elaine. "You are not what I expected, Elaine. I understood you to be a mouse."

"Even a mouse can roar. I believe there's an entire book about that."

"And speaking of books, where is it?"

"Safe."

"You said two murders," Garin changed tack. "And that you'd tell me about the other one. Do so now."

Elaine licked her lips as she sank back to her previous seat. "You haven't heard from Illyana in two days, have you?"

"I asked you to tell me about the second murder."

"I know. You don't know where she is, do you?"

"I know where she is," Garin countered.

"Liar."

No one spoke to Garin like that and survived. Though it didn't much change their current situation.

"Though in fairness," Elaine continued. "I can't guarantee her location either. All depends on bin collection."

"What are you talking about?"

Garin wasn't easily wrong footed, but Elaine had thrown him. Mac was proud.

"Well, you see, there's an alley in Samsun. Has no name I know of. But she followed me down it a couple of nights ago. Put a gun to my head, demanded to know where the book of evidence was. Then she tried to march me out of the alley. I tripped over rubbish; she tripped over me. The gun went off. Oddly, she was the one as got shot." Elaine seemed to be thinking about that. "Can't figure out how."

"What have bins got to do with anything?" Garin asked.

"I shoved her body in one," Elaine said. "One of those big industrial things. Then I chucked her gun in too. Used a wet wipe to pick it up by the muzzle, so only her prints are on it not mine. Used another bin for the wet wipes I used to get her blood off my coat. Left no obvious incriminating evidence. After all, I'm not stupid."

Mac realised that this was what she hadn't told him in Samsun. Underestimating Elaine could be a terminal condition.

"I don't like being a murderer, Mr Garin," she said quietly.

Mac thought it sounded more like accidental death than murder. Elaine was taking on unwarranted blame.

Then she smiled at Garin. "But knowing it pisses you off helps." Elaine's voice drifted off as she focused on the noise coming from behind. The scuffling and mewling suggested an uneven struggle. Very uneven: Tweedledee towered over a badly beaten Lazlo as they came to stand before the group.

"Fuck's sake." The soft-spoken curse was Jason's.

Garin stood, moving towards the boy. Not that Lazlo was a boy now. He seemed to have aged ten years since Mac last saw him. Finally, Lazlo saw the cost of this job. Shame there was no free way out. No way out, full stop.

"Leave my son alone," Elaine demanded. "He's done nothing to warrant this."

"On the contrary, his doing nothing is exactly what warranted this," Garin said. "He was supposed to fetch the notebook for me, but it was gone when he got there. He wasn't quick enough. He's also not your son."

"In every way that counts he is."

Garin sneered at her. Aware that all attention focused on the two of them, Mac flexed his fingers around the Berretta in the coat.

"Biologically, he's my son."

That stopped Mac and Elaine both.

"What?" she demanded.

Garin stepped over and put his arm about the younger man's shoulder. "Lazlo is my son."

Good God, how had they missed that?

Now the two of them were side by side, Mac saw facial similarities. The height and colouring must come from Lazlo's mother, but other than that, these two were very much alike. *Jason.* Jason had brought Lazlo in, done the background work. God, that meant the bastard had been Garin's puppet for a least ten years.

Elaine wasn't following so quickly. "Then how did he end up in Wales with me?"

"He was a plant, what you might call a sleeper. I manipulated others, agents who think themselves oh so clever. Lazlo got into all the right places for me."

Elaine nodded. "I see." Her head dipped as she focused on Lazlo. "So, you didn't betray me after all. You were never on my side. There must be loyalty before there can be disloyalty."

"You deserved what you got," Lazlo sneered. "What you'll get."

Elaine nodded. "You're absolutely right."

"Well, Elaine, you have what you came for. You found Lazlo. Now give me what I want. Where's the book?"

This time, her head tipped to the side as she looked at Garin. "You've beaten your own son because he didn't give you what you wanted. And you're right, I'm not stupid. I now know the second you get that book, or knowledge of where it is, you'll kill me. Oddly enough, that's not a great incentive."

"How's this for incentive?"

Mac watched in disbelief as the gun Garin carried shifted from Elaine to Lazlo. The proximity of the discharge muffled the shot. Lazlo groaned. Blood and lung spattered behind him. Lazlo slumped. Garin let him fall. Elaine screamed denial.

Mac pulled the gun from the coat.

Mac swung the gun, squeezed the trigger as Demko slammed into his side. The bullet went wide, missing Garin by millimetres.

CHAPTER THIRTY

Elaine watched her son crumple.

Her son, whatever anyone said. For a moment she looked into those frightened eyes and saw the scared little boy who'd come to her. She'd done her best then. There was nothing she could do now. The boy and now the man were gone. All that was left was an empty fallen shell. All dead, all dead. The words rang in her head, red mist descended.

Someone will pay for this.

Garin dodged into her eyeline. The man who had killed his own child. A lifetime spent believing that no parent could do that washed away in blood and cold hard hate.

Lips drawn back in a snarl, Elaine flew towards him. He was faster. The weight of the gun cracked across her cheek. The jolt of the hit, the rolling of the deck unfooted her, she went down.

Twisting, Garin loomed above, the gun pointed at her.

Instinct took over. She kicked out.

The gun went skittering across the deck.

* * *

Mac fell to the deck, the weight of Demko pinned him. Punches rained on his kidneys. He shifted the gun. A blow numbed his arm, he couldn't move it.

Movement behind Demko's back. Steve had slumped off the bench.

* * *

The yank to her feet felt almost like levitation, it was so fast. Tweedledee grabbed Elaine to him. With an anchor point, she kicked out. Her foot connected with the heavy table. The sudden straightening of her leg threw Tweedledee off balance. Her move, the heavy swell, forced Tweedledee to stagger back. A body lay across his path. Tweedledee tripped over Steve, fell on his spine. Elaine landed on his chest, knocked the wind from him.

* * *

Mac saw a blur of bodies fall behind Steve. Blow after blow rained down from above. Elaine rolled to the side, away from him. He raised his gun. Tweedledee sat up. Mac fired.

* * *

The shot just missed Elaine's head. The detached realisation that they had entered the rainstorm Garin mentioned distracted her. For a second her eyes met Mac's. They weren't winning. Steven shifted. He had Garin's fallen gun. Elaine pushed herself up as another shot blasted, this time through Tweedledee's exposed side into his chest cavity.

Blooded spittle spurted from his mouth as he fell back dead.

Disoriented, Elaine was helpless against the hands that dragged her back and off her feet. Dragged bumping from the outside deck inside, Elaine could get no purchase against the smooth flooring. There was only the slightest pause for a door to be opened. Her attempt to fight was futile.

She was picked up and thrown onto a bed. It occurred to her that if she hadn't lost so much weight, he wouldn't have been able to do that.

Garin's weight landed on her, pinned her down, his hand around her throat restricting her breath.

"Where is the notebook?"

Unable to answer, already light-headed from lack of oxygen, she stared at him. Light-headed but not out of it yet. Her hands free, she grabbed his earlobes. He tried to shake her off, but she clung on. She dug her nails in. They lay nose to nose, eyes filled with hate. Warmth told her she'd broken his skin, the restriction told her she was about to pass out, but she had one move left to make. Fists tight, she yanked her hands wide. He released a terrifying scream as he pulled away, hands to his bleeding ears. Coughing and dragging in breath, Elaine threw his torn lobes at him as she rolled off the bed gasping for breath.

His primal, guttural growl as he pushed himself back up, slammed into her, terrified her. Pinned tighter now, she lashed out, punched, kicked, head-butted. He grabbed both wrists. She wasn't going to get him twice the same way. Struggling just used energy she didn't have. She stilled and glared up at him, at the blood pouring down the sides of his face and onto her.

"Bitch."

"Bastard."

"Where's the book?"

"Where you'll never get it."

"Where is it?"

"Fuck you."

"No, Mrs Blake. You'll be the one who gets fucked. By every man I own. You'll be raped and abused. I'll let them do any damn thing they want, as long as it makes you scream."

"I will never scream for you."

He leaned down, and she pushed her head to the side and back as far as possible. He brought his nose a millimetre from her, blood still flowing, his neck showed the strain. Exactly what she wanted.

"You'll do—"

She bobbed her head up and sank her teeth into his neck. The muscle and sinew grated as she clenched her jaw. She tasted salt of sea and sweat, closely followed by the iron from his blood.

He pummelled her even as he screamed, but like a bulldog she would not let go. As he moved back, he dragged her with him, attached like a vice. His blood filled her mouth. She pulled her lips back, forced the flow out, her teeth not yet entirely closed as they bit into his flesh. Finally, she had room; teeth clamped hard around flesh, she jerked her head away.

Blood from his ripped jugular spurted wildly around the previously immaculate room. He moved crablike away from her. Hands frantically tried to stem the flow. There was no stopping that gaping wound. Garin's own rapid heart sped him towards death. She spat his flesh as him and stood, filling her lungs with breath, the pounding in her ears almost gone as cold calm washed through her. She pulled up the duvet, wiped her face and dropped the material.

His wide eyes filled with hate and fear. She saw the little boy from the photo.

"You were someone's beloved little boy once. I pray to God your parents did not live to see the pathetic wanker you grew into."

He tried to speak. The life fading from his eyes, he barely had the strength to hold his hands to his neck.

"Lazlo was my son," Elaine said evenly. "And no one gets away with hurting my family. No one."

Garin was still alive. Just. She stepped over him and left. He deserved to die alone.

CHAPTER THIRTY-ONE

Mac's sight blurred. He couldn't save Elaine. The hits kept coming. Much more and he'd pass out. The gun had skittered from his hand. He swung, but Demko moved faster. Laughter echoing in Mac's swirling head. He managed to get to his knees before another shot rang out. Steve.

Demko staggered. Looked at the blood appearing on his arm.

Winged.

Demko raised his foot to stamp on Steve's head.

Desperation gave Mac power.

Rage screamed from him as he rushed Demko. The unbalanced man fell to the seats. More red smeared white. He punched him in the face.

Another shot. The sound of a body falling.

Bone or gristle snapped under the blow to Demko's nose.

They were sliding.

Mac fell back, kept his feet, recovered his balanced.

He had no idea what had happened to his gun.

Something tapped his leg.

Demko was staggering to his feet.

Mac glanced down, dipping quickly to grab the gun Steve offered. Down but not out.

Focus snapped back.

Mac raised his pistol, deliberately kneecapped Demko.

Demko looked up through a swollen and bloody face. He raised his gun unsteadily.

Mac squeezed the trigger.

A small hole appeared in Demko's forehead. His features slackened. The arm dropped.

"Nice shot!" A woman's voice congratulated.

As the body slumped to the deck, Mac swung to see Elaine, drenched in blood, step out to the deck. She was smiling at him. Not her blood, then.

"Elaine!"

Mac didn't have time to move or speak before Jason turned and pulled Elaine into one almighty hug. Elation at finally beating Demko washed out of Mac seeing another man holding Elaine. And much as he wanted to shoot Jason, that was out of the question.

He sat heavily on moulded seat at the edge of the deck.

Numbly his surroundings sank in, the difference of the scene now was unbelievable. The deck was blood drenched. Tweedledum lay dead by the door to the back, slumped over Tweedledee, equally deceased. Steve curled up on the floor, beaten but he'd fought to the end, clinging to life and Garin's gun. Demko was dead. Lazlo too. At least that saved him from facing treason charges. Jason seemed virtually unscathed. Elaine stood bloodied, but safe, which meant Garin was dead. Mac wanted to lie down and give up. Victory meant nothing if he lost his Laney.

Elaine moved away from Jason and knelt over Steve, helping the injured man to rise and sit more comfortably. She checked him over.

"What happened to Garin?" Jason asked.

"He's dead."

Elaine was closest to the main deck, so she was the first to hear. Mac stood as more of the crew appeared. With guns. Expecting nothing but to be shot, he moved, but Elaine stopped him.

His head twisting to the side, he looked down at her, pale under the drying blood.

Her voice was low. "Remember your promise?"

"I do. Does it matter now?"

Her smile overflowed with sadness. "More than ever." She patted his upper arm. "Keep yourself alive."

* * *

The mob wasn't something Elaine could cope with. Nor was the prospect of Mac getting shot trying to save them. At least Mac spoke their language. She had to deal with what she could manage. At that second, Steve was all she could concentrate on. He needed help and as usual, Jason wasn't about to give any.

With careful movement and what soothing words she could offer, she checked Steve over. She didn't think there was a good prognosis.

"You know for a moment there, I thought you were really going to shoot me," Jason said.

"You know for more than a moment, I've been thinking about the inconsistency of your narrative." She eased the gun from Steve's fingers. The look they shared was full of understanding. He knew what she had to do, and he wasn't going to stop her. The strong suspicion arose that if he'd been able to, Steve would have done it himself.

"What are you talking about?" Jason demanded.

"In the container, you told Steve and I you didn't know where the evidence was." She straightened and faced the man she had allowed to own her for so long. "But Garin knew about the Berlin locker. Shame for him, I got there first."

"Good for us though," Jason tried.

Elaine didn't even try to ease the sneer from her face. "You only ever do what's good for you, Jason. That's your whole MO. If you had a gun right now, you'd shoot me, head back to the UK and try to regain the money I took from your account."

"You had no right to take what I've earned."

"Like you had no right to blame me for not having children when you'd had a vasectomy. Though god knows, I'm now glad not to have had a child of yours. You'd only have abused them too. And when you talk about what you've earned, let's think about that for a moment. How did you earn it? Playing all sides? Selling secrets? Dodgy deals left right and centre. I worked hard to make sure that all the bills were paid, all the children and the house were taken care of. I left myself short to pay the mortgage off early and all that time a tiny fraction of what you had stashed away would have seen us financially secure. But you couldn't give me even that, could you? No. Because all you ever do is take. Well, you'll take no more from me."

This time he sneered. "You were never worth giving anything too. Murderer."

"And an infidel, don't forget that." She smiled a patently false smile. "You aren't the only one who can have extra-marital sex. I may have waited until you were officially dead. But since then, I've had a wonderful time. Best ever. But then Mac is so much better than you in so many ways."

* * *

Mac was pleased to hear it as he moved back towards the open deck.

The crew hadn't exactly known what to do once they realised that Garin and Demko were dead. Mac told them all they had to do was get them to Turkish waters, and they'd leave, and the crew could do whatever they wanted, after all, there was nothing and no one to stop them taking whatever they wanted from a boat that belonged to a dead man without heirs.

"Jesus! Elaine!"

At Jason's shout, Mac focused. Elaine held a gun on Jason.

"Elaine," Jason had his hands up in front of him. "What are you doing?"

"Aiming a gun at you."

Her tone sounded oh-so matter of fact it was almost comical.

"But—"

"There's nothing left to say, Jason. Before…"

Jason's voice quaked when he spoke. "Before what?"

The crack of the pistol made Mac jump, the thump of the body was lost under the stunned moment.

"Before I kill you."

What the actual hell?

"Laney?"

Mac looked at her, as her arm lowered.

"Stay away, Mac. I'm not finished."

Without another word, she stepped backwards, to the side of the boat.

Uncomprehending, Mac stared at her looking out into the grey sheeting rain that was not only catching up with them but cloaking then, the sound of the rain growing heavier on the roof about them. One step back and she looked at him. Her left hand raised. Three fingers up like the scouts, or the Mockingjay.

"Elaine?"

Then she sat on the rail, put the gun to her head.

Mac moved, Steve cried her name, tried to stand, unbalanced. Automatically, Mac grabbed the falling man. Looked to settle him —

The shot rang out.

He turned in time to see her legs disappearing over the side. The splash louder than the slashing rain, just as quickly lost. Mac ran to the side of the boat, catching a brief flash of red dress as another body was swallowed by the hungry sea.

CHAPTER THIRTY-TWO

"You're certain he's dead?"

Madison sat in a quiet corner of the busy wine bar, Number Two sat before her, looking scraggier and older. Every care etched in the lines on her face. Her voice was monotone, void of emotion.

"Absolutely," Madison confirmed, pushing a photograph of a very dead Garin across the table, his neck an open gaping wound. Thanks to Mac, Bromstad had people intercept the *Nevermore* once it reached the Turkish waters of the Black Sea. "We also have the bodies of Ulrich Demko, Jason Blake, Lazlo Zakis, and two unidentified others."

"But not a trace of Elaine Blake," Number Two stated.

"You know from Letterman's statement why not; she went into the sea. They found strands of her hair in the room with Garin's body and the teeth marks in his neck match the impression taken by her dentist a few years ago." That Elaine had defeated a powerful Russian mafia boss filled Madison with pride. Losing Elaine had hit her hard, but at least she had finally lived before she died. "The Southgates?" Madison asked.

"Relocated. Again."

"New identities?"

"Which I can't share." The woman pushed the photo back. "And the book?"

Madison took the orange notebook from her pocket. It had arrived looking like a Christmas present, silly paper and reindeer stickers wishing a "mutlu Noeller", a Turkish Merry Christmas. It came with a note in Elaine's hand that told Madison how much she loved her, how proud she was of her, and all best wishes for her upcoming nuptials. Madison kept the note in her bedside drawer. Losing the mother she loved was proving more difficult than losing her birth mother. Without reluctance, she pushed the notebook across the table.

The woman took it and slipped it into her own handbag. "You've decoded it, of course?"

"In fairness, Mom did most of that before she posted it."

Number Two now looked at the death certificate and land transfer. "Ah, so this was how Spartek Garin got hold of that land."

"Yep," Madison agreed. "He literally stole it from his aunt. Then he dug up a couple of tonnes of titanium, apparently using slave labour, made his first fortune and went on from there."

"This is what we needed to prove that."

"Which was probably why Jason had it. His shield against Garin."

Number Two nodded.

"Why did you really give Mom that half million?"

"For the evidence. We thought she was in on it, but it appears not."

"And yet she still got you what you were after. I guess it was worth every penny."

"It saved more than that in what it would have cost us in lost operatives, broken contacts and the cost of starting it all from scratch again," Number Two said as she stowed the evidence safely away. "Congratulations by the way."

Madison looked at her hand, her ring, the soft smile came automatically. "Thank you."

"I meant the promotion."

Madison was one of five applicants, and the successful candidate. She looked back to the British agent across from her.

"Thank you, Sarah. I appreciate that. How's Agent Letterman?"

The paused before the answer suggested a lot that was going to go unsaid. "Working."

Madison sighed, slightly disappointed.

* * *

Jessica patted down the last of the earth as Keira stepped into their new garden. Steve looked over his shoulder at her. The wheelchair was a restriction he struggled with, but months of recovery still lay ahead. He watched his ever-elegant wife move towards him and their daughter.

"What's going on?" Keira asked as she stopped by them.

"We're planting a rose bush," Jessica said as she stood, wiping her hands. "It's a memorial for Aunt E."

"Right in the middle of the lawn?"

"Right where we'll see it every day," Steve acknowledged.

"Why?"

Jessica answered. "Because she was our friend, we loved her, and she saved Daddy's life."

"She did." Steve acknowledged.

Jessica turned and fixed her mother with an uncompromising gaze. Steve was amazed how much she'd grown up in the months he'd been away and in hospital. Leaving their old life behind had proved good for Jessica. Her name had changed to Maxine, a name she'd picked herself. She took one audition and an entrance exam, for the local stage school and Maxine Torres, dancer, actor, possibly singer with a few lessons, was in. And loving it. Blossoming. He smiled at his daughter, so proud of her.

"And Elaine did that, despite knowing that we all betrayed her," Jessica said, pinning her mother with a hard glare. "Especially you, since you were fucking her husband." Jessica turned and walked away. Keira merely stood there, slack-jawed, staring at Steve.

"You wanted to raise a strong powerful woman," he shrugged. "Congratulations."

"But…"

"But nothing. Keira, you betrayed Elaine. And me." Yet he reached out and took her hand. "I forgive you. Je— Maxine will in time, but right now she's still angry."

Keira nodded and looked at the plant. "In comparison I suppose that a rose in the middle of my lawn ruining the lines of the garden is nothing to put up with."

"Nope," Steve agreed. "And you will tend to this rose bush, my sweet. You'll make sure that it thrives now Elaine can't."

* * *

The memorial was well attended. Madison appreciated Neil's support, but as the last guests expressed their sympathy, she asked him to give her a moment. Guests drifted from the gardens, the wake was in a hotel two streets away, and Madison needed a moment to speak with Utku alone. He'd already wholeheartedly congratulated her and welcomed Neil to their loving, if mismatched family.

"How are you really?" she asked as they ended the embrace.

"Glad I got to make up with her before… while there was still time." Utku's red-rimmed eyes told their own story. Madison assumed hers did too.

She smiled up at her brother, a bond no one was ever going to break. "There was no way she wouldn't forgive you. Knowing her, I doubt she even thought there was anything to forgive."

He nodded, blinking back tears. "I should have known that and come back sooner. Only I never thought we'd lose her like this."

"No one could. It wasn't your fault, Utku."

"True. It was Jason's. And Lazlo's."

"And they both paid for it with their lives."

"But why did Mum have to?"

It was a question no one could answer.

"And you'll excuse me if I don't mourn Jason or Lazlo," Utku asked. "They deserved worse than they got."

Madison squeezed his hand. "Oh, I'll definitely excuse that. I feel the same."

"Not sure I can excuse Letterman for not being here though." A hardness born of pain touched him voice.

"You should," Madison told him softly. "He has the best excuse."

Utku frowned. "What could possibly excuse him? I thought she'd finally found somebody to love. A man who loved her back."

"He's dead." The finality of that weighed on her and clearly surprised Utku. Madison had seen Mac during the debrief, it hadn't been easy. "And he did love her. Like we did. Well, not quite like we did. You know what I mean." Madison wouldn't be surprised to discover his accident wasn't an accident at all. He'd confessed feeling he wasn't sure he could go on without Elaine. When Agent Smith told her he was back to working, it was clearly an attempt to act instead of feel. "His car crashed in the Urals. Line of duty. His tag team in the chase survived and brought back what they had been sent for. There wasn't enough of Letterman left to scrape up, let alone bring back." An awful and unfitting end to a good man.

"Excuse me?"

They both turned to the young woman under a hijab, who had stepped up to them. It took Madison a moment to recognise her. "Panina Binici?"

She offered a sad smile. "Indeed. You are Madison Turner?"

Madison shook the offered hand. Introduced herself and Utku. She even recognised the unwitting symptoms of attraction between the woman and her brother.

"Thank you so much for inviting me, I had to come. You see I had the very great fortune to meet your mother a second time in Ankara. She was an extraordinary person and she spoke of you both, indeed of all her children, with a great deal of affection. I know she loved you dearly."

Madison tried to speak, but it came out only as a sob. Utku's hand on her arm shook and his eyes weren't dry either.

"Wherever she is now," Panina's voice caught. "I know she will always love you."

"Thank you," Utku managed.

Madison took a moment to find her voice. "Will you join us at the wake?"

Panina shook her head. "Forgive me, no. I must go, the Ankara flight won't wait for me."

"The nine o'clock flight?"

Panina nodded.

"I'm on that flight too." Utku said. "We can share the taxi if you'd like?"

Panina nodded and smiled a thank you. The two Turks started away together.

"Another one your mother saved?"

Madison turned to find Neil at her shoulder. He always knew exactly what to say to make her smile.

CHAPTER THIRTY-THREE

London International Airport.

It was March first, St David's Day, and Laney's Ladderman was hurting. Like hell. Three months and it felt as raw as if he'd lost her yesterday.

But his Laney had always been several steps ahead of him, and this was the last respect he could pay her. And she was now his Laney, he never thought of her as Elaine anymore. Of course, he should have realised sooner that London International Airport wouldn't be near the capital of the UK. After a day of travel, he finally stood in London, Ontario. Now he was here, he just had to figure out what Laney wanted him to do. Other than hurt. Though he doubted she actually wanted him to hurt.

Then he saw it. The car-rental desk.

Hertz.

Caught out by a homophone. Sometimes, I am such an idiot.

A queue had formed after the arrival, but he had no reason to hurry. He glanced outside, ten inches of snow on the ground and temperature would be lucky to reach as high as zero. Not his favourite driving conditions, but not the greatest danger he'd ever faced.

The couple in front of him moved aside and he stepped forward to the rental agent.

"Hi," he said.

"Good afternoon, sir. Welcome to London. How may I help you today?"

He took a deep breath. He'd told Laney he understood, despite not understanding, and as hopeless as it was, he must keep the implied promise. "Do you have anything here for The Ladderman?"

The woman's eyes went wide and then she smiled. "You're the Ladderman?"

He swallowed and nodded.

"Okay. She didn't give any instruction other than only give this to the Ladderman."

She? Had Laney been here? Arranged… whatever this was? How? When? He'd seen her shoot herself, fall into the depths. He'd also not been privy to all her communications with Madison, so maybe Madison was the 'she' this woman referred to.

"How long have you had this thing?"

She looked over her shoulder. "A couple of weeks." As she straightened, she carried a small black box tied up with twine, and a buff tag. The tag said 'Ladderman only', and it was printed, no handwriting to give him a clue. The woman placed it on the counter. "It came in just before the last big storm. Have to say, we're all dying to find out what it is."

He admitted a distinct curiosity himself. He reached into his pocket and pulled out a pocketknife. He clicked the blade open and cut the string. The top came off the plastic box inside with a pop. Inside—

A parking ticket?

He picked up the slip of paper and looked at the date on it. Two weeks ago.

"That's a ticket from our car park."

The car park was right outside the terminal. Someone had handwritten 'Back right' on the face of the ticket. The writing was upright, printed, not cursive. It didn't look like Laney's handwriting; she had more flourish. Under the ticket, a car key lay in cut foam. He pulled out the key, the foam came next, just in case. Nothing more.

"Do you want me to check the cost on the ticket?"

He handed it over.

"It'll be a hundred dollars, though," she said as she put it into the machine. "Over a week and under a month always is… oh." She ejected and passed him back the ticket. "It's prepaid."

He thanked the woman and headed out to the back right of the car park, testing the remote locking key to find the right car. The lights flashed on a utility vehicle. About five years old, a couple of dings in the bodywork, average-looking enough not to draw attention. He got behind the wheel, stowed his bag on the passenger seat, and started the vehicle. A sat nav console popped up and on the screen a note that said. "Wheel chains in back". As he pulled that off, it was clear the destination had been pre-set. Another three-and-a-half-hour drive, to somewhere called Bala. The only Bala he knew was in North Wales.

This is going to be interesting.

* * *

Five hours later, he pulled up to the cabin in the woods. His memory flashed back to a night in another cabin, south of Prague. This cabin was much bigger, a cabin only by Canadian definition; anywhere else, it would be a luxury single family dwelling or detached house, with desirable views and plenty of privacy. He liked it. He was pretty sure it had greater square footage than the three-bedroom house he'd abandoned in Kent.

He switched off the engine and considered staying put, as the night had drawn in, the wind had picked up. Things looked cold and unpleasant out there compared to the nicely heated vehicle. A light, white and inviting, stood sentinel beside the door.

He grabbed his holdall, pushed the door against the wind and all but ran to the cabin, tilting into the force of the moving air, ignoring the sting of ice blasting him. At the door, he banged on the wood, wondering whether there would be an answer.

There wasn't.

He tried the handle. The wind nearly tore the door right out of his hand and into the cabin, forcing him to step in and making him fight to close the gap again. Once he'd secured the door, he turned. The centre of the cabin housed the living room, with doors off. A stone hearth rose in the middle and threw out warm golden light from the burning logs. The furniture and decoration made a homely welcome. On the far side, beside floor to ceiling bifold doors, was a canvas, 35 by 25 inches, on an easel. He eased his bag to the floor and walked over. An acrylic depiction of mountains, a dragon flew over a nest of eggs. He recognised the style.

One door opened, he turned to face her.

She stepped out.

His Laney.

Alive.

He—

She—

She saw him and stopped.

Logical thought was beyond his capacity.

After a heart stopped moment, slowly she smiled.

"It's a book cover, *Dragons of Denivor*," she said indicating the painting. "I'm being surprisingly well paid for that."

The breath left his body in more relief and wonder than he had the ability to express. He had to say something. "Nice work if you can get it."

She nodded. "And apparently, I can."

They walked towards each other, stopping shy of the hug he desperately wanted.

"Laney Armstrong," she introduced herself.

"Macte Romanov."

She shook her head. "Corbin MacDonald. I've got all the paperwork ready. Even told the folk in town that I was waiting for you to join me. I keep referring to you as Mac, hence the name."

A step closer allowed his fingers to stroke her cheek. Amazed at the soft warmth of her skin and the keen mind that put everything he needed in place. "I don't care what you call me, as long as you say you're mine. Feels like I was born to love you."

Her grin turned into a gentle laugh. "Oh, don't turn soppy on me now, my love."

He grinned too but had so many questions. "How the hell did you survive?"

"All arranged on a girl's night out. The boat on the horizon. Goker piloted the boat, Panina dived for me. When I was first grabbed, I activated a tracker they gave me. I'd taped it to my arm. Goker and Panina use the trackers for tracking fish."

Mac huffed out an impressed laugh. "Panina returned the favour for saving her life."

She nodded. "I think the quarter million to fund their research helped."

Doubtless. He nodded. "You could have told me."

She shook her head. "I couldn't be sure I'd survive, not in water that cold. I didn't want you living in false hope."

"We promised not to lie, even by omission."

"I know," she said softly, nodding. "I'm sorry, but even before I knew Madison was CIA, I knew she could spot a lie a mile off. If you'd gone back claiming I was dead, knowing I wasn't, she'd have figured it out. I needed her to believe I was dead; I wish I didn't. But that meant I needed you to believe it too. I was so afraid you'd believe it so well; you wouldn't work out my message and get here."

Mac was still struggling to believe all she had put in place. "Okay, but that's the last omission?"

She nodded. "The last omission, last lie. We have a different game to play now." She took his hand and placed it on her stomach.

He hoped to God that meant what he thought it did. Smiling wasn't going to stop any time soon, and he wanted to get to the next step of this reunion, but he knew this was the foundation on which they were going to build their life together. Everything had to be clear and agreed. "You know we're going to be lying every day for the rest of our lives?"

"Not to each other."

And that was the important point. "No," he agreed. "Never to each other."

THE END

AUTHOR ACKNOWLEDGEMENTS

As most people know, while writing is quite a solitary profession, no good book gets to market without several people having a hand in the mix. I want to thank those people who have helped me with this book.

Thanks to Ian Drury, for saying the basic idea was worth pursuing.

Thanks to Tony J Fyler, for the structural edit of the first version and telling me to get less depressing with it all. I hadn't considered it depressing, but that's why I need an editor.

Thanks to Margaret Steel and Becky Swain for beta reading when the manuscript was still one book,

Thanks to Phil Rowlands for helping me over technical issues with the submission to Diamond Books.

Thanks to Diamond Team for saying, the book is too long for us, and asking if I could cut the story in to two books. Apparently, I can and clearly, I did. It was a great opportunity and I really do appreciate it.

Thanks also to Steve Timmins for editing the book to the final polish, for pushing me on every point, and for being a pedantic wine buff, it has all added to the body and flavour.

Finally thank you to you, the reader. Without you finishing the story in your own head, the piece is only half done. For anyone curious enough, the North Gate Spell is adapted from *Fighting Fantasy: Sorcery! Kharé: Cityport of Traps*© Steve Jackson, 1984. Thanks to Scholastic books for confirming that I could use the extract.

Find out more about me and my books at www.gailbwilliams.co.uk.

DIAMOND
CRIME

Passionate about the crime/mystery/thriller books it publishes

Follow
Facebook:
@diamondcrimepublishing

Instagram
@diamond_crime_publishing

Web
diamondbooks.co.uk